Whose Body in the Library

Also available by Eva Gates

The Lighthouse Library Mysteries

Shot Through the Book
The Stranger in the Library
Death Knells and Wedding Bells
Death by Beach Read
Deadly Ever After
A Death Long Overdue
Read and Buried
Something Read Something Dead
The Spook in the Stacks
Reading Up a Storm
Booked for Trouble
By Book or by Crook

Writing as Vicki Delany
The Sherlock Holmes Bookshop Mysteries

The Devil in the Details
The Incident of the Book in the Nighttime
The Sign of Four Spirits
The Game Is a Footnote
A Three Book Problem
A Curious Incident
There's a Murder Afoot
A Scandal in Scarlet
The Cat of Baskervilles
Body on Baker Street
Elementary, She Read

The Year Round Christmas Mysteries

O, Deadly Night
A Slay Ride Together With You
Have Yourself a Deadly Little Christmas
Dying in a Winter Wonderland
Silent Night, Deadly Night
Hark the Herald Angels Slay
We Wish You a Murderous Christmas
Rest Ye Murdered Gentlemen

The Ashley Grant Mysteries

Coral Reef Views
Blue Water Hues
White Sand Blues

The Constable Molly Mysteries

Unreasonable Doubt
Under Cold Stone
A Cold White Sun
Among the Departed
Negative Image
Winter of Secrets
Valley of the Lost
In the Shadow of the Glacier

The Klondike Gold Rush Mysteries

Gold Web
Gold Mountain
Gold Fever
Gold Digger

The Ray Robertson Mysteries

Blood and Belonging
Haitian Graves
Juba Good

The Tea by the Sea Mysteries

Tea with Jam & Dread
Trouble Is Brewing
Steeped in Malice
Murder Spills the Tea
Murder in a Teacup
Tea & Treachery

The Catskill Summer Resort Mysteries

Deadly Director's Cut
Deadly Summer Nights

Also available by Vicki Delany

More Than Sorrow
Murder at Lost Dog Lake
Burden of Memory
Scare the Light Away
Whiteout

Whose Body in the Library

A LIGHTHOUSE LIBRARY MYSTERY

Eva Gates

CROOKED LANE

NEW YORK

Books should be disposed of and recycled according to local requirements. All paper materials used are FSC compliant.

This is a work of fiction. All of the names, characters, organizations, places, and events portrayed in this novel are either products of the author's imagination or are used fictitiously. Any resemblance to real or actual events, locales, or persons, living or dead, is entirely coincidental.

Published in the United States by Crooked Lane Books, an imprint of The Quick Brown Fox & Company LLC.

Crooked Lane Books and its logo are trademarks of The Quick Brown Fox & Company LLC.

Library of Congress Catalog-in-Publication data available upon request.

ISBN (hardcover): 979-8-89242-437-0
ISBN (ebook): 979-8-89242-438-7

Cover design by Joe Burleson

Printed in the United States.

www.crookedlanebooks.com

Crooked Lane Books
34 West 27th St., 10th Floor
New York, NY 10001

First Edition: June 2026

The authorized representative in the EU for product safety and compliance is eucomplyOÜPärnumnt 139b-14, 11317 Tallinn, Estonia, hello@eucompliancepartner.com, +33757690241

10 9 8 7 6 5 4 3 2 1

To Gail Cargo, my mother, who
encouraged in me a love of reading.
At 101 years old, she still reads
voraciously, now with the
help of audio books.

Chapter One

If there's anything more exciting, and more terrifying, than the first day at a new job, it's hard to imagine what that might be.

Not just a new job in an entirely new career, but a new home. Not just a new town, but a place I'd never even been to before, one that has unpleasant connotations in my family.

I was apprehensive and nervous and terrified—and bursting with hope and optimism, all at the same time.

I'd made my decision. I'd packed up my old life. I'd set off on a new path. I told everyone I knew—my friends, my aunt, my children, my brother—I was confident I was doing the right thing, and I was excited about the future.

I tried to tell myself the same. Sometimes I believed it.

I'd driven for two days, drinking too much coffee and eating too much fast food. I'd spent the previous night in a standard highway-side hotel outside a town I never did get the name of.

And now, at last, after all my planning and all the tasks, major and minor, involved in starting all over again, I was almost there. I arrived in the Outer Banks a short while ago, driven through the strangely named towns of Kitty Hawk, Kill Devil Hills, and Nags Head, and entered the Cape Hatteras National Seashore.

Following the signs, I slowed to turn off the coastal highway and went inland, down the long lane lined by well-spaced red pines. I'd caught my first excited glimpse of the lighthouse tower from some distance away, tall, strong, protective, looming over the bushes and the trees. In the daytime, the light was but a faint flash; I'd been told that at night it could be seen some thirty miles out to sea. Protecting ships, as it had for centuries, from the ever-present dangers of the so-called Graveyard of the Atlantic.

The Bodie Island Lighthouse.

The word is pronounced "body," and it's still called that although due to the shifting sands and the movement of ocean currents over the decades, Bodie Island is no longer an island but part of the narrow strip of sand making up the Outer Banks of North Carolina.

It was a Sunday morning in late August. I'd been on the road early, drinking overly strong coffee and eating an overly toasted bagel at the wheel in order to get here by ten to meet my new boss, who would take me on the grand tour. But, as has been the habit of a lifetime, I was more than a little bit early.

The library was closed today, but a few cars were scattered throughout the lot. I could see people walking the boardwalk that wended through the marsh to Bosie Creek, or studying the skies and tips of long grasses with binoculars.

The marsh, I'd been told, is a popular place for birdwatchers and other nature lovers. I was excited about having the opportunity to explore it in my leisure time.

I pulled into a parking space at the top of the path leading to the lighthouse itself. I ordered myself to breathe, and I did so.

I took another breath and studied my surroundings: the lighthouse tower, 156 feet tall, with a small viewing platform way, way, way up. Distinguishing wide bands of black and white paint, and a couple of long thin windows on alternate floors.

I'd looked up pictures of the lighthouse on the internet, and during my final interview, over Zoom, when I said to my prospective boss I couldn't imagine how they fit a library, not to mention all the other necessary rooms, into it, she laughed and said, "The Bodie Island Lighthouse Library is far larger inside than it appears from the outside. You'll see. When you join us. Will you, Nichelle?"

My heart pounded so rapidly at those words, I hoped Lucy McNeil couldn't hear it all the way from Nags Head, North Carolina. "Yes," I'd said, "I'd love to join you and your library."

And now, here I was.

My name is Nichelle Gilcrest. I'm not a Black woman, rather a mixture of an Italian mother and Irish father, which made for interesting meals when I was growing up, but I am named after the trail-blazing Star Trek actress, whom my mother adored. I'd lived all of my life in Rochester, New York. Today I was starting over in Nags Head.

A small Toyota Yaris in a cheerful shade of teal, pulled up next to me, and the driver waved, and gave me a smile as bright as the day.

I recognized the round face, plump cheeks, curly dark hair, and huge smile of Lucy McNeil, Director of the Lighthouse Library, from our Zoom calls.

We got out of our cars and met on the path. She was smaller in life than on Zoom; five foot three or thereabout, my five-ten towered over her. As well as being tall, I weigh more than I might like (who doesn't?) and I felt clunky next to Lucy's slight frame. She thrust out her hand. "I am so delighted to meet you in person, Nichelle. Welcome to the center of the universe, as we call it. Our library."

"I'm beyond thrilled to be here, Lucy. Thank you so much."

She dug in her skirt pocket and pulled out a chain from which hung two sets of keys. She handed it to me. "These are for you. This one opens the main door to the building itself, and the other is for your apartment. Let's go inside and have a quick look around. You can settle into the apartment today and tomorrow get stuck into meeting the rest of the motley crew and seeing how we do things."

She glanced at my car, the back seat piled high with boxes and suitcases. She smiled to herself, as if she was recalling a very fond memory. "We don't have a garage, I'm afraid, so your car will have to park here, exposed to the elements."

"I'm from Rochester, New York. I didn't have a garage there either, and I have plenty of experience chopping inches-thick blocks of ice off my windshield."

"I hope you'll like the weather here better. We do get something called winter, but nothing like you're used to. I'm originally from Boston myself, so I have some idea of what you mean." We walked up the path and climbed the short set of steps to the main door. I put my head back to look high, high above me at the length of the lighthouse tower stretching into the sky.

"It is impressive," Lucy said. "After all these years, I still stop to admire it sometimes." She waved her hand with a flourish. "After you. Remember, the apartment is your home, and you have all the privacy and rights that entails. I have a spare key, which I'll only use in case of an emergency. The rest of the building belongs to the town, but you're welcome to use any and all library facilities, with the exception of my and Denise's offices and Ronald's desk, whenever you like. Now, open that door, use the larger fob, and I'll show you how to disable the alarm."

I lifted the fob to touch it to the black box, but before it beeped, Lucy said, "I lived here, when I first arrived. I called the apartment my Lighthouse Aerie. I hope you'll love it as much as I did."

I smiled at her. "I'm sure I will."

"Great. Let's go. I had breakfast with my aunt and my cousin before coming here, leaving my husband with the babies, so I need to get back."

"Babies? Plural?"

"Twins. Two boys. They're three months old."

I'd noticed a stain that looked a lot like baby sick on her right shoulder, but I said nothing. Lucy was otherwise nicely but casually dressed in slim white pants and a flowing green and white blouse with white sandals on her feet. The blouse didn't quite hide the slight pudginess around her middle which suggested she'd recently had a baby and was struggling to get rid of the evidence. "I have twins also," I said, "Girls."

"Another thing we have in common."

"Although mine are considerably older than three months." I opened the door and stepped into my new life.

Chapter Two

Lucy McNeil dropped onto the couch with a grateful sigh. "Asleep. For now."

Connor wrapped an arm loosely around her shoulders. "Do you think we've finally got them both on the same sleep schedule?"

"No."

"Me neither. Let's enjoy it while we can. Can I get you a glass of wine?"

"I'd love nothing more, but better not. I have to grab my sleep when I can. Particularly now I'm back at work, even if only four days a week to start."

"How's the new employee seem?"

"I like her. I think she's going to work out fine. She reminded me of myself, the day I first arrived at the library. So nervous yet so excited. Seems like such a long time ago." She snuggled closer into her husband's warm body. Instinctively she patted the space on the other side of her. And then she remembered: Charles was not here needing cuddles and pats.

The blinds were open, giving them a gorgeous panorama of the view across the sand to the gentle surf lapping against the shoreline and the dark ocean beyond. This time of evening, only a handful of people strolled along the beach.

Lucy closed her eyes. Connor nudged her."Go to bed, hon. I'll stay up a while longer and keep an eye on the baby monitor."

She glanced at the small screen propped up on the coffee table. Isaac slept soundly, his chest gently rising and falling, barely twitching, while Lucas flopped about as best his little body was yet capable.

Connor followed her glance. "Identical twins. All of three months old, and already they have their individual personalities."

"I've barely started back at work, and I miss them so much. But at the same time, I'm happy to be back at work. Does that make sense?"

"Perfect sense. I've been known to sneak away from the office myself on occasion to run home and have a quick peek at them. Just to make sure they're okay. Although Sofia's doing a great job taking care of them. I'm so glad Josie recommended her."

"I worry about them, which I suppose is natural, but I know they're in good hands when we're away."

"Speaking of work, everything okay with your new position?"

"Overwhelming, if I'm being honest. First my maternity leave, and then Bertie announcing her retirement and saying she'd wait until I came back so I could take the job. She helped with the candidate search and the interviews for my old job, but she largely left the decision up to me, as it's me who will be working with the new assistant director."

"As it should be. What's the new person's name again?"

"Nichelle Gilcrest. This is her first ever library position. Anywhere. She's just graduated from Syracuse with her master's degree in Library and Information Science. For all that she's over fifty."

"Oh? You didn't tell me that."

"A late in life career change, she said. She was a bookkeeper, hated every minute of it over all the years she did it, and when she had a chance to take her life in a new direction, she decided she liked books, and I don't mean accounting books, and would love to work with them, so she went back to college. She had to complete her BA first, which took two years, and then she got her master's."

"Good for her," Connor said. "Why OBX though?"

"She saw the notice that we were looking for someone of her qualifications and decided if she was going to change her life, why not make it a big change? I heartily approve." Lucy gave her husband a kiss. "After all, look how things turned out for me when I moved here." Lucy had come to the Outer Banks all those years ago, all her possessions stuffed into the teal Yaris she still drove, to get away from an over-controlling family and an unwanted marriage proposal.

Connor ruffled her curls. Connor, Nags Head born and raised, descendent of a long line of proud Bankers, had never needed or wanted to get away. He was currently finishing up his second term as mayor of Nags Head, with no plans to run for further office. Instead he intended to return full time to his dental practice.

"Nichelle told me she has twin girls," Lucy said. "They're not with her, obviously if she's living in the Aerie, so I'm guessing they're at college, working, or are married. Maybe all of the above."

"She has no connections to OBX? At least when you came you had your aunt Ellen and her family and memories of childhood summers."

"Nothing she mentioned." Lucy smothered a yawn. On the monitor Lucas shifted. She held her breath until he settled down again, and then she reluctantly slipped out from under Connor's arm. "I'd better get to bed while I can. It's going to be a long day tomorrow. The start of my first full, although slightly truncated, week as Director of the Bodie Island Lighthouse Library. I should go in early, to be there when the rest arrive so I can introduce them all to Nichelle."

"One piece of advice, Lucy. Let Nichelle find her own way of doing things. As long as she doesn't make any obvious mistakes, don't be looking over her shoulder all the time and constantly telling her how you did it."

"Would I do that?"

"Yes."

"I briefed her thoroughly, but the one part of my job I didn't tell her about was helping the police solve murders. We haven't had a single incident requiring a visit from the new detective since Sam retired. Which is a good thing. The one time I met her, she terrified me. I hope Nichelle doesn't find herself involved in those situations the way I did."

Chapter Three

I awoke in a mild panic, not sure where I was. It was pitch dark; the bed was comfortable but unfamiliar. A warm, breathing lump was curled against my right hip.

Then I remembered. The apartment above the library. The Lighthouse Aerie. The breathing lump was the library cat, Charles, named in honor of Mr. Dickens. As Lucy showed me around yesterday, Charles joined us. She explained that although Charles "worked" at the library and had lived with her in the Lighthouse Aerie, once she moved out he came home with her every day. When she took time off work to have the twins, he'd been noticeably unhappy, not only at the unwelcome invasion of two squalling demanding smelly little creatures, but not going to work. She brought him back, and he settled into a bed in the staff break room. For some reason, he hadn't wanted to go up to the Lighthouse Aerie with the previous resident, Louise Jane McKaughnan. Yesterday, as we opened the door on the fourth floor, and I got my first look at my new home, Charles ran on ahead. Lucy said, "Charles might not—."

She stopped talking. The big cat had leapt onto the bed, circled twice, and settled down, paws tucked neatly beneath him. He was a lovely thing, a Himalayan, with long beige hair, expressive blue eyes in a tan face, a fluffy dark tail and matching tips on his ears.

"If you mind having him here," Lucy said, "you can show him the door. He won't stay if you don't feed him."

"I don't mind in the least. I love cats. We always had cats when I was growing up. My husband didn't care for them, so I haven't had one for a long time." That, I said but only to myself, should have been a red flag as to what sort of man he was. I eventually learned, fortunately not too late.

I'd looked around my new home. "This will be absolutely perfect, Lucy. The cat makes it even more perfect."

And it was perfect. For now. The Lighthouse Aerie was very small. Just one main room, with a kitchen alcove and a bathroom. The whitewashed walls curved following the shape of the lighthouse tower and were covered with bright paintings of Outer Banks scenes. The window seat was piled high with cushions of sage green and pale blue, making the perfect spot to curl up with a good book on a rainy day. Two armchairs provided the only seating for guests, aside from the two hardbacked chairs pulled up to the foldable kitchen table, and there was no proper dining table. Obviously, if I intended to entertain, my guests and I would have to go out. Perhaps I could get a portable barbeque, some beach chairs, and a collapsible table, and host dinners on the lawn. That might be fun. Considering that, with the exception of Lucy, I knew not one person who lived in a 200-mile radius, entertaining guests wasn't an immediate problem.

I rubbed Charles's belly. He purred and we simply lay there for a while, watching the first rays of the sun touch the long, thin east facing window. The view from here was spectacular. Across the marsh and the highway, to the long grasses, drifting sand, and wide empty beach of Cape Hatteras National Seashore, and the open ocean beyond. I never had a view like that in Rochester!

After Lucy left the previous afternoon, giving me her personal number in case I had any questions or issues, I immediately headed out to explore my surroundings. First, a walk on the boardwalk through the marsh to see the birds and ducks gathering on the creek, then I drove to the beach where I walked for ages, just breathing the salty air and listening to the sound of waves rushing to shore. I treated myself to a seafood dinner at a nice place near the pier, and I was home and tucked into bed, with a good book and a friendly cat, early. Dark clouds had begun moving in as I drove home, and I fell asleep to the comforting sound of light rain pattering against the window.

"I'm going to like it here," I said to Charles.

He said nothing in reply but jumped off the bed and headed straight for the food dishes I'd brought up from the staff break room. Finding his bowl empty he turned and faced me. If he could have put his paws on his hips, he would have. Instead he narrowed his blue eyes and gave me a theatrically plaintive meow that said, "Let's not get this living together thing started on the wrong foot. I'm about to die of sheer starvation here."

I shoved aside the covers and got out of the bed with almost as much energy as Charles. First things first, I filled his food bowl and refreshed the water dish. Before heading for the shower, I sent texts to my daughters to let them know

I'd arrived safely the night before. They had not approved of me completely turning over my life and starting again, and they never hesitated to tell me so. More than once. I assured them I knew what I was doing, and from then on I ignored their protests. Simone, who had a degree in English Lit, was getting her foot in the door at a publishing house in New York City, working as an assistant editor. Simone's love life was, to put it mildly, chaotic. Whereas Isabelle had a stable relationship with a man I didn't much care for. I could never put my finger on it, but for some reason he didn't like me, and I returned the favor. She and her partner were primary school teachers in Rochester.

I got replies almost instantly.

> Simone: *Let me know when you're ready for visitors. I'll try to get time off. Beach!*
> Isabelle: *Jonathan says if you decide to leave you can stay with us while you look for a new job. Isn't that sweet of him?*

I was most definitely not ready for visitors. I could imagine Simone's face when she saw the size of my apartment. And if Jonathan had invited me to stay with them I'd eat my book club book.

I sent texts to my mother's sister, whom I've always been close to, and to my brother's wife, Maya, letting them know I was settling in. I was looking forward to having family visiting—as long as they knew they'd have to stay in a hotel.

Texts sent, motherly duty done, I headed for the shower.

The library opens on Mondays at nine-thirty. The staff usually come in about nine or slightly before. I wanted to be downstairs, bright and perky and full of enthusiasm, to meet them. That wasn't a pretext. I was eager to meet everyone and get stuck into my first day as a real librarian.

Four years ago, at the ripe old age of fifty, I enrolled full time in college after my marriage ended and my twin daughters embarked on lives of their own. I loved every minute of it. The college atmosphere, the company of my much younger fellow students, the professors, the lectures, the assignments. I rediscovered the sheer joy of learning, and of life, which I feared had left me so long ago.

When I saw that the position of assistant director was open at this library, I jumped at it. I've never even been to the Outer Banks, and although it has a bad history for my family, I was able to dismiss it. What happened here, happened a long time ago.

I didn't expect to get the job. Why would they hire me when so many others with work experience might want the position? Nevertheless, I decided there'd be no harm in trying, and the interview would help me practice and refine my job-hunting skills.

To my considerable surprise, I got it.

One of the things I was most looking forward to was starting up a new book club. During my interview, Lucy told me the librarian-led book club had been on hiatus while she was off, but she hoped (not a very subtle hint) it could start up again under my guidance. The club's original focus, she said, had been the classic novels, but I was free to discuss whatever sort of books I enjoyed. I immediately suggested my favorite genre, mysteries of the Golden Age, and she said that would be perfect. I decided on the spot to start with *Whose Body?*, the first Lord Peter Wimsey book by Dorothy L. Sayers. I'd been rereading it, after a long time, on the journey down here, and had only a few pages left before finishing. I enjoyed it as much as I remembered.

I showered and washed my cropped black and gray hair. Although it was almost time to admit my hair was more gray with a touch of black these days. For the last ten years or more I'd been dying it blond in an attempt to keep age at bay and cover the gray. I finally gave in, had it cut and let the natural color burst forth, before embarking on the big move. No point in trying to act like one of the young ones anymore. Heavens, my new boss looked to be twenty years younger than me. She could easily be my daughter.

I'd been debating for weeks what to wear for my first day at work. I didn't want to look like a stereotypical, middle-aged librarian, nor did I want to be mistaken for a tourist on summer vacation who'd gotten herself lost on the way to the beach. The day was going to be hot, in the mid-eighties with no more rain in the forecast, so I decided on a summer dress in shades of blue worn under a peach denim jacket. I'd leave my legs bare and wear strappy black sandals with a one-inch heel. I've always tanned well, the result of my mother's Italian heritage, so by the end of summer my legs weren't too terribly Rochester-winter white.

When I was ready, I studied myself in the mirror. Was the dress too frivolous? Too colorful? Maybe a black jacket would be better than the peach? But the only black jacket I had was made of leather. Might that present the wrong image? I only had one chance to make a first impression.

Charles sat on the bed and watched me. His whiskers twitched, and he gave me a meow.

I took that as a sign of approval, and I said, to myself as much as to him, "Right. I'm ready." I straightened my shoulders and sucked in my stomach. "Once more, unto the breach dear friends." Although, I had to confess it was more like the first time unto the breach of being a librarian.

In the way of food, I'd brought nothing more than a few granola bars, which didn't matter as I was too nervous to eat breakfast, and Lucy told me the coffee pot in the staff break room would be on most of the day, as well as juice and iced tea available in the fridge. I planned to do a quick shop after work for the bare necessities before I figured out a meal routine.

I opened the door. "Are you coming?" I asked Charles.

He didn't have to be asked twice. He sailed off the bed, landing halfway across the room, ran out the door, and skipped nimbly down the railing of the iron spiral staircase. The apartment was four floors up. A mighty nice daily commute, although I would get my exercise going up and down several times a day.

Lucy told me the general public as well as library patrons were welcome to climb to the top of the lighthouse tower during opening hours, and sometimes members of the general public didn't always respect closed doors, so I needed to keep mine locked. I did so, switched the staircase light on, and followed Charles. No one had arrived before me, and I took a few moments to simply enjoy the quiet. All these lovely books in their neat rows; every one of them waiting to be read. All the worlds within, the range of people and experiences and human emotion. I had few regrets in life, even marrying Daniel had given me some happy times and two lovely and loving daughters. But I did regret not becoming a librarian long ago. I'd wanted to stay in school and finish my degree, but I was in love with Daniel and eager to get married and start a family.

And so, that's what I did.

But I was here now. Never say never, my mother always said. And she was right. As usual.

Yesterday, Lucy showed me where the refreshment things were kept and told me it was the responsibility of the day's first arrival to put the coffee on.

My initial official act as a real librarian!

I turned off the alarm and started the coffee. To mark the occasion, feeling rather embarrassed about it, I took a selfie of my beaming self with the coffee machine. I'd post it later on my graduating class's social media page. Once the coffee was brewing, I went back to the main room, said good morning one more time to the books, and unlocked the front door. I threw it open, ready to shout with joy to greet the new day.

A man lay on the steps. For the briefest of moments, I thought he was a library patron, taking a brief nap while waiting for opening hours. "Are you—?"

He did not move. Only then did my wits return, and I saw the blank empty eyes and the pool of blood seeping out from beneath his head.

Chapter Four

Lucy wanted to get to work early today, to have time to go over the library routine in detail with Nichelle before Denise, Louise Jane, and Ronald arrived, not to mention the day's patrons.

As if sensing her thoughts, the babies were well behaved this morning. She'd luxuriated in six whole hours of continuous sleep before Lucas announced to the world he was ready for another exciting day. And, as could be expected, as well as his mother he woke his father and brother. Connor helped change the babies after they were fed, then he showered, dressed, and gulped down his own breakfast. He was driving to Raleigh today for a meeting of North Carolina mayors and had to be on the road early.

"Some of the others," he said wistfully as he kissed Lucy good-bye, "arrived in Raleigh last night and are staying over tonight."

"Don't give me that sob story," she said with a laugh. "I told you, you didn't have to do the entire drive in one day but you insisted."

Connor glanced at the twins in their bouncy chairs. Lucas was bouncing, but Isaac had gone back to sleep. "Love you," he said. "Love you all."

"Go!" Lucy said.

The babies were momentarily content, so she left them and went to get herself ready for a day at the office. Yesterday, she'd been mortified to get home and discover she had baby residue on her shirt. She must have gone out like that for breakfast with her aunt and cousin and then to the library to meet the newest staff member. Not the professional image she wanted to project, but if Nichelle had twins she must know how it can be. Although, as Aunt Ellen said, the memories of the baby years are soon nothing but a confused blur.

"Ellie," her cousin Josie had added, "is two years old now, and even her babyhood is a blur."

Precisely at eight o'clock the front door opened, and Sofia's soft voice called, "Only me."

Lucy popped her head into the hallway. "I'm glad you're on time. Big day for me, my first full week as the boss."

Sofia grinned at her. "As you told me all last week."

Lucy and Connor had been lucky to get Sofia to be the baby minder. She'd helped care for Ellie for Josie and Jake's now two-year-old; they both had highly erratic schedules as Josie was the owner and head baker at a popular coffee spot and Jake was a restaurant chef. Josie had sung Sofia's praises to the sky. When Ellie started day care, Sofia landed a full-time job as a nanny, but the job ended when the couple who employed her abruptly moved to New York City. Conveniently, that meant she was looking for a position at the same time Lucy was preparing to go back to work.

"How do I look?" Lucy asked. "Calm, completely in-control professional woman, or a harried mother worried about leaving her babies all day?"

"You look like a professional who has nothing at all to worry about. I have your number. I have Connor's number. Ellen is on call, as is Josie. Not to mention Connor's mother and even his dad, although what Fred McNeil knows to do with a distressed baby, I have no idea. It's a nice day out, and I plan to take Lucas and Isaac onto the deck for some air after their morning nap. Not too much air, and no direct sun. We will be fine."

Lucas started to cry (or was it Isaac?), and Sofia said, "Go. Now. Or you never will."

Lucy grabbed her bag from the shelf by the door and went.

* * *

When Lucy arrived at the library, apart from Nichelle's, only one car, a rusty, battered old thing, was in the parking lot. As she got out of her own vehicle, the entrance to the library opened and Nichelle stood framed in the doorway. She threw her head back, and looked high into the sky, spreading her arms out as though welcoming the day.

Lucy smiled to herself. This place made the perfect start to anyone's day. Not trapped in traffic, or crammed onto crowded buses or trains. No elbowing your way down the busy sidewalk. No loud chatter or ringing phones or lineups of impatient people at coffee bars. Nothing but the light of the rising sun, the greeting of the morning birds, and the gentle sway of the long grasses in the soft breeze off the ocean.

Nichelle looked down and the bliss on her face was wiped away in a flash. Even from where she stood, Lucy could see confusion, followed by disbelief and then shock.

Something large and bulky lay on the steps at Nichelle's feet.

Lucy ran.

Nichelle saw her coming and a look of sheer relief replaced the shock.

It was a man. He was in his mid-to-late seventies probably, slightly built with still-thick gray hair, dressed in brown pants and a blue golf shirt. He lay on his back, not moving, his red-rimmed gray eyes staring up at nothing. Blood had pooled beneath his head, but it was already drying.

To her immense relief, Lucy didn't recognize him. It wasn't unusual for patrons to arrive before opening hours and go for a walk on the boardwalk while they waited or to linger by the door. But this man, she'd never seen before.

Nichelle turned her own gray eyes on Lucy. "I . . . I . . . found him like this."

Lucy dropped to a crouch and put her hand on the man's neck. Nothing moved, but she visually checked him out, searching for some signs of life. She touched nothing more, and she allowed herself a deep calming breath before standing up.

"Is he—?" Nichelle asked.

"Yes. He's dead." Lucy wrapped her arms around the other woman and felt Nichelle's deep heaving breaths. "It's okay. It's okay. You go inside, sit down. I'll call 911."

"What . . . what's he doing here? Who is it?"

"I don't know. We're a public library, right? Homeless people sometimes come by looking for shelter or a snack.

Elderly patrons get confused and try to get in when the library's not open. I don't recognize him. Do you?"

Nichelle's breathing was slowly returning to normal. She stepped away from Lucy and looked at the man while Lucy pulled out her phone. "I don't think so, but there's something . . . something very familiar about him. What's that in his hand?" Several tiny pink beads strung together escaped from his tightly clenched right hand.

"Looks like a child's bracelet. Don't touch it." Lucy spoke into her phone, trying to keep her voice calm and steady and her information succinct. "This is Lucy McNeil. I'm at the library. A man has died. I don't know anything more. We need an ambulance and probably the police."

The 911 operator told Lucy assistance was on the way.

Nichelle spoke in a voice so small, Lucy could barely hear it. "I'm not entirely sure, but he might be . . . my father."

Chapter Five

Lucy stared at me, the phone in her hand forgotten. "Your father? What does that mean? How can you not know?"

"He . . . disappeared a long time ago. It happened here, in the Outer Banks."

"Mrs. McNeil, Lucy, are you still there?" came the distant voice from Lucy's phone.

"Yes, yes." Lucy said. "I'm hanging up now. Tell the medics the man has no vital signs and he's . . ." she swallowed, "cold and the blood looks to be dry. I don't know how long he's been here."

She shoved her phone in her bag and took my arm. "Let's get you inside. You've had a shock. Do you want a glass of water?"

I struggled to recover my wits. It had been a shock, but Lucy's presence was a comfort, and the authorities were on their way. "Charles! You told me not to let him out."

"I'll handle Charles," Lucy said. The big cat had stepped outside and was cautiously sniffing at the dead man's hand. "I'll put him in the storage closet. He will not be happy about that, but the police won't thank us for letting a cat spread hair all over their crime scene. Not to mention he'll soon get bored and go in search of birds to play with." She bent over and scooped the cat up. "You go inside and sit down, Nichelle. Leave the door open so we can hear them arrive."

I did as I was told. Lucy and Charles disappeared down the hallway, but she was soon back with a glass of water and without the cat. I'd dropped into a chair at the computer tables and she pulled one next to me, sat down, and handed me the glass. "Drink that."

Once again, I did as ordered. When I finished, Lucy said, "You said he might be your father. What did you mean by that?"

I shook my head. "Just a thought. The shock."

"I thought—" Lucy began.

"Thought what?"

"It's likely nothing, but his eyes are very much like yours. An unusual shade of gray."

"Yes. I have my father's eyes. I might as well tell you the whole sad story while we wait. When I was sixteen, my father went on a fishing trip to the Outer Banks with a group of friends. He disappeared."

"Disappeared? You mean . . . completely?"

"As in not seen nor heard from ever again. My parents' marriage was a rocky one, since I came along anyway. My mother loved my father a great deal, and because of that she put up with a lot. He was a heavy drinker. He was never abusive or violent, in fact the opposite. When he drank, he was the life of the party. Everyone's pal. When I was little he was the best dad. Always ready to play, always with the jokes and the pranks. He'd show up at school in the middle of the day to take my brother and me out for ice cream. The teachers didn't much care for that, but he had a way of convincing them to let us go. But fun and ice cream can't be all of a man's life, can it? He had trouble holding down a job because he'd come in late and hung over or go out to lunch and not bother to come back. He never let minor details like that worry him. My mother worked all the hours she could to keep us afloat. He stole from her purse sometimes, to go out drinking with his pals. Maybe even to buy ice cream. If he did happen to have some money on him, he'd buy Mom frivolities she didn't want rather than adding to her grocery money, or he'd hand over cash to anyone with a sob story, and the next day he'd forget who he lent it to."

"Hard for a kid to deal with," Lucy said.

"Yeah. He could have his down times too, but not often. Then he'd be listless, unmotivated, have trouble getting out of bed. At those times, he didn't even want to go out for ice cream. Those mood swings didn't help the work situation much."

"It sounds as if he might have been bipolar," Lucy said.

"I know that now. My mom just said Dad was 'sad,' without ever explaining what he had to be sad about, so we were to let him be. She said it would pass, and it always did. Then—ice cream time again."

"I hope you don't mind me being somewhat critical," Lucy said, "but it sounds as though your mother enabled him."

"She did. That was the sort of family she herself had been raised in. Father knows best. No questions, no arguments. Plus, as I said, she loved him a great deal, and if he was happy, she could be happy too. When I was sixteen, my grandmother, my dad's mother, died. She was the exact opposite of him: downright miserly. Because of that, she had a not-inconsiderable amount of savings, and as he was an only child, he naturally inherited it. His barfly buddies convinced him to take them on a fishing vacation. They called it fishing; my mom knew it would be little more than a drinking holiday. Fortunately, before he left, Mom talked him into opening a joint savings account with her in which to deposit his mother's money. It was enough to get us through after he disappeared." I thought back, memories tumbling all over themselves in my mind. Getting the news. My mom's shock. The days of uncertainty. Mom's increasing agitation. My own failure to understand how someone could simply . . . not be there anymore. My brother was only a year older than me, and he was getting increasingly angry at Dad for his failure to support us. Then his anger at Dad for what he called "walking away."

"My mother kept a picture of him prominently displayed in the living room until the day she died. Every time I visited her, I saw that picture. Which might be why that man outside reminded me of my dad. I don't know what happened to the picture when Mom died. Brad, that's my brother, might have it, though I don't know why he'd want it. He and Dad were constantly at odds in the . . . final months. Sentiment, perhaps. Memories of what might have been but never was."

"What did the police say about your father's disappearance? Any theories?"

"None that I know of. I was only sixteen, remember, not involved in many of the details. Mom came down—down here, I mean—but Brad and I stayed at home. Like I said, Dad was the life of the party, always up for a good time. His friends told the police they had dinner on their last night, plenty of drinks of course, hit the bars later, more drinks, and then they went back to their hotel. Dad didn't show up at breakfast, and his bed hadn't been slept in. The group was an odd number; the rest of them shared, but Dad had a hotel room to himself. The only thing that appeared to be missing was the clothes he'd last been seen in and his bathing suit, so the police concluded he decided to go for a late-night swim, and under the influence of drink, he wasn't careful of the riptides and got carried out to sea. They never found his clothes or the slightest trace of him."

"That's so hard." Lucy put her hand lightly on my arm. From the back room, Charles called to let us know he'd been "accidentally" locked in. In the distance, sirens approached. Lucy stood up. "Company's arriving. I'm sorry this happened, Nichelle. And on your first day too. At least I had a couple of days here before I tripped over my first body."

"What does that mean?"

"I'll let the others fill you in. The detective will be wanting to talk to you as soon as she arrives. You can use the break room or Bertie's . . . I mean, my office. No matter how much Charles insists, do not let him out."

Lucy went outside, leaving the door open. Blue and red flashing lights flickered between the trunks of the red pines as the vehicles approached. I sat quietly, knowing it would be some time before I got the opportunity to be alone with my thoughts once again, and remembered. I told Lucy I thought the man outside might be my father, but that wasn't exactly right. I knew for a certainty he was either my dad or his twin, and I'd never heard about any long-lost brother. The face was older than the one in the picture in my mother's living room, naturally. A network of lines and deep folds around the mouth and eyes, a few dark patches on the time-and-sunworn skin. But the thick curly locks were still there, although now totally gray. The proud straight nose still straight although less proud in death and lined with touches of rosacea. If it was Dad, why had he come here, to where I was now living, and on the very day after my arrival?

And why on earth would he be holding a cheap pink bracelet of the sort a little girl would wear?

At first glance, it looked as though he'd tripped coming up the stairs and bashed his head into the concrete of the landing. That was possible, particularly if he'd been drinking. But if he tripped, wouldn't he have fallen forward, his face and forehead colliding with the solid surface? Not the back of his head? I shoved speculation aside. The police would handle it.

As for me and my memories, all I know is after my dad disappeared, we had more money. Mom was able to quit one of her jobs, and although she mourned her husband for the rest of her life and never remarried, that ugly black cloud of constantly worrying about finances was lifted from her face. She was obviously much happier, and she could even afford the occasional treat for herself or her children. She died five years ago, of cancer.

It might have been the thought of my mother's life, full of regret, that convinced me to pursue my own dreams. My brother, who at seventeen had been on the verge of turning into a real troublemaker, calmed down, finished school, and went to college. He was now a chartered accountant for a major national firm, with a wife I liked and a family of his own.

Would the mystery of where my dad had been for the past thirty-eight years now be solved, or would I be left with even more questions? I should call Brad, let him know, but on the off chance I was mistaken, I decided to hold off. Same with my daughters. They'd offer to come down to be with me, but I wanted to start my new life on my own two feet. Strange how life sometimes works out—after twenty-five years of mothering, I didn't want my children to think they needed to start mothering me.

Chapter Six

I've never seen a police investigation other than on TV, and despite myself I found it fascinating. The medics arrived first, and tended to the body. Yes, it was a body. There had been little doubt in Lucy's or my mind, but I could tell by the glances and nods they exchanged and how they acted with no sense of urgency, the man—Dad?—was dead.

The police arrived soon after, a couple of uniforms first, who began stringing up crime scene tape to block off the steps and the main entrance to the library. They ordered Lucy and me to stay inside and wait. We kept the door open and watched the activity. The police seemed to know Lucy quite well, and one big handsome guy even asked her how Isaac and Lucas (presumably the babies) were doing and if she and Connor (presumably her husband) were getting enough sleep.

Shortly after, three vehicles that didn't look like they belonged to the authorities turned into the lane. People jumped out and ran up the path. A tall, thin woman with bony hips, flat chest, large nose, and sharp cheekbones. A woman older than me, dressed in a slightly below-the-knee skirt and a blouse with a bow at the neck. A short man in his forties with a wild mane of white curls, dressed in a short-sleeved white shirt and a brightly colored tie.

These people were my coworkers. I recognized them from their pictures on the library web pages.

"Louise Jane," the big cop called. "Stop right there. You'll have to go in the back way. This entrance is sealed off, as you can see, and the library closed for the rest of the day, if not longer."

"Surely you don't mind letting me have a peek, Butch," the tall, skinny woman said. "I know everyone around these parts, you know that."

"I know as many people as you do, probably more, Louise Jane. Go inside by the back way, or I'll arrest you for interference."

Louise Jane harrumphed. She didn't look all that frightened at the threat, but she did halt her approach.

"I cannot believe this has happened, not again," the older woman said.

"The day after I move out!" Louise Jane said. "It's increasingly obvious my calming presence is all that controlled whatever unfriendly forces are at work in and around this building."

"Do not repeat that," the man said as they walked away. "I'm sure there's nothing malicious about what happened here. A birdwatcher had a heart attack most likely."

Lucy and I were still standing in the doorway, watching the activity. "You go to the break room, Nichelle," she said. "I'll unlock the back door to let the others in, and we'll join you. Not the most auspicious of circumstances to meet your new colleagues, but it can't be helped."

I walked away as she called, "Butch! Anything you need from me?"

"Not right now. Detective's been called. She's at a meeting in Kill Devil Hills, but she'll be here soon as she can. You know the drill."

"Sadly yes," she said.

Drill? Were these people so accustomed to police activity they had their routine down pat? Before I was first interviewed for the job, I did my research on the library. It was extremely popular among the locals. It had an excellent reputation, a dynamic and active children's program, an extensive academic library, even a collection of precious old maps and rare books. I love nothing more than people gathering to discuss books and literature, and I'd been particularly attracted by the library's events schedule, packed with information about upcoming and prior events. Not only book festivals and author readings, but among other things, several years ago the library hosted an exhibit of Jane Austen first editions, and last year they curated an art show in conjunction with a traveling exhibit of works of American Impressionism.

Satisfied this library had everything I wanted in a job, I hadn't thought to search any deeper. Along with preteen book clubs and toddlers' story time, was it a hotbed of criminal activity?

As in almost every office I'd been in, the break room was stark and functional. A long table with room for six chairs, a small fridge for storing lunches and cold drinks next to the milk and cream, a sink beside a drying rack containing one mug. Chipped linoleum floor and cheap wooden cabinets with a handful of mismatched mugs and plates as well as a big bag of coffee beans and some tea bags and sugar. Kettle and a large coffee pot. I'd put the coffee on when I first came down, but I hadn't had any yet. I eyed the coffee before taking a seat, but my stomach rolled over, and I decided best not to.

"I had hoped," Lucy was saying as the group joined me, "to introduce you to Nichelle in more favorable circumstances. But here we are."

"Once again," the older woman said.

I stood up and tried to smile. "Hello."

"This is Nichelle Gilcrest," Lucy said. "She'll be taking on the role of assistant director. Nichelle, welcome to the Bodie Island Lighthouse Library. This is, in no particular order, Ronald Burkowski, the best children's librarian in the state." He stepped forward, and I held out my hand. His in return was as warm and soft as his smile. No prizes for guessing Ronald was the children's librarian, not with that tie featuring a drawing of the USS Enterprise NCC-1701 streaking across a star-filled background. Yes, I do know my *Star Trek*.

He saw I'd noticed the tie and said, "I hope you don't mind. I wore this today in your honor. You must get a lot of comments about your name."

I grinned at him. "That would be an understatement. It's not only an unusual name, but all the Trekkies in the world want to ask me about it."

"You can have your private meeting of the *Star Trek* fan club later," Lucy said with a smile. "This is Denise Robarts, our academic and research librarian."

The older woman, who appeared to be in her mid-sixties, said, "I'm looking forward to working with you, Nichelle."

"Denise is part time," Lucy said. "She calls herself semi-retired, and we were very lucky she decided she wasn't ready for complete retirement yet."

"Looks like coffee's on," Ronald said. "Can I pour you a cup, Denise?"

"Thanks."

Ronald went to the pot while Lucy continued the introductions. "Louise Jane McKaughan, Denise's assistant and general dogsbody."

"Great to meet you. Lucy told us you're not from around these parts. Anything, anything at all, you need to know, feel free to come to me. I'm an amateur, although highly knowledgeable, historian specializing in the Outer Banks. I have a particular interest in the paranormal, as well as a great deal of sensitivity, which I inherited from my grandmothers before me. You might not be aware but this lighthouse—"

"A story for another time, LJ," Denise said as she accepted the steaming cup.

"One for me too, thanks, Ronald," Louise Jane said.

"A story for maybe never." Lucy gave me a wink. "We don't want to frighten Nichelle away, do we?"

"Nichelle? Coffee?" Ronald asked. "I should have asked you first."

"Not for me, thanks. I'm feeling slightly queasy. I'll be okay in a few minutes, but it was a hard way to start a new job."

"One advantage of the library being closed for the day," Denise said. "You can have a slow day to get to know your way around."

"As well as general information, any tips you need on living here, so far from town and everything," Louise Jane said, "just ask me. An ancestor of mine was a lighthouse keeper here in the days when they needed one, and in later years my family's worked tirelessly to raise funds for upkeep and maintenance. That proud family tradition continues, as I myself was the resident before you. I left only yesterday as it happens. I loved it here, but my living arrangements are getting complicated, and I need more space. Not to mention the requirement of remaining under the radar in the event of the arrival of a visitor I cannot mention."

I blinked in confusion. By visitor did Louise Jane mean one of the spirits she seemed to believe in? Surely she wouldn't be so blunt if she was entertaining a married lover? And what was on the radar about the Lighthouse Aerie anyway?

"I look forward to chatting to you more, Nichelle," Denise said as Louise Jane paused to take a breath, "but for now, what's going on outside, Lucy? That looks uncomfortably like a body under that blanket by the door and the police ordered us to keep away."

"Sadly, it is." Lucy went on to explain what had happened, what little we knew at any rate, and I added my own perspective.

"You didn't recognize him?" Ronald asked.

"No," Lucy said. "I did not. I'm positive I've never seen him here at the library or anyplace else."

I said nothing.

"You all know the routine by now," Lucy said. "We'll be closed for the rest of the day at the minimum, if not tomorrow. Gives us a chance to get caught up on that pesky paperwork. Stay out of the way of the authorities as best you can but be available for an interview if you're needed."

The routine? How many times was this place closed for a police investigation anyway?

"It'll be strange," Denise said. "Not having Sam Watson around."

"I'm sure the new detective will be equally competent." The look on Lucy's face indicated she wasn't entirely convinced of the veracity of what she was saying

"Lucy will be tied up after work and on her days off with her babies," Louise Jane said. "If you need any help, Nichelle, once again you can call on me. I know just about everyone who lives within a hundred miles of here, and if I don't know them, I know people who do."

"Thanks, but why would I-?"

Lucy stood up. "That won't be necessary, Louise Jane. Connor tells me the new detective is proving herself to be highly efficient, and he and the chief are very pleased with her."

"Sam Watson was highly efficient, but he still relied on you sometimes."

"Relied on Lucy to do what?" I asked.

"Lucy, and I must modestly admit, I myself, helped him solve some of his cases," Louise Jane said.

I was getting confused. "I have no experience in the legal profession or in law enforcement. I was a bookkeeper before I became a librarian."

"Neither do—"

"Enough," Lucy said. "Please, Louise Jane. Let's let the police handle this. That unfortunate man was probably enjoying an early morning stroll on the boardwalk when he felt a heart attack or stroke coming on and tried to get help. Sadly, help didn't arrive in time. Now, if we've nothing further to discuss . . . good. Ronald you might want to contact the parents of your regular group participants and let them know activities are canceled for today. No point in them driving all the way out here for nothing. Nichelle, I'll help you get familiar with the computer system while we're waiting."

"Waiting?"

"For the detective. She will have questions for you."

"Uh . . . okay."

"As I'm free all day," Ronald said. "I'll be happy to show you around the children's library. Come up any time."

"Same for me," Denise said. "My office is on the third floor. The rare books and maps room is accessed by the back staircase. The door is kept locked, but I'd love to show it to you any time. We have some wonderful and valuable items."

Ronald topped up his coffee, and he and Denise left. Reluctantly, Louise Jane pushed herself to her feet. "Very well. I owe, I owe, it's off to work I go."

Once she'd skipped merrily out the door, I asked Lucy if she'd mind if I made a phone call before starting work. "I might have spoken too soon, when I said that man could be my dad. It's been a long time. I want to call my brother and ask if he has any pictures."

"Of course. Take all the time you need. I forgot to tell you yesterday, cell phone reception in the lighthouse tower is poor to nonexistent. That's why there's still a landline in the apartment, although if the wind is blowing from the right direction and you stand on a chair and stick the phone out as far as you can stretch, you might get a bar. Or not. We have wi-fi throughout the lower floors, but if I have to make a personal call, I usually use the library's line or just go outside. Much quicker than trying to find a signal in here."

I did as Lucy suggested and took my phone outside. The wind caressed my cheeks, and birds called from the marsh grasses. The scent of salt in the air was strong. I could hear the buzz of conversation as men and women did whatever they were doing at the front of the building, and of cars as they came and went. More came than went, so I assumed the forensics people were arriving.

No people were strolling on the boardwalk or hiking through the marsh. The police must have closed the laneway to the public. A small motorboat chugged past on the waters of the creek, but it kept on going. Fishing, most likely.

"Hey, Nichie. What's up? Are you settling in okay? How's the new job?" My brother's deep cheerful voice answered the first ring.

"More exciting than I expected. I'm sorry, Brad, but I don't have time to explain. I might . . . I might have news of Dad."

Silence.

"Brad?"

"Dad? You mean—"

"I don't know what I mean. I don't. I'll explain later, one way or another. Do you have a picture of him?"

"I'm at the office, and I've got nothing here or on my phone. Maya's home today." My sister-in-law was an ER nurse. "I'll give her a call and ask her to dig around in the box in the basement. I think I know where the picture Mom kept in a frame is. Would that do?"

"Yes. The most recent you can find."

"Recent is thirty-eight years ago, Nichie. You know that, right? People change."

"Thanks, Brad. If she could do it right away, I'd appreciate it. Cell phone reception's poor in the library, so if you need to talk send me a text, and I'll pop outside to make the call. I'll fill you in later on what's going on."

I tucked my phone into my pocket and stood still for a few minutes, thinking, remembering. I hadn't come to the Outer Banks hoping to somehow find my dad. Had my dad instead found me? Maybe the idea of reconnecting with his only daughter after so long did cause his heart to fail. If he continued drinking all these years in the amounts he had when he was with us, his heart couldn't have been in any sort of decent condition, and he was well over seventy.

Louise Jane claimed to know everyone worth knowing in the Outer Banks. I wanted to show her a picture and ask if she knew the man who had been my dad. If it was him, and not some sort of doppelganger.

Lucy opened the door. "Sorry to bother you, Nichelle, but the detective's here, and she wants a word."

Chapter Seven

Detective Rhonda Thomas did not smile when Lucy and I came into the break room. "Thank you, Mrs. McNeil. I'll talk to you later."

Lucy gave her a nervous smile. "Nichelle's new here, not only to the library but she moved to Nags Head yesterday. I'd like to stay."

"That will not be necessary. Please close the door on your way out."

Lucy's shoulders sort of slumped, and her head dipped. I wasn't entirely surprised. Rhonda Thomas was one intimidating woman. Her accent was straight out of the Bayous of Louisiana. She was even taller than me, easily five feet eleven, maybe six feet, of long lean muscle, her hair a halo of wild black curls tipped a light golden color. Her cheekbones were sharp, her eyes almost pure black, the smooth skin of her face a deep brown. She wore no makeup; her only jewelry a gold stud in her left ear lobe. Her pantsuit was plain dark brown worn over a white blouse done up to the top button. Low-heeled black boots were on her feet.

I felt hideously underdressed in my light summer dress.

"Mrs. McNeil, one thing," Detective Thomas said as Lucy turned to go.

"Yes?"

"I recall telling you on the previous occasion we met, I don't want or need civilian assistance on my cases. I hope you understood that."

"I did. Perfectly."

"Good. Then we have nothing to worry about, do we?"

Lucy closed the door behind her.

Thomas turned to face me. She took a notebook and pen out of her jacket pocket.

I slunk into a chair. I'd been a good student in school, never in any trouble. But there had been that time MaryJane Mallone dared me to throw a pencil at the teacher's back as she stood facing the board. The teacher turned just in time to see the projectile leaving my hand and heading her way. If she hadn't ducked it would have got her in the face. I was sent to the principal's office. The principal was bad enough, but when my mom was called away from work to come and get me because I'd been suspended, the look on her face had me truly terrified.

Almost as terrified as facing Detective Rhonda Thomas.

Obviously not one for introductory pleasantries, the detective said, "Mrs. McNeil informed me she arrived at the library at approximately eight-fifteen this morning to find you standing over a dead body on the front steps."

"I wouldn't say standing over."

"What would you say?"

"Finding? Discovering? Coming across?"

"But still standing next to. With. Over. In the presence of."

"Yes," I admitted.

"Mrs. McNeil said you are not from around here. Today's your first day at this job."

"That's right. I lived in Rochester, New York, until the day before yesterday."

"Why did you leave Rochester?"

"To take this job." I attempted to lighten the mood. "I wasn't fleeing the police."

She tilted her head to one side. "Why would you say that?"

"Sorry. Just making a joke."

"If you have any more jokes to make, please do so now, and then we'll get on with the business at hand."

"Sorry," I repeated. "I'm divorced, my children are adults and living on their own. I went back to college and earned a degree in library science. I came here to take this job. That really is it."

"Take me through the events of this morning. How you came to be finding or discovering this body."

I first explained why I'd been at the library so early in the morning, and why I opened the door from the inside.

"You live in the library?" She looked around the break room as though searching for a cot tucked away somewhere. "What, you sleep on the couch?"

"An apartment on the fourth floor. It's small but big enough to suit one person very comfortably. It goes with the job."

"Seems odd to me, but everything I've been told about this library leads me to believe the entire place is odd. Never mind. Continue."

There wasn't much to tell, and it didn't take me long to tell it. I finished, saying, "then Lucy arrived, and she called 911."

"You were in the building all night, yet you didn't hear anything?"

"Nothing. And I mean nothing, other than the cat moving around. I heard rain at some point, hitting the window. The walls are solid stone, and I was four floors up."

"What time did you last pass through the door to the outside?"

"I went out to explore in the late afternoon. I had dinner at a restaurant, but I didn't linger. It had been a long day. I got back here around seven, seven thirty. I went directly to my apartment and sent emails to some friends to tell them I'd arrived. I read for a while, and I went to sleep at nine-thirty. I know the time for sure, because I remember thinking I was getting old if I had a nine-thirty bedtime."

"Of the vehicles in the parking lot outside, only one hasn't been identified to me. The ownership of that car matches the ID found in the dead man's wallet. Name of Brian Saunders; address in Nags Head."

"Brian Saunders?" My dad's name had been Bradley Sanderson.

"Do you know anyone by that name?"

I shook my head.

"Did you recognize this man? Anything familiar about him?"

I must have hesitated because those eyes focused on me, and she said, "Ms. Gilcrest. I asked you a question."

I let out a long breath. "I . . . might have. I can't be sure. My father disappeared when I was sixteen. That man, outside, reminded me of him. The name you just said is . . . similar to his."

For the briefest of moments her impassive expression faded, and she blinked in surprise. "Is that so? What was your father's name?"

I told her, and she said, "You were sixteen? How long ago was that?"

"Thirty-eight years. My father has never been heard from since."

She blinked again. "Thirty-eight years? Tell me about your father's disappearance. Where did it happen?"

I told her what little I knew. "I phoned my brother shortly before you got here. He's going to send me a picture of our father. In case my memory's faulty. Can I check to see if it's come in?"

"Go ahead."

I had a message from Maya, Brad's wife. My fingers hesitated over the icon.

"Ms. Gilcrest?" Thomas said.

"This is tough, you know. If it is . . . was . . . my dad."

"I understand. But it has to be done." The first note of anything approaching warmth I'd heard in her voice.

I opened the message. I saw the picture I remembered from my mom's living room. My parents married young, and they had Brad almost right away and me a year later. When Dad disappeared, he'd been only thirty-nine, Mom a year younger. My father had been a good-looking man, although I hadn't realized it back then. His eyes were the same dark gray as mine, his smile wide and easy, his curly black hair thick and not yet touched with gray, but even then the signs of drink were starting to draw lines across his nose and put redness in the eyes.

Thomas held out her hand, and I put the phone in it. She studied the picture for a long time, and then she nodded. “Might be. Might not be. Lotta years have passed. The same eyes though.” She looked at me. “Your eyes.”

I nodded.

“Send me this picture, please.” She told me her number, and I did so.

“I understand you only had a quick glance at the deceased. Would you be willing to come to the hospital and take a better look?”

“If I must. Yes, I will. If it is . . . him, I need to know.”

“Do you know if your father had ever had any charges laid against him? Before he disappeared that is?”

I remembered my mom grabbing her things and running out of the house more than one late night. She never wanted to worry us, so she didn’t say what was happening, but Brad and I knew Dad had been taken down to the police station. He was never one to get into a fight, but he sometimes frequented the sort of bars where an impromptu brawl was considered part of the night’s entertainment, and he found himself caught up in the action. In those instances he was released to my mom and nothing more was said. He’d once been charged for drunk driving, but as it was his first offense, and he hadn’t been in an accident, he was lucky to be let off without jail time.

“Once I know of,” I said.

“Was this in Rochester, under the name Bradley Sanderson?”

“Yes.”

"Rochester might still have his prints on file. If so, we can do a comparison with the man you found here."

"My brother is also Bradley Sanderson of Rochester. I don't know if he's ever had any contact with the police."

"I'll mention that to them. Mr. Saunders was holding a small child's bracelet in his right hand. Did you see it?"

"I noticed some pink beads, yes. It seemed an unusual thing for a man to carry."

"I'm going to show you a photograph of it. Tell me if you recognize it."

I studied the photo carefully. A mass-produced, cheap child's trinket made of shiny pink beads on a string. I tried not to look at the open hand it was held in. "Nothing," I said at last. "It looks like a standard little girl bracelet of the sort you can get at any dollar store. If you're asking if it's mine, I might have had one like that when I was a child, but I have no memory of it. I don't own anything like that now, and there's no reason I should. My daughters are adults so they'd never want a gift like that. I don't have any grandchildren. Do you think it's more than it appears?"

"That is to be determined. As for now, I'm going to pay a visit to the address on his ID. If someone's there, I'll break the news and take them to identify him. If Mr. Saunders has a life history they can confirm, which doesn't match what you've told me of your father, I'll let you know. If not, then I'll need you to join me."

"Okay."

"In the meantime, I have to ask you not to leave Dare County without notifying me."

"I just got here," I said. "I'm not going to do a runner. I mean . . . I don't mean . . . I have no plans to go anywhere."

"See that you don't. If you remember anything more, such as leaving your apartment at any time during the night, you might want to consider telling me about it. Before I find out on my own."

She walked away. I stared after her.

Surely she didn't consider me to be a suspect?

She might. If my long-lost father had knocked on my door after thirty-eight years and said, "Surprise!" I would have laughed and cried and hugged him and demanded to hear everything. But Thomas was a police detective. To do that job she had to have a suspicious mind. Did she think instead of hugging him, I bashed him over the head, left him on the steps, and then pretended to find him the next morning in time for my new boss to witness my distress?

Not a good way to start my new life.

Chapter Eight

"Are you okay, Nichelle? If not, you can take the rest of the day off. Maybe go to the beach or explore the town. We have no patrons coming in today."

The newest employee of the Bodie Island Lighthouse Library sat in the breakroom, her head in her hands. She looked up and gave Lucy a weak smile. She wasn't crying but her eyes were wet.

"Thank you, but no, I'm fine. I have to make a good impression at my new job, right?"

"Right," Lucy said. "Don't worry about it, Nichelle. I have to confess, it's my first day too. Last week Bertie, Albertina James, the previous director, was here, and she helped me get myself sorted and settled in. Yesterday, she and her friend Eddie left for Italy. Starting her retirement in style she said. I'm on my own from now on. Coffee?"

"Thanks. I should be able to manage it now."

The pot had been recently refreshed, so Lucy took two cups out of the cupboard and poured. She took cream out of the fridge and held the container up in a question.

"Yes, please," Nichelle said. "Cream, no sugar."

Lucy handed the other woman the cup and sat down. “Honesty forces me to confess that regarding my new job, I have an advantage you don’t. I know the people I’m working with, and I know how we do things around here. They’re a good bunch, none better. We all have each other’s backs, all the time.” She chuckled. “Even Louise Jane.”

“Louise Jane. Was she serious about that paranormal stuff?”

“She was very serious. She has plenty of stories about all the different ways this lighthouse is supposedly haunted, but in all the time I lived here, I never sensed anything out of the ordinary. Well, maybe that one time.” Lucy decided not to expand any further on that and continued quickly, “But it happened around Halloween, so that doesn’t matter. Probably more to the point, Charles never appeared to sense anything out of the ordinary. They say animals have strong senses, right? Not that there’s anything for him to sense.”

“I guess,” Nichelle said, not sounding all that convinced.

“When Bertie first hired Louise Jane, she told her quite firmly that on no account is any of her so-called paranormal research or activity to be done on library time. I didn’t think she could stick to that promise, but she has. To her credit. The point I’m trying to make, and very badly it would seem, is you can count not only on the library staff but the volunteers and the patrons to be on your side. We all want you to succeed here.”

“Thanks. That means a lot to me. I ran my own business as a bookkeeper, doing the books for small and medium-sized companies. Not only did that mean I usually worked alone, but if anything showed up on the books the owners or managers didn't like, they were on the hunt for someone to blame. Who better than the messenger?"

"One of the nicest things about working in a library is the people we encounter in the day to day are genuinely friendly, part of the community, and wanting to be here. Having said that, obviously troublemakers can be found anywhere and everywhere, even here."

"I'm looking forward to getting to know people." Nichelle changed the subject suddenly. "I have a picture on my phone. Can I show it to you? In case you've seen him before?"

"Your dad?" Lucy asked.

"Yes. The most recent photo of him we have. My sister-in-law sent it to me. I gave it to Detective Thomas. It's obviously way out of date, but if you've been living here for a while you might . . ." Her voice trailed off.

Lucy held out her hand. "Let's see." She took her time studying the old photograph before handing it back with a shake of the head. "Unless he's changed a great deal, and more than as a result of age, I've not seen him before. I notice some definite resemblance to the man we found outside, but it's hard to be sure."

Nichelle nodded. "I don't know what to think. I guess all I can do is wait until the police positively identify the man. Maybe he just happens to look like my father."

Lucy said nothing; she let Nichelle think. The other woman had a lot to deal with right now. How hard must it have been for her family to simply lose their husband and father? To have him disappear without a trace. Obviously that was uppermost on Nichelle's mind right now, but what Lucy was most interested in was what had brought the man to the library steps so early in the morning. She reminded herself she didn't intend to start investigating. She had more pressing responsibilities now.

Hard not to think it all over though.

"What was that talk earlier?" Nichelle said. "You're all on a first name basis with the police officers, and everyone kept mentioning something about earlier incidents?"

"I was hoping you'd at least get a full day in here before hearing that," Lucy said. "In the past, the Lighthouse Library has had more than its share of involvement in police cases. As in any place so freely open to the public, stuff happens, but we've been particularly unlucky. As Louise Jane mentioned, I sometimes found myself trying to help. That is absolutely not a part of your job description. Which gives me an idea." She got to her feet. "If you don't mind sending me a copy of that picture, I'll ask Sam Watson, he's recently retired from the NHPD, if he remembers anything about your dad's case. What was your father's name?"

"Bradley Sanderson. Senior. My brother's name's the same."

"It would have been before Sam's time, but when he started working here some of the older officers might have still been talking about it. I assume the case was never closed. Sam might be able to find out some things your mother never told you." Lucy studied the face of the woman in front of her. "If you want to know. Do you?"

"I've spent a lot of years wondering, so yes, I think I do."

Chapter Nine

Before Lucy could move, a uniformed officer tapped lightly at the open door. "The detective's just called. She wants me to bring someone named Ms. Gilcrest to meet her at the hospital."

"That's me," I said.

"Let me introduce you," Lucy said. "Butch Greenblatt, this is our newest library staffer, Nichelle Gilcrest. Nichelle's from Rochester, New York, and she's taking my old job."

Butch stuck out one huge paw. His eyes were warm and his smile sincere. "Nice to meet you, Nichelle. You've got mighty big shoes to fill."

"So I fear," I said taking his hand. His grip was firm but not an attempt to crush any bones.

"Would you like me to come with you?" Lucy asked. "As moral support, I mean."

"Thank you, but no. I'll be fine. Detective Thomas said she might want me to have another look at the body." I counted my blessings the detective didn't want me brought to the police station.

"I'm here if you need me," Lucy said. "While you're doing that, I'll make the call I mentioned. If you need to talk after hours, feel free to call my personal number."

"But only before 8PM," Butch said. "Lucy has two brand-new babies and when they're that age, sleep is only thing their parents can think about. So my brother tells me anyway."

"Butch's brother, Jake, is married to my cousin, Josie," Lucy said. "You'll find we have all sorts of crossing relationships around here. Butch, it's almost noon now. If you have time, on the way back why don't you take Nichelle to Josie's to pick up some goodies for the staff and any of your colleagues who happen to pass through the library. My treat."

"We'll do that," Butch said. "You ready Ms. Gilcrest?"

"I guess I'll have to be," I said. "Please, call me Nichelle."

* * *

Josie's Cozy Bakery turned out to be one of the must-visit Nags Head destinations. A Seattle coffee house combined with OBX beach culture, it was full of great scents and loud conversation. The line to be served was long, but no one seemed to mind. Espresso machines hissed, staff called orders, wonderful scents drifted out from the back. The display counter was crammed full of plump, fruit-filled muffins, Danish pastries, cookies and tarts, and an assortment of packaged salads and sandwiches and wraps. As we shuffled forward, several people greeted Butch by name. More than a few gave me curious looks, obviously wondering what I was doing in the company of this young, handsome cop.

The ones who looked at me but didn't give me curious looks probably thought I was his mother.

When I'd arrived at the morgue, before going into the viewing room, Thomas told me no one had been at home at the address on Brian Saunders's ID. She had officers knocking on doors in the area, asking if anyone knew the man, but it was the middle of the day on a Monday, and most people wouldn't be home until evening.

The visit to the morgue had been unsetting, but not as bad as, despite my assurances to Lucy, I'd feared. Fortunately I didn't have to go into a stark white room and stand over the actual body, but I was able to view the face on a TV screen while Butch, Detective Thomas, and the pathologist watched me.

I spent a long time studying the face on the screen. The expression was calm, the eyes closed, for which I was grateful.

"I can't be absolutely sure," I said at last. "A lot of time has passed since I last saw my father. But, yes, it is possible. The resemblance is there." That was not entirely true. I was just about positive this man was my father. More than the looks, now faded with time and age, something about him spoke to me. I didn't say so. The police would have no interest in my instincts and emotions.

"Thank you," Detective Thomas said. "We'll be running the picture you gave me through aging software and that might help us determine if it is him. I contacted my colleagues in Rochester, and they're doing a search of their records for old fingerprints. That'll take some time."

"Do you know how he died?"

"I'm not at liberty to say at the moment. Let's let the pathologist finish her work first. Thank you, Officer Greenblatt. You can take Ms. Gilcrest back to the library now." She'd walked away before I could ask any more questions.

When Butch and I were back in the car, cardboard container of take-out coffee cups on my lap and a bag of cookies, tarts, and squares in the back seat, I asked him, "What happens now? About the scene at the library, I mean. When can we open?"

"That's up to the detective, and she'll make her judgment based on what the forensics people have to say. They're working in the main room now. If they find evidence the guy was inside the building last night, they'll want to search the whole place. If not, they might not need access much longer."

"Let's hope," I said. "What sort of evidence are they looking for?"

"It rained during the night, and the ground's muddy. He had some mud on his shoes. They'll be looking for things like lumps of that mud, shoe tracks, fingerprints on the furniture. They'll check his clothes for cat hair from Charles or a strand that matches carpet or furniture fabrics. Change of subject, about the book club."

"That is a dramatic change of subject. What about it?"

"My girlfriend, Steph, and I are members. Lucy sent out an email last week saying you were taking over and letting us know what you'd chosen for the inaugural meeting."

"Yes, she copied me on it."

"It's just . . . not another of those blasted Lord Peter books, please."

"Oh. You don't like classic mysteries?"

"I don't like Lord Peter Wimsey, to put it mildly. What a pompous idiot. We read *Busman's Honeymoon* a couple of years ago, and it was bad enough. Lucy explained that he has some residue of what we now call PTSD from his experiences in the war, so I cut him some slack, but I've started to read *Whose Body?*, and . . . let's say it's not making me like him more."

I struggled for something to say. I wanted my book club to love the books I chose as much as I did. Before I could ask if Butch wanted me to suggest another book, he said, "Just my opinion, for what that's worth. Steph's further on in the book than I am, and she says she's enjoying it. The plot's intricate and engaging. Me, I don't know if I can stand listening to the guy prattle on any longer to appreciate the plot."

"Perhaps that's something we can talk about at the meeting. Whether people today can relate to the style of writing of decades, even centuries past. Charles Dickens and many of his contemporaries were paid by the word, so they had a reason to drag it out."

"Plus people back then didn't have as many other distractions competing for their reading time—TV on and cellphones constantly beeping." Butch slowed to turn into the laneway. An officer was posted at the entrance, turning people away. Butch gave her a wave as we passed.

Two vans and a couple of police cars were still in the parking lot, along with the vehicles belonging to my colleagues. A woman was walking along the boardwalk, head down, moving slowly. I guessed there wasn't much left to search for on the front steps, so the investigation had gone indoors, as Butch told me it had, and spread throughout the immediate area. Yellow police tape posted at the bottom of the front steps fluttered in the wind.

"I'll help you carry our loot," Butch said. "We'll have to go around the back."

We put the treats on the break table and Butch opened the top box. "I'll let you in on a secret known only to everyone in the Outer Banks. Josie's pecan squares are just about the best thing you can get anywhere." He helped himself to a glistening, nut-studded pastry. The look on his face was one of blissful anticipation. Clutching his treasure, he made a move to leave, and then he abruptly turned around to face me. He hesitated.

I waited for him to compose his thoughts.

"This might seem way out of left field, but I meant it when I said Lucy has to have time with her family now."

"I know that."

He lifted a hand, still holding the pecan square. "You don't, not really. She had this way of getting involved in murders that happened around here. It wasn't a matter of being nosy or self-important, as some people implied, but she's smart and observant, and Detective Watson trusted her. He always said she had good instincts."

"And?"

"I don't really know what I'm saying, Nichelle, but if you notice anything or if you think of anything that might be important, talk it over with Lucy, after telling the detective, of course. But, please, don't let her go tearing off on a trail. She's put herself in danger more than once. Detective Thomas looks fierce, I know. I'm not saying there's a softie under that toughness, but she's a good detective, and her primary interest is going to be in solving this case. Oh, you better grab something for yourself. That mob out front would have seen us arriving with these bakery boxes, and soon enough they'll happen to find themselves needing to come in for a glass of water or something."

The plaintive sounds of Charles, begging to be released, came from the storage closet. "Would it be okay," I asked, "if I take the cat upstairs? You, the police I mean, aren't wanting anything there, are you?"

"I'll say one thing for Charles, and that's that he can be mightily persuasive," Butch said with a laugh. "He won't be any happier alone upstairs; he likes to be at the center of the action at all times, but go ahead."

Chapter Ten

My father disappeared before there was much in the way of social media, so I had no pictures, other than the one Maya sent me, to go through, trying to remember him. I didn't even have all that much in the way of memories. I'd been sixteen years old when he left, and when I look back on it now, to my regret I realize that I tried to simply forget him. Deep down, I always suspected he'd run out on us. It was tough for my mom—no death to mourn, no funeral to have, no certainty about what happened, always waiting, always wondering if he'd throw open the kitchen door one day and yell, "hey, gang I'm home," in the way he always did.

I spent Monday afternoon getting up to speed on the library's computer systems; taking care of social media and community information portals would be an important part of my job. Thankfully that gave me something to concentrate on so I could try to ignore the sounds of the police going about their duties. They didn't spend much time inside the building, which was a good thing—they found no indication the dead man had been in here at any time.

I worked at the table in the break room, keeping out of the police's way. Louise Jane popped in every now and again for a glass of tea. She gave me her personal phone number and told me to call her at any time—day or night—if I needed an "intervention."

I didn't want to ask what sort of intervention I might need in the middle of the night. I've never believed in ghosts, and I've never been the sort to be nervous when I'm on my own. I didn't want to start now, but I didn't know how to tell her I didn't want to hear about anyone (anything?) that might be haunting the lighthouse.

Shortly before quitting time, she came into the break room bearing a book, cover worn and tattered with use, pages yellowing with age. She put it on the table in front of me. "This is one of the best sources we have about historical hauntings in this part of the world. You can skip most of it, if you don't have a lot of time, but be sure to read the part about The Lady."

"What lady?" I asked, despite myself.

"The Lady. I always think of her with a capital T, capital L." Louise Jane tapped the cover of the book with her index finger. "She's the inhabitant most intimately connected to the apartment on the fourth floor. Her name was Francis, and she was brought here in 1872 after her marriage. A marriage she was forced into by her cruel father, to a man she didn't love, and when she objected to her confinement, she was locked inside that room by her much older and very jealous husband. The children of the town asked why no one would help *The Lady*, but the times were such—"

"Louise Jane." Ronald came into the break room, empty coffee cup in hand. "You're not supposed to be repeating those stories on library time."

"That was Bertie's rule," Louise Jane said. "Lucy hasn't mentioned it."

"I think we can safely assume, unless we hear otherwise, that what Bertie said and did, Lucy will continue doing. Same salary, same hours of employment, same rules against gossiping and spreading rumors." He took his cup to the sink and rinsed it out.

Louise Jane huffed. "I'm just giving our new arrival a book that might be of interest. OBX history, if you like. We are a library, Ronald. We exchange books. That's what we do here."

Ronald gave me a wink. "Books are fine, but don't try to personalize the stories, is all I'm saying. None of those treats left?"

I gestured to the trash can, from which the corners of a white box peeked out. "They were gone in a flash." Good thing I'd taken Butch's tip to heart and helped myself before the rush began. He was right: that pecan square was beyond amazing. "I am interested in learning more about the history of this area. I've been reading up on it since getting the job, but there's so much to learn. I'd love to talk to you sometime about that history."

Louise Jane gave Ronald a smirk. "See. The story of The Lady is intimately connected not only to this building but to the history of women's rights in previous centuries. She was confined here, by her husband, and she was powerless to do anything about it other than—"

"Other than throwing herself out the window," Ronald said. "Yes, we know the story."

I smiled to myself. Ronald and Louise Jane were clashing, but I sensed no animosity between them. Clearly, they were fond of each other, and equally clearly they were rehashing old territory. I got the sense of camaraderie from everyone I'd met so far, and it went a long way toward making me feel I'd made the correct decision in coming here and taking this job.

"Louise Jane gets a mite carried away sometimes," Ronald said.

"I do not."

"Up to you to listen to her or not, Nichelle. My wife, Nan, and I would love to have you around for dinner one night soon. Nan's away visiting her mom this week, so how about next week? Any day you're free?"

"I'd like that. I'm free every night, as it happens."

"Great idea," Louise Jane said. "It's sometimes hard to get to know people well in a work environment." She whipped out her phone and consulted the calendar. "How about next Thursday? Wednesday's my regular dinner with my great-gran at her residence, and Tuesday I'm giving a talk at the library in Duck. They, at least, have no objections to learning about paranormal history."

Ronald grinned at her. "You don't work for them, Louise Jane, and it's a one-time thing." He turned to me. "Now that we have Louise Jane's schedule, is Thursday next okay for you?"

"Great."

Louise Jane made a note on her phone.

Lucy came into the room. "I've had a call from Detective Thomas. She says pending no new developments, we can open the library tomorrow. They can find no evidence Brian Saunders," she gave me a quick glance, "or whatever his name is—was inside the building last night."

"That's good news," Ronald said.

"Why did you say 'whatever his name is'?" Louise Jane asked. "Is there some doubt?"

"That's a matter for the police to determine," Lucy said. "Nichelle, can you update the library's website, letting people know regular hours and activities will resume tomorrow. And then, I think we can all go home."

* * *

Following Lucy's directions, I went to a supermarket to pick up things I needed to stock the kitchen and pantry and make a start at turning the Lighthouse Aerie into my home. I was unpacking the groceries when my phone rang. I'd given my brother the landline number in the apartment for when he wanted to actually talk, not just text back and forth.

He got straight to the point. "How's it going? Any further news? Has the man been identified yet?"

"I've nothing to report," I said. "I haven't heard from the police again about the identity of the person I found. I'm starting to think I might have overreacted." That was true. As the day progressed, doubt began creeping into my mind, shoving aside the earlier confidence that I'd been correct about the man found on the library steps. I hadn't thought about my father for a long time, not until I decided to take this job and move to the Outer Banks. Had I been too eager to finally put an end to all the questions? Except, of course, whether he was my father or not, all I had now were more questions.

"First impressions are usually right," Brad said. "The ones our instinct tells us are true before we let the doubts crowd in. I'm coming down."

"You don't—"

"I know I don't have to. If this person turns out to be our father, I want to be there, and I don't think you should be dealing with it alone, that's all. I'm about to leave. Car packed, wife kissed, dog told to guard the house. I'll spend the night somewhere along the road and get to Nags Head early afternoon. You said your place is super tiny, so I've already booked a hotel for myself. Three nights at first, and then we'll see."

"I'm glad you're coming," I said, meaning it.

"Yeah," he said. "Me too."

Chapter Eleven

I didn't hear anything to the contrary, so the following morning, Charles and I were downstairs shortly after nine to switch off the alarm, put the coffee on, and boot up the computers.

That is, I turned off the alarm, put the coffee on, and booted up the computers. Charles investigated every patch of carpet in the main room, checking out evidence of the police's presence. Last night, I thought he might be mad at me for locking him in the apartment during the day, but as soon as I filled the food bowl and refreshed the water dish, any lingering resentment disappeared. Charles attended to, I'd heated up the take-out meal I bought for my dinner, and then he and I snuggled together in a comfortable armchair to watch a movie before bed.

Lucy arrived at the library not long after I came down. "You'll soon find that the majority of our patrons are fiercely loyal to the library," she said. "My office phone was ringing nonstop all yesterday, and when I got home, my own phone got so many calls, I had to switch it off. Word of what happened spread, as it does, and people care, so they want to know what's going on. This is by way of warning you I expect we'll be particularly busy this morning. If anyone asks you—and they will—about the police investigation, tell them you don't know anything."

"Which won't be difficult to do, as I don't know anything."

She smiled at me, her tired eyes full of concern. "Did you hear anything more from Detective Thomas about the possible identity of the man in question?"

I shook my head. "No. Nothing."

"These things take time."

I glanced past her out the window. "Some cars are pulling up outside."

"We can go ahead and open a few minutes early. As well as those wanting to hear all the news, many will be coming in to meet you. If you start to feel overwhelmed, ask Louise Jane or me to take the desk and escape to the break room for a few minutes."

"Thanks. I'm sure I'll be fine. I'm looking forward to getting to know everyone."

Lucy unlocked the door and two people walked in. Judging by their ages and the strong facial resemblance they were mother and son.

"Lucy," the man said. "I tried calling you last night but your phone must have accidentally been turned off."

"Strange how that happens sometimes," she said.

The woman snorted. "I told Teddy a new mother has better things to do with her evenings than talk on the phone."

"But it might have been important," the man protested. Her accent was pure North Carolina, but his was a strange sort of posh English that didn't sound entirely right.

"You haven't been in for a while, Mrs. Kowalski," Lucy said. "It's nice to see you."

The older woman didn't get a chance to reply before the man said, "Word's all over social media as well as the radio news. Brian Saunders died here. At the library."

He was rather an odd duck, I thought. Late thirties at a guess, but trying to look older. *Who does that?* He was slightly taller than me, very thin, with small dark eyes, dressed in a Harris tweed jacket, despite the Southern summer day. The stem of a pipe protruded from one pocket and an ironed and folded handkerchief from another. A strong aura of tobacco clung to his clothes. He looked past Lucy and studied me through thick lenses. "Ah hah, you must be the new librarian. Excellent. Welcome, welcome to our jolly little community." He marched toward me, smiling broadly, hand outstretched. I stood and took it. Wet fish came to mind.

"Theodore Kowalski," he announced. "Of Nags Head. Allow me the honor to present my mother, Loretta Kowalski." The older woman gave me an informal wink. Her eyes danced with amusement.

"I'm Nichelle Gilcrest," I said. "Pleased to meet you, ma'am, Mr. Kowalski."

"We don't stand on formality here, Michelle," he said. "Isn't that correct, Lucy?"

"That's right, and her name isn't Michelle but Nichelle. With an N."

He blinked rapidly. "Oh. Please accept my apologizes."

Loretta laughed. "*Star Trek* isn't one of my Teddy's areas of expertise, but it is mine. Were you named after the actress?"

"I was."

"I heartily approve! It's lovely to meet you. I hope you enjoy it here. I've lived in Nags Head my entire life, anything you need to know, I'm happy to help."

"Everyone's been so kind," I said.

"We've come in for a reason," Theodore said. "Apart from meeting Nichelle, of course. We find ourselves in need of your sage advice, Lucy. I insist Mother should go to the police, but she's reluctant. She doesn't want to bother them."

"It isn't bothering them if you have something they need to know," Lucy said. "About what?"

"Brian Saunders. Mother knew him."

That caught my attention. "Did you know him well, Loretta? How long for?"

"Not well, no, and not for long, and that's why I don't want to bother the police. We . . . met on one or two occasions, that's all."

Lucy lifted her hands. "My days of involving myself in police matters are over. I don't have any advice, sage or not, to give, except that if Brian Saunders lived in Nags Head, which it seems he did, he would likely know a great many people. Do you know something in particular that might be relevant to his death?"

"No, I do not. And that is my point exactly," Loretta said triumphantly. "See, Teddy, I told you so."

Theodore looked as though he was about to argue, but before he could get another word out, the door opened, and a woman came in. Something approaching panic crossed Lucy's usually cheerful face before she quickly replaced it with a smile. "Maureen. How nice to see you."

"Not another murder," the new arrival said. "Really Lucy, I dared to hope that with you in charge, things would calm down around here."

My boss's smile remained firmly fixed in place. "Maureen, please let me introduce you to our new assistant director, Nichelle Gilcrest. Nichelle, Maureen Peterson is one of our most dedicated volunteers."

The new arrival nodded to me. "Nice to meet you, Michelle. Now, Lucy, what -?"

"Are you on the roster today, Maureen? If so, speak to Nichelle, that's with an N, about your duties. She'll be in charge of the friends of the library group."

"I don't have a shift today, no, but I have some ideas about programming for the early teenagers to run past you and Ronald. It's so hard to keep their attention, isn't it? My Phoebe will be part of that cohort this year, how time passes. Call Ronald, will you and we can have a quick chat."

"He's not due to come in until noon today," Lucy said.

Maureen's face fell, but she didn't let that small matter deter her. "Never mind. I'm here now. I'll tell you what I have in mind, and you can tell Ronald what we've decided. Nice meeting you, Michelle. Loretta, we must have that coffee date one day soon." She almost dragged a reluctant Lucy out of the room.

Loretta Kowalski said, "Not if I have something to say about it."

"I'm looking forward to the book club," Theodore said. "I approve of the switch to classic mysteries. I myself love little more than the classics. By the way, here's my card." He pulled a square of paper out of his breast pocket and handed it to me: Theodore Kowalski. Rare and Collectable Books, Maps, and Papers. "Some modern readers, no names of course, find the classics too long and too dense, and as a result the club has been slowly losing members. I trust you'll get it firmly back on track. Lord Peter Wimsey has always been a favored character of mine. Such a man of his times, hovering uncertainly between the ancient aristocracy and modernity, yet managing both smoothly. *Whose Body?* is the first in that series, did you know that? It's about not one but two men who disappear and there is some confusion over—"

"She suggested the book, Teddy," Loretta said. "Of course she knows. I put a hold on the new Vicki Delany book last week. Is it going to be much longer, Nichelle?"

"I'll check," I said. "But first, if I may . . . you said you knew Brian Saunders. Were you friends?"

"I wouldn't say friends, not really. We . . . uh . . ." she fumbled for the words. "We went out, together I mean, on a couple of occasions. Nothing important, mind. A casual and very short-lived relationship. I don't mind saying, that was enough for me."

I blinked at the sudden sharpness of her words. "How so?"

She colored slightly. "I'm a bit embarrassed to say, but we met on a . . . dating app."

"Entirely against my advice," Theodore said.

"As you never fail to remind me, dear. Why don't you run along and have a look through the books while Nichelle and I get acquainted."

"Perhaps I'll join Lucy and Maureen. I have some knowledge of books young people might enjoy, they'll appreciate hearing." He toddled off.

"Not that many teenagers are likely to want to read the adventures of Lord Peter Wimsey," Loretta said. "Never you mind my Teddy, Nichelle. He puts on that ridiculous English accent and dresses that way thinking it makes him look more like a serious rare book dealer. He doesn't smoke either, but occasionally he lights that pipe and waves it around his closet to capture the scent."

I laughed. "I'm going to like it here."

"As for your question. Yes, I went out on a date, twice, with Brian Saunders. We didn't exactly hit it off. He's considerably older than I am, but at my age one can't be fussy."

Loretta was in her early to mid to sixties, ten years older than me, maybe. I didn't take offense. I'd learned that dating detail as soon as my divorce was finalized, and I cautiously dipped my toes into the dating pool. Where they didn't remain for long.

"Although," Loretta went on, "it does look as though I can afford to be fussy after all. He wanted to see me again, but I decided best not to."

"May I ask why? I know it's none of my business, but . . . I'd rather not say, not yet, but I might have a personal involvement with the matter."

"Not a problem. I never married; Teddy's my only child, and I've always been happy on my own. But Teddy's getting older, he has a lovely lady in his own life now, and I thought I might like to meet someone to spend my later years with. I can't really say, not exactly, why I didn't want to see Brian again. He was a good-looking man and perfectly pleasant company. We had dinner at a couple of nice places, each paying our own bill, although I did think he took rather too long before pulling out his wallet. Something was just . . . off about him. Too pushy maybe. I sensed an aura of desperation around him."

"Desperation?"

"Desperate to connect. I might have been wrong, but my instincts told me he'd settle for any woman with a pulse, and that's not exactly flattering, is it?"

"It most definitely is not. How did he react when you told him you didn't want to see him again?"

"In a way that surprised me. As though he was almost relieved. Obviously I was wrong about the desperation, but I don't regret my decision. As I said, he was nice enough, but . . . off."

"I'm a great believer in trusting your instincts," I said, remembering what my brother said to me only last night. "You did the right thing. When was this?"

"Little under a year ago. I remember because the restaurant we went to the second time was quiet, and the waiter said it was nice to see the back of the summer crowds."

"Mid-September then," I said.

"Nags Head's a small town, but not that small. I never saw Brian again. It came as a shock to hear his name on the radio yesterday morning. For all that we no longer had contact, I was sorry to hear about his death. If you hear anything regarding funeral arrangements, Nichelle, can you let me know?"

"I don't know if anyone will tell me, but if I do hear, I will." I wanted to ask Loretta if she'd ever been to Brian's house, what he shared with her about his life and his family, but I didn't get the chance. The door opened once more and people began streaming in. A few asked for Lucy, and I told them she was in a meeting. Several introduced themselves to me and said they were pleased to meet me. Some asked what I knew about what happened to Brian Saunders, and I was able to truthfully tell them I didn't know anything.

A woman dropped a laden book bag on the circulation desk with a puff of effort.

"Obviously you have work to do," Loretta said to me. "I'll leave you to it. Now, where did that boy of mine get to?"

Chapter Twelve

I enjoyed my first day of "real" work. As Lucy had warned me, we were busy for a Tuesday. People wanted to meet me and that gave me a good feeling.

I was going to like it here. I just knew it.

And then, mid-afternoon, Detective Thomas paid a call.

She was dressed in another plain, dull suit, not in uniform, and she hadn't brought an officer with her, but no one would ever have any doubt she was with the police. She walked with determination, and she held herself as though ready to leap into action at any moment. She kept her face expressionless, and her dark eyes moved constantly around the room, watching everyone and everything.

Heads popped out from behind book racks, ears lifted to hear better. A rush of people suddenly needed to look at the books closest to the circulation desk. Even Charles appeared out of nowhere and sniffed at her boots. The detective looked down, and the slightest of smiles appeared at the corners of her mouth before she recovered and wiped it away.

"Good afternoon," she said to me in that smooth Louisiana accent. "I wonder if I can have a few minutes of your time, Ms. Gilcrest."

I felt myself blushing at the sudden attention everyone in the room was giving me. "I'm . . . working . . . I . . . uh . . ."

"I'm sure you can get one of your colleagues to take over here. If not . . ." she glanced around her, "it will be necessary to close the library for the remainder of the day."

"But I haven't finished looking through the books that came in since I've been away." A patron pointed to the wall of shiny new hardcovers. "I spent most of the last two months visiting my daughter. She lives in Las Vegas now, why anyone would want to live there, I cannot imagine. But never mind that now, her decision. Anyway she—"

Thomas focused her intense brown eyes on the speaker. She didn't say a single word, but the woman ducked her head and crept away saying, "I'll have a quick glance at the display, shall I? Won't be long."

"Detective Thomas." Lucy came into the room. "What can we do for you?"

"I need to have a private talk with Ms. Gilcrest."

"Not a problem. Nichelle, I'll take over the desk. Mrs. Cunningham," she said to a hovering woman, "do you have a problem you need assistance with?"

"No, no, nothing at all. Just wanting to welcome the new staff person." Mrs. Cunningham had introduced herself not more than five minutes ago. She scurried back to the safety of the shelves.

"You can use the break room if you like," Lucy said. "Louise Jane made a fresh pitcher of tea not long ago. Help yourselves."

I stood up. Detective Thomas indicated I should proceed her. I did so, conscious of her firm steps behind mine and the eyes of everyone in the library on me. I didn't know why I was so nervous. I had nothing to fear. I didn't kill the man.

I took a seat at the table. Thomas closed the door, but not before Charles slipped nimbly around her legs.

"Nice cat," she said.

"He is," I replied, trying to begin the conversion in a light and friendly manner as befits someone who doesn't have a thing in the world to worry about when speaking to the forces of law and order. "Do you have a cat?"

"I am not here to discuss preference in pets." That put me firmly in my place. "First, Ms. Gilcrest, I need to inform you that the fingerprints we got from Rochester of one Bradley Sanderson Senior match those of the man we have identified as Brian Saunders of Nags Head."

Her words came like a punch to the gut. I sucked in a breath. I felt tears in my eyes. I shouldn't have been surprised; I'd thought the man I found on the library steps was my long-lost father. But it was a shock to actually hear the words, to know the questions that had hung over me all of my adult life were finally being answered.

No, not answered. Only one question was answered. All the whys and the hows were still to come. I thought of my mom, never knowing, always wondering. For years, she'd see the back of a man's head walking swiftly through the mall, or catch a glimpse of a profile driving past, and be sure it was her husband. On more than one occasion, she ran after the man, only to be embarrassed when it turned out to be someone else.

And here he'd been all the time. Living—happily or not—in Nags Head, North Carolina.

I was so wrapped in my thoughts, I hadn't heard the detective open the fridge and get out the tea. "Take this," she said in a voice that might have contained a touch of sympathy. She handed me a glass. I accepted it with a nod of thanks. Charles jumped into my lap, and I stroked the soft fur with my free hand. He didn't purr, and he didn't settle down for a nap. He sat up straight and kept his eyes focused on Detective Thomas.

"We ran the picture of your father you sent to me through aging software, and it created a good likeness of this so-called Mr. Saunders, but the fingerprints are definitive enough. I have to ask again, you didn't know your father was here, living under an assumed name?"

"Not a clue." I dug my fingers into Charles's warm thick fur. He purred.

"I trust you'll want to inform your family."

"I spoke to my brother last night." I hadn't said anything to my daughters yet. I wanted to be absolutely positive before doing that. "He'll be arriving soon. My mother died five years ago. My paternal grandmother died only a few weeks before Dad disappeared; my grandfather long before that."

"Is that so? Did anyone ever think it might not have been a coincidence that his mother died and then he disappeared so soon after?"

"It wasn't a coincidence at all. He used some of the money she left him to go on the fishing trip that brought him here."

"We've been asking around about Brian Saunders, speaking to his neighbors, people at places he regularly frequented. He lived in Nags Head for many years. He never married.

Until very recently, he worked at Gardner's Beach Supply store in town, where he'd been employed for five years. His landlord reports that he was a reliable tenant, paid his rent on time. His employer said much the same, although the job was casual, with not many hours in the off season. He has no police record, which makes sense if he was pretending to be someone he wasn't. He'd keep his nose clean as he couldn't risk being printed. He kept himself largely to himself, but he did have some friends. Drinking buddies, mostly, people he hung out at a bar with. Single men of that age don't really have friends otherwise, do they?"

I didn't know anything about the living habits of single men my dad's age, but I shook my head anyway. The person Thomas was describing didn't sound anything like my father—friend to everyone, the life of the party, always spreading around whatever money he had. He'd been living on the pay from a seasonal retail job at seventy-seven?

"No one we've spoken to can say what brought him to the library on Sunday night. His girlfriend told us he wasn't a reader; he would have had no reason to visit the library, particularly not late at night when it was closed. He wasn't, according to people we spoke to, any sort of nature lover or birder, so he wasn't here to look at birds."

That, at least, sounded like Dad. My mom had been a voracious reader. Dad glanced at the sports pages in the newspaper now and again, but that was about it. Then I realized what else the detective had said.

"His girlfriend? He had a girlfriend?"

"A woman he was dating. According to her, at any rate. They didn't live together; she heard we were inquiring about him on social media and contacted us. She said they each liked their own space." She watched my face as she spoke, looking for clues, watching for lies, judging me.

"Did you tell her about . . . his real name?"

"Not yet. I wanted to inform you first."

"Thank you for that. Do you think I could meet her?"

"I'll be speaking to her again, now that we have this further information. If you'd like me to, I can tell her about you. Ask if she wants to meet."

"Maybe not right away. This is all just too much to handle, and I'd like to talk things over with my brother first."

Thomas's dark eyes stared into mine for what felt like forever. I tried not to shift in my chair. The cat firmly planted in my lap gave me something to do with my hands. At last the detective said, "Do you still maintain you haven't seen your father for many years, and you never met the man calling himself Brian Saunders here in Nags Head or anyplace else?"

"No. I mean yes. Absolutely, I maintain that."

"I'll want to talk to your brother when he arrives. Please give him my number."

I nodded. "This girlfriend. How long have they been together?"

"Why are you asking?"

"I'm wondering if she's the reason he left us." Did he meet her on his fishing trip and decide not to come back to Rochester? To cut his wife and family adrift and run off with another woman? Without so much as a word?

"Obviously, as we have no idea at this time what happened to your father all those years ago, I can't say why he decided to disappear. But I can tell you the woman we spoke to says they've been together a little over a year. She's not old enough to have known your dad back then, anyway, Nichelle. She's younger than you. Forty-nine."

"Really?"

"No accounting for taste," the detective said. Although she might have been talking to herself as much as to me.

"How did he . . . my dad . . . How did he die? Did the autopsy say?"

"Blunt force trauma. He was hit on the back of the head with a metal object."

"So he was murdered?"

"I am working on that assumption, yes. No defensive wounds, so it would appear either he didn't hear his attacker coming or that person was someone he knew and willingly turned his back on."

"He was . . ." I swallowed, "face up when I found him." Those gray eyes, staring at me without seeing me.

"Likely his assailant needed to make sure he was gone. I'm sorry to have to give you those details. It can be hard to deal with, I know."

"You have your job to do."

"I do."

"There's no chance it was an accident, then? That he tripped and fell, or something?"

She shook her head. "None. We've extensively searched the grounds around the lighthouse for the object used, but found no sign of it. I have little expectation it will be found. Almost certainly the assailant took the weapon with them and tossed it into the sea at the first opportunity where, if it's heavy enough, it will sink to the bottom. If it, whatever it is, does eventually wash up to shore, whoever finds it will likely put it in the trash with all the other debris collected every day. Blood was on the library steps where he fell, but that fall did not cause the initial injury. I'll be off. Make sure your brother calls me as soon as he gets to town."

"Did he have a phone on him? Or in his car?"

"Yes, and our techies are at work on it now. I have no updates as to what they've found, not yet."

"What about that pink child's bracelet? Any significance to that?"

"Not that I know of. At first, I thought it might be of some value, maybe containing real stones under the beaded covering, but nope. Just a trinket you can buy at a dollar store any day of the week for a buck ninety-nine."

"Can you tell how old it is?"

"It's cheap enough it would have started to disintegrate after a few months, so not old by any means. We're keeping that detail under wraps for the time being, so I'd prefer if you don't discuss it with anyone."

"I won't."

"Thank you for your time, Ms. Gilcrest. I'll be in touch when I have further news."

She left. I cradled the cold glass of tea in my hands. This was all so overwhelming. I was glad Brad was coming. We needed to be together.

Charles jumped off my lap and headed out the door. I started to push myself to my feet. I had a job to do, and I needed to get back to it. I could take the time to analyze what I'd learned later.

But one thought had me dropping back down.

If this Brian Saunders had been in a relationship with a forty-nine-year-old woman for more than a year, why on earth had he'd been on a dating app where he connected with Loretta Kowalski eleven months ago? Loretta said he seemed almost desperate for a relationship, yet relieved when she told him it was off.

I sighed. Unlikely I'd ever know.

Chapter Thirteen

Brad texted me later in the afternoon to say he'd run into bad traffic on the route and would be delayed. He'd let me know when he arrived in the Outer Banks.

Not long after that a man came into the library. He was in his well-preserved—very well preserved—mid-fifties, tall and lean, with a square face and a lantern jaw, graying hair cut very short, and a nose like a hawk's beak.

Not only because of his good looks, he caught my attention because men of that age don't often come into a library on their own. They're usually with their wives or in the company of children.

I most certainly had not come to Nags Head to meet a man, but almost despite myself, I fluffed my hair and sat slightly straighter behind the circulation desk.

"Sam, hi! So nice to see you." Ellen O'Malley, introduced to me as Lucy's aunt and a staunch supporter of the library, wheeled the empty returns cart back to the desk. She abandoned the cart and gave the new arrival a big hug. "How's retirement suiting you?" she asked once she released him.

"CeeCee tells us you're loving it, but I don't know if she's an impartial witness."

"I won't say loving it, but it's all good. So far. We had a great trip to Australia over the winter. Lifetime dream of mine to see Australia, and it was great to be able to spend all the time we wanted on the vacation without having to hurry back to work." He grinned. "All the time we could afford, I should say. Not always the same."

"What brings you here today, Sam?"

He turned toward me with a smile that almost had my heart aflutter. I smiled back and tried not to touch my hair again. "Lucy called me. She thought I might be able to help your new assistant director." He took a step forward and held out his hand. "Sam Watson. You must be Nichelle. Welcome."

I stood up and held out my own hand and we shook. "Thank you. I'm pleased to meet you." Sam Watson. This must be the retired detective Lucy said she'd contact on my behalf.

"I'll let Lucy know you're here," Ellen said.

"No need," Lucy came into the main room of the library. "I'm here."

I was beginning to wonder if Lucy had either highly developed senses or had secret cameras installed around the library. Her office didn't face the parking lot or the front path, but she seemed to be able to pop up whenever she was needed. "Let's go to my office. Ellen, can you take the desk?"

"Happy to."

Sam Watson and I followed Lucy to her small, overfurnished, crowded office and took seats. A painting of a woman doing a downward dog on the beach at sunset hung on the wall behind the desk. The desk itself was piled high with folders and documents, books, accounting ledgers, scraps of scribbled-on paper, two empty coffee mugs, and a half-full glass of water. A single photo occupied pride of place amongst the clutter. Lucy and a handsome man about her age, beaming smiles competing with tired eyes, each of them holding a sleeping baby wrapped in a blue blanket.

"You kept Bertie's painting," Sam said.

"I did. She offered it to me. I love it, and it reminds me of my first day here. Sitting where you are now, while she invited me to take the job, and all I could do was look at that picture. Here I am talking as if I'm the one who's recently retired and remembering my glory years, but it wasn't that long ago when I first came here, was it?"

"Plenty of things have changed since then. Before we start a long stroll down memory lane, and bore Nichelle silly, let's get to the point of my visit."

"Go ahead," Lucy said. "Nichelle, Sam was the lead detective for the NHPD for many years. I asked him to find out what he could about your father's case."

"Thank you for doing that," I said.

"Happy to help," he said. "Despite trips to Australia, retirement does have its drawbacks and boredom can be one of them."

"I hear something about an art tour to Italy in the fall," Lucy said with a smile.

"Australia was my dream. The great art museums of Italy are CeeCee's. That's my wife," he added redundantly for my benefit.

I tried not to look too disappointed. As I said, I didn't come here looking for a man.

"First, Nichelle, I need to ask if you really want to dig into all of this. I am aware that the man who was found dead here yesterday, going by the name of Brian Saunders, is almost certainly your father, Bradley Sanderson Senior, reported missing to the NHPD back in 1988. Before I continue, I'll mention that nothing in the police reports from that time indicates he was suspected of being involved in any illegal activity, but hearing the details can be distressing all the same."

"I'm aware of that," I said. "And I thank you for your concern. Before yesterday, I would have said no, I didn't come here to Nags Head for any reason other than to take a promising job. I had no intention of trying to find out anything to do with my dad. I put his disappearance behind me a long time ago. But," I took a deep breath, "considering he was here, literally on my doorstep when he died, I can't help but think he was coming to see me. And thus, maybe he wanted me to know what happened all those years ago." I said nothing about the child's bracelet he'd been holding, but I couldn't help but think it was intended to be some sort of peace offering to me. I am not ten years old anymore, but it's possible I once had a similar one, long forgotten by now, but my father still remembered it, all these years later. If I did own such a thing, it would have been nothing more than one small piece of all the clutter little girls gather and soon throw out when something else attracts their attention. It no longer had the slightest significance for me. Had it for my father?

"I understand." Sam's smile was kind. "Okay, all this happened well before my time on the force, and there's no one around anymore who worked on the case. People retire and die or move away, but the records remain, so I was able to have a look through them. Bradley Sanderson Senior, age thirty-nine, and four male friends of approximately the same age, all of Rochester, New York, came to Nags Head supposedly on a fishing vacation. They booked three rooms for four nights at the Sportsman's Motel, which no longer exists. On the first full day of their visit, they went out on a chartered fishing boat. The crew of the boat reported nothing of note happened, except that they thought the men were more interested in beer than in fish, but that's not entirely unknown."

"My mom was surprised when Dad said he was taking his friends fishing. He'd never fished before, far as we knew."

"It's an important male bonding experience," Lucy said. "Or so I've been told."

Watson chuckled, and continued, "The second day, according to the friends, they went their separate ways. Three of the men, including your father, used the car they'd rented and drove down to Ocracoke. That's an island, only accessible from here by a regular ferry from Hatteras. We never found any evidence they'd done anything other than visit the island, have lunch, and come back. The other two men said they hung around near their motel, had a beach day, which they openly admitted included lunch and a lot of drinks at a pier-side bar. The men met up around six for dinner and some barhopping; all five of them were together for the rest of that day.

"Day three, another fishing charter. The crew of that boat reported the same as the earlier one had. Not much fish, lots of beer. The crew were interviewed separately, and they all claimed the five men left the boat together. They'd noticed no tensions or arguments between the men. And they would have if such had happened on one of those small charter boats."

"Was there any question that one of his friends, or all of them, might have done away with Sanderson?" Lucy asked.

"It's always a question, Lucy, but nothing the investigating detective found pointed to it. They questioned the staff at the hotel where the men were saying and some of the bars they visited. No disagreements, no fights. If anything, the men appeared to be enjoying their vacation. The friends all reported that nothing seemed to be on Sanderson's mind but having a good time."

Lucy threw me a look, before reluctantly saying, "I have to ask, and I'm sorry Nichelle, but was there any indication any women . . . shall we say . . . joined the party?"

"None. The question was asked. The men stated that they didn't interact with anyone, male or female, on a personal level, other than to exchange sports news with a bartender or two, and they spent no time with anyone who hadn't come from Rochester with them.

"One thing of note—the full cost of the trip, the flight, the car rental, all the hotel rooms, boat charters, and much of the meals and bar tabs went on Sanderson's credit card."

"He'd recently inherited money from his mother and used some of it to treat his friends," I said.

"Yes, your mother told the detectives about that. They were initially suspicious of her, I have to point out. Wondering if she might have been angry that he spent the money on himself and his friends. Your parents were not well off financially."

"They were not," I said.

"A murder investigation," Lucy said, "and I suppose one into a disappearance, churns up a lot of muck the family would rather not know."

"I remember Mom going down to Nags Head when she got the news. She came back, as you'd expect, very upset. It was a tough time. I was sixteen, not exactly the best age to be sympathetic to what my mother was going through." I didn't mention that, thanks to Dad putting his inheritance into a joint account, Mom didn't have money worries any more. The bank froze the assets for a while, but eventually it released them when the police report concluded accidental death while under the influence.

"Your mother was almost immediately cleared as a suspect, Nichelle," Sam said. "Her alibi was solid for the time your dad disappeared. She was a night attendant at a seniors' home, right?"

"One of her jobs, yes."

"She was at work that night—other staff members and several residents confirmed that. It was speculated that she could have hired a hit man, but never seriously. The provenance of your grandmother's inheritance was clear, and nothing had been withdrawn from it. Otherwise, your mother clearly didn't have that sort of money. Or any way of getting it."

"The police were thorough," Lucy said.

"Might have been some political pressure. Never looks good when a tourist simply walks into the water and disappears. Back to events. On the last night of their vacation, the men went out barhopping once again, but they didn't stay too late. They had an early start the next morning to catch their flight. Sanderson's four friends told the detectives they said goodnight in the lobby of the hotel and went to their rooms. The next morning, he didn't come down; he didn't answer the phone in his room, so they had the hotel check. The bed wasn't slept in. His clothes were still in the closet, his toiletries in the bathroom, his wallet on the dresser. All that seemed to be missing was the clothes he had on earlier and his bathing suit, along with the room key. The police closed the investigation saying he went for a late night swim and, under the influence of alcohol, he was swept away by the rip tides. The coast guard searched but, as we know, he was not found."

"Does that happen?" I asked. "Rip tides?"

"It does. They can be strong here."

"What about his clothes?" Lucy said. "If he went swimming he must have taken them off. Were they ever found?"

"No. He might have worn them into the water. If he left them on the beach, someone might have grabbed them. They might have drifted out on a wave and never reported found."

We were quiet for a long time. I thought of the sea and the beach as I saw them from my fourth-floor window. Open, wide, windswept, largely empty, surf pounding the sand. Dark, dark nights.

"And now," Lucy said, "it's a murder inquiry. All these years later. Do you know anything about how that's going, Sam?"

"Not officially. I don't ask and Detective Thomas doesn't tell me. I hear things though, and they're looking closely into what Brian Saunders has been up to in the last thirty-eight years. From what I hear, not much. He lived alone and never came to the attention of the police, not officially anyway."

"Unofficially?"

"I didn't mean that, no. I just meant no charges were ever laid. As for the ongoing case, early days yet."

"I hate not knowing," I said. "Not knowing *again*. For thirty-eight years, I haven't known what happened to my father. And now, I don't know who killed him or why anyone would want to."

And I still didn't know why he left us, without saying a word.

* * *

While I'd been with Lucy and Sam Watson, my brother texted to tell me he'd arrived on the Outer Banks and was heading to his hotel. Before relieving Ellen, I slipped outside to return the call. Brad answered on the first ring.

"I'm pulling up to the hotel now," he said. "What time do you get off work?"

"I finish at five today, and I can leave right away. Send me the directions to your hotel, and I'll come there."

"Okay. I have to say, don't expect too much. I went online and grabbed the first room I could find. It's not far from the beach, though."

"This isn't a vacation, Brad."

"I know, Nichie. I know."

"I have something to tell you, and I might as well do it now."

"They've confirmed it's Dad?"

"Fingerprints on the dead man match Dad's from back in Rochester."

Silence came down the line. I said nothing, letting him process the news. Then he said, "I'll send you those directions," and he hung up.

Chapter Fourteen

Brad and I went to dinner at a nondescript beach bar not far from his hotel. The restaurant was noisy with rock music turned up too loud, young men and women in surfing shorts and beach dresses calling for more drinks and shouting at each other. But we didn't care. We had serious things to talk about and didn't want to be overheard. Brad ordered a hamburger and a beer, and I asked for a white wine and hush puppies. He wiggled his eyebrows at me when the waitress left with the menus. "Going native? Already?"

"Might as well try the whole OBX experience. Hush puppies are supposedly a regional specialty, and they do sound good." I smiled at my brother, and he smiled back.

"You okay, Nichie?" It struck me at that moment how much Brad looked like our father in the picture I'd recently seen. Good looking men, both of them. Dad had been approaching forty, and Brad was now fifty-five, but they looked closer in age as Brad was thinner and fitter, and he didn't have the slightly puffy face that marked our father as a serious drinker. But he did have the same thick curly hair, although his was turning gray now, the same strong jaw, and wide mouth. The eyes were different though. I got my dad's eyes, but Brad's were the soft hazel of our mother's.

"I'm okay," I said. "Obviously this is all unexpected and unsettling but I can cope. It was one thing when we thought Dad was dead, even though Mom always refused to accept it, but now . . . I keep wondering why, why he left us, but I'm old enough not to take it personally. If he and Mom had issues I didn't know about, it wasn't me . . . you and me . . . he left."

"Have you spoken to Isabelle and Simone?"

"I called them each after work, before leaving to meet you. I didn't get Isabelle, but I spoke to Simone, and she said she'd tell her sister what's happening. She offered to come down, but I said no. What could she do? Hold my hand? For how long? It might be another thirty-eight years before we find out what happened to him this time."

"Maya said much the same to me. If my father abandoned Mom and us, it's all on him. Not Mom. Not us."

"How's Maya doing?" I asked. "Is she managing okay with all her new responsibilities?" My sister-in-law and I had been close even before she married my brother. I'd wanted to spend some extra time with her before I left Rochester, but things simply got ahead of us, as they do. My packing up to leave; her promotion. My kids. Her kids.

"Fine." Brad's eyes slid away from mine, and he looked almost relived when the waitress put our drinks on the table.

"To new beginnings." Brad lifted his glass and we clinked. I decided I must have been imagining the wariness that had briefly come over him at mention of Maya.

When Dad had still been around, my brother had been an angry young man, determined to set himself on a path my mother worried would come to no good. Even then, I knew he was rebelling against Dad. He'd get furious when Dad bought me or Mom treats he couldn't afford, or when he came in late at night from being with his so-called buddies. About six months before he disappeared, Dad lost his job at a hardware store. Brad was so angry, I thought they'd come to blows. They likely would have, had not Mom stepped between them. Brad stormed out of the house and didn't come back for three nights.

He was seventeen, running with a bad crowd, and failing all his classes. The despair of his mother, but all Dad could say was, "Boy'll come 'round. Reminds me of me at that age."

That was exactly what Mom had been afraid of.

Then Dad disappeared, and Brad changed almost overnight. No one ever asked him to be the "man of the house" but he took on that role. The sullen, angry teenager left and the responsible young man took his place. He dropped many of his friends, finished school with good grades, and went to college, much to Mom's pride. He landed a good job, married a nice woman, and they had two great kids.

He looked at me across his beer. He looked twenty years older than when I'd seen him last, and likely he was thinking the same about me. Grief, they say, ages you. Delayed grief compounded by shock can only age you faster.

"Have you ever thought, Nichie, how lucky we were that Dad left us?"

Many times, I thought. "Of course not," I said.

"He was a loser. A complete and total loser. Mom, to her credit, I guess, loved him. And so she stayed with him. That money we inherited from Grandma. You know Dad would have squandered every last penny on things like that stupid fishing trip. Rounds for everyone at the bar. Someone would have come along with a sob story about medical bills for a sick kid or needing a loan to get out of a jam, and Dad would have handed it over without checking the story and not worry that he never got paid back. Mom would have kept on working those soul-crushing jobs and crying in the bathroom at night when Dad was out, yet again."

"Please, Brad. I'd rather not go over all that."

"His friends, the guys who came here with him, they figured he killed himself, you know. That he went on that swim with the full intention of never coming back."

"What? Why? How do you know that?"

"After it happened, we never saw those guys again. They didn't drop over to ask Mom if they could help with any maintenance around the house, run errands, give us a few bucks until the bank unfroze the accounts. Just as well. Anyway, I ran into one of them about ten years or so later. He came into a bar where I was having a drink after work, recognized me, and came over. It was something like seven o'clock, and he was already plastered. Started going on about what a great guy Dad was and how much fun they'd had on that fishing trip. Basically saying he was sorry our father died because he wasn't able to take his friends fishing any more. Jerk. Anyway, I was about to finish my drink and leave—I didn't much care for the company—when he said he wanted me to know that if he'd known what Dad was planning he would have stopped him."

"Meaning?"

"That's what I wondered. So I stayed. I bought him another drink and let him talk. Basically, Dad hadn't been having a great time on the trip, not like they told the cops. The other guys thought he was being a downer. He talked a lot about Mom, how he didn't deserve a wonderful woman like her. How his kids didn't respect him. Meaning me, not you, I know. He said his family would be better off if he was gone."

"Whoa!" I said. "That's heavy stuff."

"The guys figured Dad was depressed, and he killed himself. Went for that swim with no intention of ever coming back."

"He was almost certainly bipolar," I said. "What they just called moody back in Mom and Dad's day."

"Yeah, likely. Anyway they never told the cops, and they never told Mom the things he'd said. They made up some story about how Dad told them before going up to his room that last night he was going to miss the ocean. Making it sound as though he only wanted to enjoy one last swim. He wasn't anywhere near as drunk as they told the cops he was."

"Here you go. Burger and hush puppies." The waitress put two laden plates in front of us. I waited for her to leave before asking, "Why would they do that? Lie, I mean?"

"To protect us, most likely. Although I don't know if anything could have protected us. Mom anyway."

"They might have been thinking about financial matters. Insurance companies don't pay out for suicides, do they? Thoughtful of them, I guess."

"Another thing I never told you." He lifted his hand, and indicated to the waitress he'd have another beer. I declined. All this talk was getting very deep, and I needed my wits about me. "I've come down a few times over the years."

"Down? Here?"

"Yeah. Here. Stayed at the same motel as Dad had, when it was still standing. I asked the staff about Dad and his friends. They remembered, of course, because of the police activity around his disappearance, but they couldn't tell me anything. Same thing with the fishing boat crews, even the bartenders at the places they'd been drinking. I walked along the beach, maybe hoping to see Dad swimming to shore. Don't know why, really. Nothing I could accomplish the cops couldn't."

"When was the last time you were here?"

"Thanks." He accepted the beer. He avoided looking at my face. "About six months ago."

"And you never told me? Did Mom know? What about Maya?"

"Mom knew. I asked her once if she wanted to come along, but she never did. It's never a fun time. When we were first married, I told Maya, but she didn't come with me. She said it's my way of dealing with the trauma of my past, and it's better than taking drugs. I started to get the feeling she was losing patience with what she'd call clinging to the past, so the last couple of years, I haven't mentioned it. Lately, some of the times I told her I was in New York for meetings, I was here."

He kept his attention on the plate in front of him and ran a French fry through the puddle of ketchup. Talking about such emotional things can be hard for guys of my brother's age.

I didn't have much of an appetite, but I picked up a hush puppy and dipped it into the spicy sauce provided. Yummy.

"Good?" Brad asked.

"Very good. How's the burger?"

"Okay." He chewed like a man not paying any attention to his food. Behind me, a woman yelled, "Watch it!" Another woman screamed; a tray full of glassware and cutlery fell to the floor in a cacophony of shattering glass and bouncing metal.

A table of young men burst out laughing.

"I'm sorry, I'm so sorry!" A young woman in a short tight dress lifted her hands to her mouth, her eyes wide with shock. The waitress glared at her as the bartender brought out a mop. "You," he said to the customer. "You're cut off. Get lost."

The men at the table hooted, and the woman burst into tears before running into the night.

"Reminds me of my ill-spent youth," Brad said.

"Sadly, for me, I never had an ill-spent youth," I said.

"Okay, we've talked over the past. Tell me what's happening now."

"Dad's death is—"

"Don't call him Dad," Brad said. "Our Dad left us a long time ago. Brian Saunders was his name now. His choice. Not ours."

"Okay. Brian's death is being investigated as a murder, the police have no doubt about that. I know nothing more. I don't know if someone specifically followed him to the library to prevent him from talking to me, or it just happened to be their best opportunity. It might have even been a random thing, but . . . I mean I work there now, and I live alone out there, so I'm not considering that to be a possibility."

Brad had finished his burger and shoved most of the ketchup-sodden fries to one side. He put down his beer. "What do the police say? Are you safe?" My mother's eyes looked at me, and I swallowed heavily.

"They say nothing, but my boss assured me she lived in the apartment for a number of years before moving out when she got married. It's probably safer than a lot of places. It is in a lighthouse. No one can climb through the window. Plus, I have an attack cat."

"A what?"

"A joke, Brad. I have a cat now. Well, the library has a cat. Do you . . . do we . . . want to find out what Dad . . . he . . . Brian's been doing all these years?"

"Do I want to? No. Do I think I should? Yeah. I can't let it go that easily."

"Me neither. Detective Thomas told me he had a girlfriend. Maybe we can meet her?"

"A girlfriend?" He appeared taken aback at that. "You don't think—?"

"He didn't leave Mom for her, no. The detective said she could put us in touch with this woman if I wanted, and if she wants to meet me."

"I think we should," Brad said. "I doubt we'll get any answers from her, but if she and Brian were close, she deserves to know he wasn't as he appeared."

"Maybe she knew all along."

"Maybe she did."

Chapter Fifteen

As Brad and I were leaving the restaurant, I said, "When are you meeting with Detective Thomas?"

"Why would I do that? I came down here to be with you."

"You didn't call her? I told you she wants to speak with you. I gave you her number."

"Yeah, well, she can find me if she's so inclined."

"Is that wise?"

"I don't much care if it's wise or not," he snapped.

The restaurant we'd just left was ablaze with light and laughter and music. All along the coast lights shone from houses, while in the darkness the sea rolled steadily to shore. A few flashlights bobbed slowly along the beach. Traffic on the road was heavy but moving steadily. I clicked my fob and the headlights of my car blinked in greeting. I'd picked up my brother at his hotel to come to dinner together. "When I call her to tell her we'd like to speak to the girlfriend to get more info about Brian, she'll ask where you are."

"So let her ask. I'll talk to her when I feel like it."

"I don't think it works that way," I said.

* * *

I was right—it didn't work that way.

When we got to the long-past-its-prime cheap motel a couple of blocks from the beach where Brad was staying, a police car was parked at the front door. I pulled up behind it, and Brad put his hand on the door before getting out. "Do you have work tomorrow?"

"Yes, I do."

"If you send me the address where Brian lived, I might poke around his neighborhood during the day. See if I can talk to anyone who knew him. We can try to meet with the girlfriend after you get off work."

Detective Rhonda Thomas came out of the motel. She looked directly at my car.

"Busted," I said.

"What?"

"That's the detective, on the steps. She's seen you."

He sighed. "Couldn't be helped, I guess. Nothing to worry about, Nichie. I had a few run ins with the cops in my wild youth, and I don't care to spend any more time in their company than I have to."

Is there anything more inclined to make a person worry than when someone says, "nothing to worry about"? Until this minute, I hadn't been at all worried as to why my brother didn't want to talk to the investigating detective. I assumed he was being his usual stubborn self. How many times in our youth had I heard, "You're not the boss of me!"

We both got out of the car.

"Good evening, Detective," I said, trying to sound not at all worried.

"Ms. Gilcrest. Mr. Bradley Sanderson Junior, I assume." Thomas's tone was cool. She did not smile, and she did not offer to shake hands. A uniformed officer stood behind and slightly to one side of her, watching, saying nothing. At his feet, a clump of weeds was trying to force itself through a crack in the pavement. The hedges lining the path to the door were overgrown and weed-choked, and two very unhappy looking geraniums drooped limply in cracked terracotta pots. A group of laughing college-age girls burst out of the motel and ran off into the night, not sparing us a glance.

"I am," Brad said.

"Did your sister not tell you I wanted to speak to you as soon as you arrived in town?"

"She did," he said. "But we had things to catch up on. I was going to call you in the morning."

"Not tonight?"

"I wouldn't want to presume to call after office hours."

Her eyes narrowed. Detective Thomas didn't care to be toyed with. "Fortunately, I do not keep office hours, although I am going to the office now. You can come with me, and we can talk there."

I didn't like the sound of that. She'd never asked me to come to the police station to be interviewed. "Now?" I said.

"Now," she said.

"Have there been any developments since we last spoke? Have you learned anything new?"

"Nothing I need to share with you. Are you coming, Mr. Sanderson?"

The uniform stepped forward.

"Sure," Brad said. "Always happy to be of help to officers of the law."

"Are you arresting him?" I asked. "What for?"

"I am not arresting him. Just wanting a chat."

"A chat? About what?"

"About what he was doing in Nags Head on Saturday last."

Chapter Sixteen

I wanted to follow Brad to the police station, but he told me not to. He'd call me later, he said.

I drove back to the library in a state of shock. Brad had been in Nags Head on Saturday? He told me he came to the Outer Banks occasionally, seeking some sort of resolution to our father's disappearance, and he'd last been here about six months ago. Was that a lie? Why would he lie to me about something like that? I thought back to his behavior at the restaurant as he talked about visiting the Outer Banks. I thought he'd been hiding his emotions, but maybe he was lying to me and feeling a twinge of guilt about it. Was he hiding something? I feared finding out what that something might be.

The library was closed; only a few soft internal lights left on, as well as the one over the door. Far overhead, the 1000-watt beam of the First Order Fresnel lens shone in what I'd learned was its regular pattern: 2.5 seconds on, 2.5 seconds off, 2.5 seconds on, 22.5 seconds off. A lighthouse light is as individual as its paint design, a way of identifying one from another in the days before interactive maps, satellites, and GPS.

No cars were in the parking lot. I lit my way to the door using my phone, conscious of my earlier question if the murder of Brian—of my father—had been a random attack. I assured myself that random attackers did not strike in the same place twice. That wouldn't be random, now would it?

Nevertheless I was glad when I was safely inside and the door firmly shut and locked behind me. I went to the panel in the break room to reset the alarm and then climbed the hundred steps to my apartment, feeling every one of them.

Charles greeted me effusively when I came in. He purred and rubbed up against my legs. I decided to interpret his greeting as "welcome home" rather than "feed me." I picked him up and held his firm little body close to mine. Enough cuddles and he indicated he was ready to get down. I fed him and topped up his water dish, and then I pulled up a stepstool and sat next to him while he ate. I felt better already. Brad could be quiet and sometimes distant, but he had his reasons for everything he did. Sometimes no one else knew what those reasons were; he rarely shared what he was thinking.

I debated if I should call his wife, Maya, but soon decided not to. I wouldn't want to worry her unnecessarily: it was likely nothing more than a case of mistaken identity. Someone who vaguely resembled my brother had been in Nags Head on Saturday. It would get itself sorted out soon enough.

I FaceTimed my daughters instead.

"I still think I should come down there," Simone said. "You shouldn't be dealing with something this momentous on your own, Mom."

"Uncle Brad's here," I said. "So I am not alone."

"Some help he's going to be."

"What does that mean?"

"Uncle Brad's still hung up about stuff, Mom. You moved on, particularly after Grandma died, but he didn't. Maybe it's a guy thing—he has unresolved issues about his missing father."

"He is my brother, honey. He'll be supportive of me and me of him. Besides, I can't put you up." I lifted the iPad and swung it around, giving her a full view of the entirety of my apartment. "Unless you want to sleep on the floor. Do you?"

"Maybe not. Have you spoken to Dad?"

"I have not."

"You should, Mom. He never knew your father, and I don't know how much you talked about the situation with him when you were first together, but he was fond of Grandma, right, and he'd like to know."

"I'd rather wait to see how it all turns out. I'm not quite up to speaking to your father now. You can tell him if you like. I'm not keeping it secret from anyone."

She dipped her eyes to her keyboard, and I knew she already had. "I suppose you're right. I can't take the time off work now anyway. I'm working on the advance promo for what's going to be the biggest domestic thriller of the year. This brother and sister, who've been estranged for years find out that—"

"I'll look forward to the book," I said. "When it comes out." That might explain why my daughter was eager to psychoanalyze my brother's relationship with his father. She'd been reading about a situation she'd decided was similar. Not that Brad and I had ever been estranged, but out of the blue, my life had suddenly turned into the stuff of a domestic thriller. "Did you speak to Isabelle?"

"Not in person, but I texted her."

"I'll let you know if there are any developments."

"Love you, Mom," she said.

"Love you too."

I next tried Isabelle, and she answered as the connection was about to close. "Mom. Can't talk for long. I'm at tennis. Jonathan's playing now."

I could hear the thud of a ball hitting a racquet. Isabelle's neat brown hair was tied back with a sweat band, and the bright lights of the court shone over her shoulder.

My daughters are identical twins. As babies they were virtually indistinguishable, but as they grew and developed individual personalities, they began to look less and less alike. Simone's face is chubbier, her cheeks pinker, her eyes wider, and she always seems to be on the verge of breaking out laughing. She likes to experiment with make-up, jewelry, and hair color. Today her hair was so pale as to be almost white, the tips dyed a fluorescent pink. Long feathered earrings dangled from her ears. Whereas Isabelle is much thinner, sleeker in a way, hair cut sharply at her chin, the color left its natural brown, subdued make-up, small gold hoops through her ears.

"Simone told me what happened," Isabelle said. "Wow, that's really something. Imagine your dad popping up out of the blue only to drop dead at your feet. Thud."

I pulled back slightly. "I wouldn't quite put it that way."

"Jonathan says it's tough, yeah, but it's long past time you got over it, Mom. He says it was one thing when Grandma was alive, right? She was obviously remembering him all the time. Even when she pretended not to."

"Hard not to get over it when, as you so delicately put it, the man dropped dead on my doorstep."

"Don't get involved, is all I'm saying."

"How can I not get involved? I—"

"Be right there!" she shouted to someone I couldn't see. "Gotta run, I'm up. If you need anything, Mom, let me know. Bye."

I was left staring at my own face.

I closed my iPad with a smile and a shake of my head. How could identical twins be so different?

Whose Body? by Dorothy L. Sayers sat on my nightstand. I had about twenty pages left to go. I was looking forward to the book club meeting tomorrow night. I'd already heard contradicting opinions on the character of the amateur sleuth protagonist from Butch Greenblatt and Theodore Kowalski. Nothing gets a book club discussion going better than literary dissent amongst the readers. I got myself ready for bed and crawled under the covers with the book and a pen and notepad. As I finished reading, I made notes about possible topics of conversation. Butch mentioned that the group had earlier read another Wimsey novel, and I was slightly disappointed to hear that: he and his author wouldn't be new to the club. But *Whose Body?* was Sayers' debut novel, and her style changed over the eleven books and the twelve years between *Whose Body?* and *Busman's Honeymoon*, the final.

When the phone rang shortly after eleven, I leapt to answer it and felt a wave of relief at hearing my brother's voice.

"I'm leaving the police station now. Much ado about nothing. Talk tomorrow."

"Wait. What did she want? What did she mean, you were in Nags Head on Saturday? How do the police know that? Is it true? Why?And why didn't you tell me?"

"Hard to deny it. Yeah, I was here. I told you I came now and again."

"But you said the last time was six months ago, Brad."

"Leave it, Nichelle," he snapped. "What does the date matter?"

"It matters—"

"I said leave it. I got a speeding ticket on Saturday. Stuffed it in the glove compartment and forgot about it. That's how they traced me, and how they found me tonight. I said we'll talk tomorrow. How about I drop by midafternoon? I'd like to see this library in a lighthouse. Sounds intriguing."

He hung up. I was not left with a warm and fuzzy feeling.

* * *

Over a boiled egg and a piece of toast, I scanned the morning news and social media updates. The police said an arrest was expected shortly in the Brian Saunders murder. In the meantime, they were asking people who'd been in the vicinity of the Bodie Island Lighthouse and Bossie Creek marshes late Sunday night or early Monday morning to come forward.

I hadn't asked Detective Thomas to put me in touch with Brian's—Dad's—girlfriend. I wasn't sure I wanted to talk to either of them right now. Not while my brother was being secretive.

After speaking to Brad, I fell into a restless sleep. As I had book club tonight, and that was part of my job, I didn't have to be downstairs until noon. When I woke, Charles was already at the door, whining to be let out. Lucy told me he loved his job, so I held the door open for him. He dashed out with the sort of eagerness I wished I could muster on a working day.

After catching up on the news and getting ready for the day, I poured myself a fresh cup of coffee and went over the notes I'd made for the book club discussion. I didn't want to control the meeting too closely, and I hoped the members would have a lot they wanted to say. But in case they didn't, or they started to get way off track, I needed to be prepared. I considered inviting Brad. He was no more a reader than our father had been, but he might like to meet the members and enjoy the discussion. I decided to see what happened today. I closed my computer, washed up my few dishes, and went to work.

Chapter Seventeen

"I'd like to go to the book club meeting tonight," Lucy said to Connor over breakfast, "but I'm not sure if I should. I don't want Nichelle to think I'm micromanaging her or I'm not sure if she's capable of handling it."

"It'll be okay if you don't try to run the meeting yourself. Don't talk over her to make helpful suggestions."

"Would I do that?"

"You would."

"I think I'll go. I read a lot of Dorothy L. Sayers in college, but nothing other than *Busman's Honeymoon* for the book club since. I managed to get a few pages into *Whose Body?* while I was nursing the babies, and it bought some of the story back."

Isaac and Lucas, fed and burped and changed, were sitting in their baby chairs, watching their parents have their own breakfast. Isaac's eyes were drifting closed, but Lucas's darted around the room, taking it all in. Everyone and everything. All at once.

"I'm not going to work until noon today," Lucy continued. "Sofia's fine staying with the boys until you get home."

"Which indicates to me, in my role as Lord Peter Wimsey, that you've already decided to go, and you simply wanted me to tell you what you want to hear."

"Pretty much," she said.

* * *

Lucy walked into the library as Nichelle was taking over the reception desk from Maureen Peterson, today's volunteer. The new employee was looking tired, Lucy thought. Understandable, considering the emotional trauma she must be going through with all that happened since she arrived. "Everything okay?"

Nichelle gave her a weak smile. "Fine. I've heard nothing new about the murder case and the news this morning just repeated what we already know. My brother arrived last night, and the police had some questions for him."

"What sort of questions? If you don't mind my asking."

"It seems as though he's been to Nags Head several times over the years. He wasn't entirely honest with me about the last time, and Detective Thomas caught him out."

Maureen Peterson was running bar codes into the computer, checking books back in and stacking them in piles to go onto the returns cart to be reshelved. She was, Lucy couldn't help but notice, working exceptionally slowly and standing so far away from the bar code reader she had to stretch to reach it.

"Maureen, do you mind taking the desk for a while longer?" Lucy asked. "I have some routine personnel issues to discuss with Nichelle that didn't get done earlier."

Maureen tried to hide her disappointment at missing out on the gossip-worthy conversation. "Perfectly fine, Lucy. You go right ahead. Before you go, did you tell Ronald of my suggestions?"

"Suggestions?"

"For the next batch of early teen programs."

"Oh, right. That. Uh . . . not yet. Been so busy you know. Coming, Nichelle?"

Lucy almost ran to her office, Nichelle hurrying after her. When Lucy had shut the door behind them and sat down at her desk, she put her purse into a drawer and then said, "We're a very close-knit community here at the library. Too close-knit sometimes if you get my meaning."

Nichelle smiled. "I suspect I do."

"If Maureen ever starts to get nosy about your personal affairs, all you have to do is ask her something about one of her daughters, and she'll switch to the new subject immediately. Although, be warned, you might not be able to escape. As for now, do you want to talk about it? About what's bothering you? No problem, if you'd rather not."

Nichelle let out a long sigh. "I won't say I'm not worried. I wasn't worried, not until last night. Whatever happened to my dad . . . to Brian Saunders . . . didn't affect me, not in any way other than emotionally. But now, this about Brad, my brother . . . I don't know what to think. Why would he lie to me? If he was here on Saturday, as the police say he was and he's not denying, why would he go home, knowing I was due to arrive the very next day?"

"I don't know, Nichelle. But I can tell you I do understand what you're going through. Being involved in this sort of thing on a personal level can be extremely difficult to deal with. Did you ask your brother those questions?"

"I tried. He wouldn't talk about it. I'll try again later."

"Are you and your brother close?"

"Not particularly, no. After our dad disappeared, he tried to take on a father role, but as he is all of one year older than me, I didn't take it too well. Time passed, we went to college, got married, had families, drifted apart. We lived in the same city, until I came here, and when our mom was alive we usually got together for Thanksgiving, Christmas, and birthdays, the usual sort of thing, but we didn't put any effort into keeping in contact. After Mom died . . . not so much. I got divorced, went to college. I hadn't seen Brad for over a year until yesterday. I'd say I'm better friends with his wife, Maya, than I am with him. No one's fault, really. Just the way it happens."

"I have three older brothers," Lucy said. "I probably wouldn't even know if they're still alive, except I expect my mom would tell me if they weren't."

Nichelle smiled weakly.

"What do you want to do now?" Lucy asked.

"Do?"

"About this case. Your father's disappearance and death. If you have questions, and obviously you do, you need to find answers for your own peace of mind, do you agree?"

"I do, yes. I'd like to talk to people who knew him as Brian, but I'm not sure if that's appropriate right now. The detective might think I'm interfering in her investigation rather than minding my own business."

"You're trying to find the truth about your father's life. No one can say that's not your business."

"Thanks, Lucy. I needed someone to tell me that."

"If I may make a suggestion, the best place to start is where he lived. Do you have his address?"

"It was on the news; the police released it as part of their initial statement."

"Why don't you go there now?"

"Now, but it's working hours?"

"You have book club tonight, right? The last of the stragglers don't normally get away until well after nine, so I figure you can take an hour off this afternoon." Lucy read the hesitation on Nichelle's face. "If you don't want to go alone, I'd be happy to come with you. Or would you prefer to wait and go with your brother?"

"I'd like that. If you came. I'm nervous about it and until my brother tells me straight up what's going on, I don't know that I can entirely trust him. Not with my emotions."

Lucy stood up. "Understandable. Ronald and Denise are in, and I'll let Maureen know she has the desk for a while longer. She won't mind. The circulation desk is the best place to see everyone coming and going. It's the epicenter of all OBX gossip, as you will soon discover."

"They didn't teach us that in college."

Lucy laughed. "A lot of things they didn't teach us in college. Investigating murders, most of all."

Chapter Eighteen

We took Lucy's car into town, and I was glad of it. My mind was a churning morass of conflicting thoughts. As we drove, I texted Brad: *You okay? When will I see you?*

He didn't reply.

Lucy had punched the address we were after into her phone, and the cheerful voice directed us north on Highway 12 to meet the Croatan Highway. Traffic increased at Whalebone Junction with cars and vans sporting a wide variety of out-of-state license plates, loaded with kids and beach equipment, surfboards on roofs, bicycles and fishing poles mounted on backs. Past the outlet mall, burger joints, motels, and tourist attractions of all sorts. Before long, Lucy slowed down, turned left, and we entered a residential area.

I knew Brian worked part time at a beach supply store, and as we slowly drove through the quiet streets, I wondered how he could afford a house in this area. It wasn't high end, but not low-end either. Just a quiet street of small, older houses on scruffy lots, sitting close together in varying degrees of upkeep. Few of the yards had anything approaching a garden. Little more than sand and tangled beach grasses, weeds, and a few scruffy trees.

"This place gets insane in the summer," Lucy said. "Many of these houses are most likely vacation rental properties. The owners spend exactly what they have to on them in order to attract the level of rent they want, and not a penny more. Hard sometimes for people with low-income or seasonal jobs to find a nice place to live." The phone announced that we'd arrived, and Lucy said, "This must be it."

It wasn't far from the beach, which isn't hard as everything in Nags Head is close to the water in all directions.

She pulled up to the curb. I looked at the house. Perhaps Brian could afford to rent this particular place as it was very small and badly in need of some maintenance. Like many, if not most, of the houses in the Outer Banks, the living area was above the ground, the building resting on stilts, offering protection from hurricanes and high water levels; the front door accessible via a steep staircase. One story tall, no garage, the wood siding painted a dull turquoise, air conditioning unit resting in a side window. A deck, barely five feet wide, paint peeling off it in long strands, sat off to one side, the only furniture two aluminum-frame chairs with chipping paint and cushions so weather-worn the pattern and colors were barely recognizable. The property was unfenced; weeds poked out of cracks in the paved driveway; the yard was nothing but sand and more weeds. An unpainted metal mailbox on a wooden pole sat next to the street. The flag was not up. Today appeared to be garbage day, as bins were out at the end of many of the driveways on the street, but not the one we were interested in.

I got out of the car, but Lucy stayed behind the wheel, letting me have some time alone with my thoughts. Maybe I was trying to find some imprint of my father's personality on the house, such as the way he painted our garage door a hideous lime green one summer, just for a laugh, or the time he covered the front yard with thirty-five life-sized pink flamingos for Mom's birthday. But nothing—it was nothing but a small, nondescript rental house in a working-class neighborhood. I stared at it for a long time, the sun hot on my face, trying to imagine my father living here, coming and going from work, having friends over for a barbeque, taking out the trash. But nothing came. My father, Bradley Sanderson Senior, had never been here. Just Brian Saunders, whom I met only in death.

The occasional vehicle drove by, but no one was out walking the dog, biking to work or school, washing the car, playing catch.

"The police will have gone through the house." Lucy came to stand next to me. "I doubt they found anything of significance as the crime scene tape has already been taken down. If you want to talk to the neighbors you might have to come back in the evening or on the weekend. Most of the vacation renters will be at the beach and many of the permanent residents are at work at this time of day."

"I don't know what I'd say to them. Hi, did your friend ever tell you he had a family he ran out on and why he did that? No, I don't need to talk to anyone. I don't want to go to the place where he worked either. I'd like to know why he came to the library that night, if he had something he needed to say to me. Why he brought me a stupid childish bracelet. I'd like to know who killed him, and why. But as for all the rest—I've lived thirty-eight years without knowing. I can let it go. I don't want to see any more. Let's go back to work." I changed the subject. "I'm looking forward to the book club tonight, although you made it sound terrifying."

"All I meant is the club members are dedicated and opinionated readers," Lucy said. "You can manage them. Would it be okay with you if I come? As a participant only. My husband's minding the kids tonight."

"I'd like that, yes. Some moral support, maybe." I turned to go back to the car.

A Honda Civic drove up and turned into the sandy and weedy driveway of the house we'd been watching. A woman got out. She was in her late forties, dressed in slim-fitting, white, fashionably shredded jeans, a tight blue T-shirt adored with sparkles that fell just short of the tops of her pants, and sandals with three-inch heels. Giant sunglasses were perched on her face. Her blond hair hung loose, long and tussled, scraggly at the ends, black roots intruding on the blond. Her lips were a bright red slash. She gave us a brief, uninterested glance as she walked the few feet across the yard. She climbed the steps. Put a key in the lock.

I looked at Lucy, asking her what she thought I should do.

"Trust your instincts," she said. "Always."

"Hello!" I started up the driveway. Lucy kept close behind me.

The woman turned, door open behind her. "Yes?"

"Sorry to bother you," I said, "but . . . I . . . I knew the man who lived here. Brian Saunders, right?"

"Yes." She lowered her sunglasses. Her voice was cool, her eyes wary.

"I assume you know . . . you know . . ."

"He died. Yes, I know that. Who are you?"

"I'm . . . his daughter. Nichelle."

Something flashed behind her eyes. She glanced at Lucy, and then back at me. Her lips turned upward in what she might have intended to be a smile. "Sorry. You must be thinking of someone else. Brian didn't have any children."

We remained at the bottom of the steps. Lucy said, "I'm Lucy McNeil, and this is Nichelle Gilcrest. May I ask your name?"

"Why?"

"To be polite?"

"Melissa Archibald, if you must know. Why are you asking about Brian?"

"My friend isn't mistaken, and she isn't lying. She is the daughter of the man you knew as Brian, but we understand if he didn't tell you about his family. She's only wanting to—"

"Extend my condolences to his friends," I said.

"Condolences accepted. Anything else I can do for you?"

"Do you live here?" I asked.

"No, I do not. Brian and I were good friends, and I have a key. The cops called to tell me I can pick up some of the things I left here. If that's all, I'll ask you to leave me alone in my grief. Good-bye."

I didn't see any noticeable signs of grief, but before I could say another word, she went into the house, slamming the door behind her.

I stared at the door. When it didn't open again, Melissa having changed her mind, wanting to invite me in for a glass of tea and to get to know me better, I turned to Lucy. "Detective Thomas told me my d—I mean Brian had a much younger girlfriend. That must be her. The age matches, and she has a key to the house and keeps some things here."

"Let's go," Lucy said.

As we walked back to the car, I said, "Does she seem a bit young, and trying too hard to look even younger, to be involved with a man in his late seventies? A man without a lot of money, at any rate?"

"Yes," Lucy said. "She does."

Chapter Nineteen

Brad called me in the midafternoon, suggesting we meet. I'd already taken time off to go to Brian's house, so I didn't want to ask Lucy if I could leave work again, and my brother and I could hardly talk about our family business while I staffed the circulation desk and half the population of Nags Head tried to listen under the pretext of returning or checking out books.

"This is only my third day at this job," I said. The library was busy this afternoon. Denise and Louise Jane had a group of high school students visiting to learn about conducting historical research; Ronald was upstairs with his toddler's story time, while mothers, and a couple of fathers, either browsed the shelves or gathered in the magazine nook chatting.

At the moment no one was in need of my assistance. "I can't ask for more time off, Brad, and I'm working late tonight. I have book club at seven. How about you come around after and we can talk things over? I have something to tell you."

"What?"

"Let's leave it until we can talk in person. I can show you my apartment."

"Is your book club open to anyone?"

"Yes, it is. We serve refreshments."

"Why don't I come to that? I've got nothing else to do around here, other than spend the evening in a bar, and that's probably not a good idea."

"No, it's not."

"Detective Thomas didn't exactly tell me not to leave town, but it was strongly implied. I've been ordered to notify the police station if I do go home."

At that moment a stream of small, excited children tumbled down the steps from the second floor, laughing and clutching books to their chests. Maureen Peterson tried, and failed, to keep them under some degree of control, while Ronald followed the hordes, and parents went to greet their kids.

"I have to go," I said. "Book club's at seven, at the library. We're discussing *Whose Body*? by Dorothy L. Sayers."

"Don't think I've ever heard of it or her," my brother said. "But I can pretend."

"No, you can't." I hung up the phone and put on my cheerful librarian face.

* * *

After the library closed, Lucy, Louise Jane, and I began laying out chairs and refreshments in the third-floor meeting room. We would provide jugs of water, tea, and juice, along with glasses and napkins, and Lucy's cousin Josie would bring treats from her bakery.

"Josie says they're leftovers," Louise Jane said, "but everyone knows she bakes specially for the book club."

"I trust we pay her."

"We do," said Lucy.

"I hope we've put out enough chairs," Louise Jane said. Charles had claimed his place immediately, front row center. He was now having a brief nap before the event began. "I'm expecting an awful big crowd tonight, not just because the club is restarting and people missed it, but folks who haven't been in already want to meet our new librarian."

"I'm going to my office to finish up a few things," Lucy said. "At quarter to seven, Nichelle, you and Louise Jane go downstairs to meet the arrivals and let them in. The library is closed, but anyone who's here for the meeting is welcome."

I suspected Lucy was deliberately taking herself out of the hostess role tonight as a way of making sure people knew I, not she, would be running the meeting.

I was nervous, so long before the appointed time, we went downstairs and stood on the front step waiting for our guests.

It was a lovely evening, the sun low in an orange sky, birds calling to each other as they flew home to nest for the night. A soft breeze carried the scent of salt off the ocean.

"So? Anything?" Louise Jane asked.

"Nothing new. I haven't seen or heard from Detective Thomas all day."

"Not that. I mean have you sensed anything in the library, after dark in particular? Although some of our other-worldly residents can appear in the daytime. As well as The Lady, who can admittedly sometimes be shy, a lightkeeper's little son, who climbed to the top against his father's orders and fell to his death, sometimes comes out to play with the children when story time's finished if their parents haven't picked them up yet."

"I don't believe in that stuff, Louise Jane," I said.

"Doesn't matter if you believe in it or not," she said calmly. "Did you get a chance to read the book I gave you?"

"I haven't exactly been bored in the past twenty-four hours," I said, perhaps a bit too harshly.

The first of the cars turned into the laneway and that was, thankfully, the end of that conversation. I was not comfortable talking about these things with Louise Jane. I wanted to get on with everyone I worked with, and Louise Jane was trying to be friendly, in her own way. But I was afraid she'd soon imply my father might become the newest "resident" of the lighthouse.

"No hurry," Louise Jane said. "Looks like Josie's car. She usually comes early to lay out her offerings. Tip to the wise, don't be polite. If you don't grab a pecan square as fast as you can, Butch will scarf them all up. If not him, then Mrs. Fitzgerald. Have you met Mrs. Fitzgerald yet?"

"Don't think so."

"Chair of the library board. Not nearly as frightening as she first appears. Although . . . I have heard stories of unwary librarians never being seen again."

I looked at her.

Louise Jane laughed. "You should see your face. She didn't chase Lucy away, so you're probably safe. Have you ever been to France?" she asked apropos of nothing I could tell.

"Yes, but a long time ago. When the man I eventually married and I were dating, we backpacked around England and France for a few weeks. I've always wanted to go back. The time never quite seemed right."

"I go fairly regularly," Louise Jane said. "For no particular reason, mind, just that I like it there. I considered moving to France at one time, but my mother, my grandmother, and my great-gran are still alive and kicking, and I don't want to leave them."

"Do you speak French?"

"Not much, but I've learned a bit. I'm part-time here, and I can take time off without pay as and when I need. Although, lately, occasionally, France has come to me."

"Huh?"

"Here she comes," she said, leaving me absolutely befuddled as to what, if anything, she was trying to tell me. "Chin up. Back straight. You're on, Nichelle."

A beautiful young woman, tall and slim, approached us, two bakery boxes stacked in her outstretched arms.

"I'd give you a giant hug of welcome, but as you can see my arms are currently occupied. You must be Nichelle. I'm Josie Greenblatt."

"I went to your place yesterday," I said. "I was with a police officer by the name of Greenblatt. A relative?"

"If you mean Butch, he's my husband's brother."

"Oh, that's right. Lucy told me that. Sorry, I've met so many people over the last couple of days I'm having trouble keeping everyone straight."

"Totally understandable. We can be an overwhelming bunch at first."

"Josie is Lucy's first cousin," Louise Jane pointed out. "Their mothers are sisters. We have a lot of intertwining relationships around here."

"So I'm coming to understand. Your baking is fabulous, Josie," I said. "I'm looking forward to your place being a regular haunt of mine."

"Thanks. I'm not staying tonight. Just dropping these off. Ellie, that's Jake's and my daughter, was home from day care today because she wasn't feeling well. She's already back to bouncing on every piece of furniture that has any give, but my mom spent the afternoon at our place, so I need to relieve her." She shoved the boxes into Louise Jane's arms. "Have fun!"

Theodore Kowalski arrived next, still dressed in his tweed jacket, still surrounded by an aura of tobacco, accompanied by a woman his own age wearing a soft, flowing summer dress.

"My mother phoned the police," he said to me after introducing the woman as Lorraine. "My girlfriend," he added proudly.

"Nice to meet you, Lorraine. Thanks for coming," I said. "What did the police have to say?"

"They didn't ask her to come in," Theodore said. "They thanked her for her call and said a note would be made on the file in case they had further questions. I'm looking forward to tonight's discussion, Nichelle. As no doubt you intend to ask for recommendations from the club of what we should read over the next several months, I've gone to the trouble of preparing a shortlist." He dug in the large leather bag tossed over his shoulder and came up with a single piece of paper. Type filled the page. Bullet points, in twelve-point font, one-inch margins, single spaced.

"Teddy has strong opinions on what's worth reading and what is not," Lorraine said. "Not everyone, and that includes me, always agrees. Don't let him browbeat you, Nichelle."

Butch Greenbelt and his diminutive girlfriend, Steph, were next, and then a stream of people whose names I'd never be able to keep straight. One of the last to arrive was my brother, Brad.

After I introduced him to Louise Jane, he said, "This place truly is out in the middle of nowhere. Are you sure you're safe living out here, Nichie?"

"She's safer here than a lot of places," Louise Jane said. "Thick walls, high windows, limited points of access." Then she added, not at all helpfully, "Lucy was attacked once, not far from this very spot, and none other than The Lady saved her. I've been telling Nichelle about The Lady and our other residents of a spiritual nature."

The only word in that sentence my brother, not to mention me, heard was "attacked."

"Attacked?" Brad said. "You mean by a person?"

"Don't worry about it, either of you. It wasn't a random thing, it was personal. Lucy does have a way of attracting trouble, although that seems to have stopped since she had the babies. Good thing too."

Brad and I exchanged nervous looks.

"You take your brother upstairs and make friendly." Louise Jane shoved the bakery boxes at Brad. "No better way of making friendly than to give people cookies. I'll stay another few minutes in case of any stragglers. If anyone comes after that, they know to ring up, and we'll buzz them in."

Brad took the boxes, and we went into the library. "Impressive," he said, admiring the long rows of book-filled shelves disappearing into the darkness at the back of the main room, the magazine nook, the alcove where we featured special promotions, the computer desks and chairs. "This place seems a lot bigger inside than it first appeared."

"I'll give you the grand tour after book club."

"Does that woman, Louise Jane, seem a bit odd to you?"

"Odd, yes. But she's trying hard, in her own odd way, to make me welcome."

We climbed the twisting spiral staircase. A wave of conversation poured down from the third floor, but the moment I entered the meeting room, it stopped. Everyone looked at me. The faces were nothing but friendly, everyone smiling, everyone welcoming. Every chair was taken, and Butch and Theodore were standing against the wall.

Then again, maybe they were looking at Brad and the boxes he was carrying.

"Why don't I lay these out?" Butch stepped forward. He gave Brad a nod and took the boxes. "Welcome."

"Thanks." Brad found himself a place next to the wall where he nodded to Theodore. One woman sitting near the back nudged her companion and jerked her head toward my brother. Her friend looked, giggled, and nudged her friend back. I had absolutely no idea what that might be about, but I didn't have time to consider it.

The group was a nice mixture of ages and types. The big gruff cop, the tiny woman with him. Theodore in his tweed jacket, complete with paisley cravat around his neck and handkerchief in his front pocket. A pretty young woman in ragged shorts and a T-shirt. Mrs. Fitzgerald, in her eighties the terror of librarians everywhere, had taken the front row center seat with Charles comfortably settled on her lap. She was next to an unkempt man in his sixties, who looked as though he'd just stepped off his fishing boat, and a small nervous woman about the same age beside him. Maureen Peterson had brought one of her daughters, Phoebe, age thirteen, who couldn't look more bored if she tried. I took a guess the girl was trying very hard indeed. Lucy was seated off to one side, taking herself out of the limelight, next to an elderly gentleman.

"For those of you I haven't had the privilege of meeting yet, I'm Nichelle Gilcrest," I announced. "I'm the new librarian here."

Cries of welcome and pleased to meet you, rang throughout the room.

Most of the people had introduced themselves to me when they arrived, but it all passed in a blur of names and faces, so I suggested we go around the room so people could tell me a bit about themselves. When that was over, I cleared my throat and said, "I hope you all had a chance to read this month's book, *Whose Body?* by Dorothy L. Sayers. I suggested it myself because I hadn't met any of you yet, so I didn't know your tastes, but I'm hoping as we go forward you'll feel free to recommend other books that fall within our mandate of classic mystery novels."

"As long as there's no more of that Peter Wimsey," Butch said. "Geez."

The diminutive woman next to him, a defense lawyer named Steph, gave him a poke in the ribs.

"Lord Peter Wimsey," Theodore said, "is one of the all-time greats of crime fiction."

"Exactly," the man next to Lucy said. "Much of what we read today in the way of mystery novels owes a great deal to Mrs. Sayers and Lord Peter."

"Doesn't mean I have to like him," a woman said. "I agree with Butch. The man's a pompous idiot."

"He is most definitely not an idiot," Mrs. Fitzgerald said. "In any way. He so cleverly deduced that the body couldn't have been that of Sir Reuben Levy because he wasn't an orthodox Jew."

"Yeah, I wondered about that," Phoebe Peterson said. "How could he tell when the guy didn't have any clothes on?"

"I'll explain later," Maureen said, blushing to the roots of her carefully styled helmet of dyed brown hair.

I needn't have worried about keeping the discussion going. They leapt eagerly into an argument about whether or not to accept the attitude and prejudices of people of past times and if Lord Peter Wimsey was, indeed, an idiot.

"Never forget," Theodore said, "the book was published in 1923. Mrs. Sayers was obviously writing not for us in the twenty-first century, but for her contemporary readers. This book, and her following ones, proved to be highly popular."

"About the murders," Louise Jane said. "Can we talk about the story? How cleverly Sayers twisted the two supposedly unrelated disappearances together to make one case and how Lord Peter realized what was going on."

Brad caught my eye. Maybe *Whose Body?* wasn't the best pick for the inaugural meeting of my book club. Although the book concerns two men who have been missing for only a matter of days, not one man missing for thirty-eight years.

Josie's treats were all gone, the jugs contained little more than melting ice, Charles had gone to sleep, and the members of the Bodie Island Lighthouse Library Classic Mystery Reading Club had discussed in great detail the investigative prowess of Lord Peter Wimsey, as well as his relationships with others in the book, and how he and they fit into their world. It was almost nine, and I was wondering how to bring the meeting to an end, when Mrs. Fitzgerald said, "Enough fictional murders. Once again we have one on our own doorstep. Lucy, what do you know about that?"

Lucy stood up. "Nothing. I know nothing more than any of you know from what information the police have made public. We don't even know what brought that man to the library that night. He was not a patron here. None of the staff had ever seen him before."

"Butch," Mrs. Fitzgerald asked, "anything to report? Nothing you say will leave this room."

"I'm not falling for that one again," he said with a smile. "The investigation is ongoing."

Brad threw Butch a look. He hadn't known the other man was a police officer.

The official reports had concentrated on details of the killing and had not mentioned that Brian Saunders had once had a different identity. No doubt the news would come out soon enough, but I was glad to have a breathing space before being bombarded with questions and sympathy.

"Brian Saunders," said the man next to Lucy, who'd introduced himself as Tim Snyder, retired high school teacher. "I knew him. I shouldn't speak ill of the dead—"

"Whyever not?" Mrs. Fitzgerald said. "They'd be quick enough to speak ill of you, Tim."

"No one has anything ill to say about Tim," the thin, nervous woman named Jo Harper said.

"I am simply making a point," he said. "And, if I may continue with that point, Eunice, Saunders was a nasty piece of work. Take it from me—he was on library property, at that time of night, for no good reason."

I avoided looking at either Lucy or my brother.

"What does that mean?" Brad asked.

"I never trusted the man. Always figured he was up to something."

"Something like what?" Butch asked. "Illegal activity?"

"No, nothing like that. Not that I knew of anyway. He lived not far from me, and he was popular with a certain crowd, guys my age, the sort as disappointed in retirement as they were in life. I don't go to Blackbeard's Cave much anymore, partly age creeping up on me, but mostly that my friends aren't going for one reason or another."

"What's Blackbeard's Cave?" Brad asked.

"A neighborhood bar," Tim Snyder said. "Stupid name, but when the place started up they were trying for tourist dollars. Never got them. Not exactly the sort of establishment you find on the tourist trail. I knew Brian from there. He was a moody sort of guy. Sometimes kept himself to himself, sometimes up for a party, and he'd occasionally offer to pay for a round of drinks."

"I know the place," Butch said. "It's not popular with the tourists, like you said, but it's no criminal hangout either."

"I never said it was. Never said Brian was a crook either, not far as I knew. I'm just saying I didn't trust him, that's all. On the few occasions we met, I found him either morose or too jovial by half."

"Not that your opinion on the matter is entirely unbiased," Ralph Harper, the scruffy guy who looked like a fishing boat captain, said with a laugh. "I doubt you had such a bad opinion of him before he asked Jo here out on a date. You didn't like that."

"Darn right I didn't," Tim snarled.

Everyone turned to look at Jo Harper sitting beside Ralph. She gave the room a shrug and dipped her head. "Nothing came of it." Her voice was very low. She hadn't said a word while the group discussed the book, but she had appeared to be listening.

"You dated him?" I asked her.

"No, I didn't. He suggested we go out to dinner or a movie one night. I don't usually do things like that, so I said no."

"Did he push the point?" I asked.

She shook her head; her unkempt brown and gray hair fell further over her eyes.

"Where did you meet him?" Brad asked.

"At the Shrimp Shack."

"My usual breakfast place," Ralph said. "Near Manteo. Best breakfast in OBX, if you're ever looking. A real seaman's breakfast, not that granola and avocado toast stuff the tourists like."

"Let Jo finish her story," Tim said.

"Ralph always goes there for breakfast if he's got an early charter," Jo said. "He forgot his wallet one morning, so

I called a cab and took it down to him. I caught Ralph just as he was leaving. It was a cold rainy day, so I decided to treat myself to breakfast out. I haven't done that in . . . years. I don't know if I've ever had breakfast in a restaurant before. I had the pancakes with bacon. It was good. While I was eating, Brian came to my table and told me he was a friend of Ralph's."

"Not a friend," Ralph said, "Just someone I'd see around town and say hello to. He didn't come to the Shrimp Shack much, from what I heard he went to Blackbeard's Cave mostly, like Tim said."

I must have looked confused, and maybe a bit embarrassed because Louise Jane burst out laughing and said, "Gosh, didn't you realize, Nichelle? Ralph and Jo are brother and sister. Neither of them ever married so they live together."

I winced inside. So much for jumping to conclusions.

"When did this happen, Jo?" Theodore asked.

"Three months ago, maybe. Early spring. I told Ralph, and I guess Ralph told Tim."

"What's an old guy like that want with a woman as young as Jo?" Tim snorted.

"He went out with my mother a couple of times before that," Theodore said. "She turned down any suggestion they do so again, because she said she wasn't comfortable in his company. Although she couldn't put her finger on why."

"What of it?" Louise Jane said. "He was a lonely old man, looking for companionship. Maybe he got word of a dating club for old folks and mistakenly thought it was being held at the library Sunday night." She laughed heartily. A few other people joined in.

"Lonely old man," Tim snorted. "Dirty old man, more like it, if he's after women like Jo here and Loretta Kowalski."

I glanced at my brother. His lips were pinched into a tight line.

I looked at Lucy, and she gave me a nod. I stood up. "Thank you all so much for coming to the inaugural meeting of the Bodie Island Lighthouse Library Classic Mystery Reading Club. I'd like to propose an email discussion of what books we should consider reading over the next few months."

Theodore pulled his sheet of paper out of his shoulder bag with a flourish and waved it over his head. "I have a few suggestions, listed here in order of preference sorted by relevance to the history of crime novels, then status of the author's work and reputation, then subdivided into status of that particular book, and last, reading pleasure. I'll give—"

"Why isn't reading pleasure first?" Steph asked.

"Could this get any more boring?" Phoebe asked her mother.

"I've had just about enough of you, young lady. I'm considering not bringing you again."

The girl's eyes lit up. "Promise?"

"Email me a copy of that list, please Theodore," I said. "I'll distribute it along with other people's suggestions as initial discussion points."

"No need." He fumbled in his bag and took out a stack of papers. His glasses slipped down his nose, and he shoved them back with one finger. "I took the liberty of making enough copies for everyone." He began passing them around.

Lorraine smiled at him fondly. Mrs. Fitzgerald rolled her eyes, but she accepted one when it was her turn.

"Now remember everyone," I added, "a classic mystery novel, for our purposes at any rate, is one from the nineteenth century to roughly 1950, emphasis on the 1920s and 30s, the so-called golden age of crime fiction, translated from any language, by an author of any country. I'm excited about seeing your suggestions."

One by one people began to leave, calling goodnight to everyone, thanking me for the discussion. The two women who'd been eyeing Brad at the beginning of the evening glanced at him as they passed and nudged each other again.

"Such an interesting evening, Nichelle," they said with another round of giggles as they passed me.

I glanced at Brad. He didn't react to the women in any way other than to smile as vaguely politely as he had to everyone else tonight. I suppose Brad was a good-looking man, for his age, and for a brother.

Louise Jane followed them downstairs in order to show everyone out.

Soon only Brad, Lucy, and I remained in the meeting room. Brad gave me a questioning glance and jerked his head toward Lucy.

"She knows," I said. "About what happened to our dad and that he's Brian Saunders."

"Okay," Brad said. "What was that about the old guy suddenly dissing on Brian? Do you think they have a history? Should we talk to him?"

"Tim Snyder's very fond of Jo Harper and highly protective of her," Lucy said. "Jo spent many years as a total recluse. For decades she only ventured off her own property occasionally to walk the streets or the beaches at night, avoiding contact with almost everyone."

"I did wonder why she'd never had breakfast in a restaurant before," Brad said.

"That's why. And it's why she lives with her brother, Ralph. Because of events that happened not long ago, and the involvement of Mr. Snyder and his friendship and encouragement, she's emerged from her shell enough to come to book club, never mind staying at the Shrimp Shack to have breakfast after Ralph left. I'm not surprised Mr. Snyder reacted so strongly to someone he thought might threaten Jo's new-found peace-of-mind." Lucy smiled. "Maybe even a bit of jealousy on his part. For a while I thought Mr. Snyder and Jo might get together, be more than friends, but I suppose the age difference was just too much."

"All the more reason for him to get angry if he thought Brian was interested in dating Jo," I said. "He looks to be about the same age as Brian. Speaking of age differences. I have some news, Brad."

Lucy headed for the refreshment table. "I'll clean up, and you can show your brother around the lighthouse. You'll want to talk in private."

"It's okay," I said. "Please stay. You were there when I met her."

"Met who?" Brad asked.

"Met whom," I said instinctively.

Footsteps on the stairs and Louise Jane and Charles appeared. "All gone," Louise Jane said. "Good meeting, Nichelle. Everyone told me they enjoyed it." She looked from one of us to the other. "What's going on? What are you bunch talking about? Not classic mysteries at a guess."

"Nichelle?" Lucy said.

"Louise Jane might be able to help us," I said. "If she knows as many people as she says she does."

"I know more." She dropped into a chair. Charles sniffed under the refreshment table. Disappointed no one had dropped a cookie or a piece of pastry, he leapt onto my lap.

"He's accepted you," Lucy said. "I'm glad. It can be hard for much-adored pets when babies arrive on the scene, and they're abruptly pushed out of what they see as their rightful place in the family hierarchy."

I rubbed behind Charles's ears. He purred in return.

"Okay, spill," Louise Jane said. "What do you need help with? That guy who died here, I assume. Couldn't help but notice that you two got very uncomfortable very suddenly the moment his name came up."

"Brian Saunders," I said, "had a past life under the name of Bradley Sanderson."

"Which not-at-all-coincidently happens to be your name," she said to Brad.

"Not a coincidence, no."

As briefly as I could, I told Louise Jane the bare bones of the story.

"Wow!" she said when I finished. "He must have come here on Sunday to see you, Nichelle."

"I have to assume so. It's not so much the why of why he came here that matters—he likely read about me in the notice in the paper or online and decided too many years had passed—but why someone killed him."

I said nothing about the police questioning Brad, and my own thoughts as to why Brad had been in town on Saturday, and why he hadn't told me about it. "Loretta Kowalski says she dated Brian twice, but she decided not to see him again because she had an 'off' feeling about him, although she couldn't describe anything in particular. As we heard tonight, he asked Jo Harper out. Both of those women are in their sixties. Brian was seventy-seven. I'll admit that isn't too ridiculous of an age gap."

"A single man of that age with an income and in full command of his faculties, not to mention a driver's license, is considered a valuable prize in some circles," Louise Jane said. "I'll ask my mom and my grandmother if they know of him."

"It's the income, I'm wondering about," Brad said. "He worked at a beach supply store, as a salesclerk. I can't imagine he made much there."

"He used to work at a beach supply store," I said. "The police told me he left there recently."

"Even worse. A job like that doesn't pay well, and it tells me if he was working at his age, he needed what little money the job paid. He wouldn't have much, if anything, in the way of benefits or retirement income. Remember, he disappeared when he was thirty-nine. He would have had to start over completely, and he needed to avoid contact with any sort of government agency that might have searched his records."

"Lucy and I went to the house he was living in today," I said. "It's an average small house in an average neighborhood in an expensive town. He was only renting, but he clearly wasn't totally down and out."

"If you want to dig into what happened, you need to ask Detective Thomas some questions, Nichelle," Lucy said. "Questions about his source of income, his financial situation, to begin with. If he was into something not on the level, that might be what got him killed."

"Do I want to look into it? That's what I'm wondering. You tell me to follow my instincts, and my instincts say yes, but I'm not sure. Maybe I'm afraid of turning up things I'd rather not know."

"They're looking at pinning it on me, Nichie," Brad said.

"You think so? Because of you being here Saturday?"

"Yeah. Detective Thomas paid me another visit earlier, not long before I left for the library. She's interested in why I was in Nags Head, and why I've been coming down over the years. She asked me about that last night, at the police station, and followed up today."

Louise Jane and Lucy watched my brother but said nothing.

"What did you tell her?" I asked.

"I . . . This is hard for me to say."

"Would you like us to leave?" Lucy asked.

"No need," Louise Jane said. "I never repeat information told to me in confidence."

"Since when?"

"It's okay," Brad said. "Might as well tell you all. It'll come out soon enough. Hopefully it won't get back to Rochester, though. Yeah, I was here, in Nags Head, on Saturday. I arrived on Wednesday. No point in denying it as I got a speeding ticket early Saturday morning. On my way *out* of town I might add. I was back in Rochester that night. My wife can testify to that, but Detective Thomas implied that a wife isn't considered to be a reliable alibi. In particular, my wife won't be a reliable alibi, not if the cops tell her what city's asking about me. Maya thought I was in New York City for business on Thursday and Friday."

"Oopsie," Louise Jane said.

"Oopsie is about right. Over the past several years, every time I've been in Nags Head, I told Maya I was having meetings in New York."

"Why?" I asked.

"Why else?" Brad twisted his hands in his lap. His head was down, avoiding my eyes.

"Okay, moving right along," Louise Jane said. "Will this person you were visiting in Nags Head give you an alibi?"

"No. She's . . . It's complicated."

"For heaven's sake, Brad!" I said with so much force I startled Charles. "We do not need that. How long—"

"Can we talk about that later, please, Nichie?"

I ignored him. "All that stuff you told me about some admittedly foolish idea of hoping to find Dad, when no one else could, of wanting to come to grips with your emotions around his disappearance, of searching for answers. You're telling me now that was all pure bunk?"

"No, Nichie. That's true. At first, over the years, that's why I came. Then, time passed, and my reasons changed."

"How much time passed before your reasons changed?" I said.

"Why don't you two come to grips with that at another time," Lucy said calmly.

"Now's good," Louise Jane said.

"It is not," Lucy said. "Back to the matter at hand. What did the detective have to say about your most recent visit?"

"Suffice to say I'm in the police's eye because I was here not long before my long-lost father died. How much anger did I have toward him, Thomas asked me. How many years of built-up resentment was I holding onto. Did I come here with the intention of killing him, or did I snap when I finally did confront him."

Chapter Twenty

Lucy had no intention whatsoever of getting involved in the latest murder case at the library. She had her family now, two precious babies who needed all the attention she could give them. Connor, who worried when she unwittingly put herself in danger, but always supported her when she needed to follow her instincts or satisfy her natural curiosity.

She sat quietly in the third-floor meeting room while Nichelle's brother told his story. He looked like a dog who'd been caught scarfing up the remains of the Thanksgiving turkey left on the kitchen counter not quite out of range. Was that because he'd been caught having, presumably, an affair? Or because he'd been caught trying to track down his father, and perhaps succeeded. Brad lived in Rochester, a long way from Nags Head. Detective Thomas had to be asking why he'd be having an affair here, of all places, so far from his home. If Brad wouldn't give the police this person's name, for whatever reason, they'd be doubly suspicious of his story.

Lucy's mother had once been a murder suspect, and Lucy had felt compelled to do all she could to do clear her. She'd advised Nichelle to follow her instincts and that was all she could do. If Nichelle wanted to take it further, Lucy could make some suggestions—most of all, speak to Sam Watson.

"Did you do it, Brad?" Louise Jane asked. "Did you kill your long-lost father?"

Brad's head jerked up. "No. I most emphatically did not."

"Great, now we've got that settled, Nichelle, you need to start by asking Sam Watson what he knows of what the police know."

"Louise Jane, why don't we let Nichelle decide for herself what she wants to do," Lucy said. "Sam tells me he's happy with Detective Thomas, and Butch says the same. She's a good detective."

"She's got a bee in her bonnet about men who fool around on their wives," Brad said.

"What makes you say that?" Nichelle asked. "Did she say something."

"Not in so many words, but I could tell."

"Are you saying the detective will not be impartial?" Lucy asked. "That she'll railroad you for the killing, not because you were in Nags Head killing anyone but, as you put it, fooling around?"

"That's exactly what he's saying," Louise Jane said. "As for what I say—"

"Why don't we let Brad speak for himself," Lucy said.

Louise Jane harrumphed, but she said no more. Nichelle kept her head down, stroking Charles. Charles watched them all.

"I don't know what I'm saying," Brad said at last.

"Okay." Nichelle lifted her head. "That's your problem, and I'll leave it up to you to handle it or not. In the meantime, we have another avenue we can explore. Lucy and I went to Brian's house earlier. We met his girlfriend."

"Sounds like he was quite the man about town," Brad said. "Her, whoever she is, as well as your book club lady and the mother of that guy in the weird suit."

"I find something highly concerning about that entire situation. The woman we met told the police she and Brian had been together about a year. Yet less than a year ago, and then a few months ago, he was in pursuit of, as far as we know, at least two other women. Loretta Kowalski and Jo Harper, respectively. Both of whom are considerably older and substantially less flashy than this girlfriend. The name she gave us is Melissa Archibald."

Lucy watched Brad's face as Nichelle spoke. He seemed amused at the mention of his father having a girlfriend, but not shocked at hearing the name. Unlikely, unless he was a very good actor or the woman had given him a different name, it was the same woman he was coming to Nags Head to see. Lucy had never been one to believe in coincidence.

"Don't know anyone by that name," Brad said. "You say the other women he dated are older than this Melissa. How old is she?"

"Late forties, almost fifty. She dresses like she's trying to be ten years younger."

Brad laughed without humor. "You must be kidding me. Let's be honest here. Women of that age don't go out with a guy almost thirty years older than them unless he's rich. Sure doesn't sound like Brian was anything near that."

"Don't make assumptions," Louise Jane said. "It does happen. Why, my great-great-uncle Eb fathered two children in his seventies, and he was dirt poor."

Lucy was about to interrupt and, as politely as possible, say she didn't give two hoots about Great-Great-Uncle Eb and his progeny, when Louise Jane continued, "Back to the matter at hand. You're asking about someone named Archibald. My cousin Ricky married an Archibald girl from Duck, I think. Her name wasn't Melissa though, and considering Cousin Ricky is actually my father's older cousin, and they married about fifty years ago, I'm guessing it's not her. I can ask around."

"You think all this is significant?" Brad said. "Why?"

"Why indeed," Nichelle said. "I have a question. When I have a question, I need an answer."

Both Charles and Nichelle turned to Lucy. "Do you agree?"

"I do," Lucy said.

Chapter Twenty-One

My ex-husband called me indecisive. He'd get angry at me, accuse me of never being able to come to a decision.

He'd been wrong about that, among many other things. I am not indecisive, I simply like to think things over, to examine all the angles. I don't act rashly or leap into uncharted waters. I think long and carefully before eventually coming to a decision.

But once I reach that decision—to divorce him, to go to college at age fifty to get the degree I'd long dreamed of, to investigate my father's murder—I was all in with everything I had.

Louise Jane volunteered to use her contacts to find out what she could about Melissa Archibald as well as Brian Saunders. Lucy placed a call to Sam Watson and left a message telling him I'd like to speak to him when he was available.

"What can I do?" Brad asked.

I couldn't think of anything I wanted Brad to do. Admittedly, my own marriage hadn't been doing too well for a number of years, but it was when I found out Daniel was cheating on me, I finally realized the time had come to do what I needed to do. And so I made that final decision, and I left him. He tried to get me to come back but, decision made, it was made. In light of that, I wasn't exactly having warm feelings toward my brother at the moment.

"Ralph mentioned that Brian sometimes went to the Shrimp Shack, which is where he met Jo," Lucy said. "Why don't you drop in there, see if anyone can tell you anything about him. I know the place. They open early to cater for charter boat and fishing crews and workers at the docks. They do a great all-American breakfast."

The look of relief on my brother's face at being given a task almost made me feel sorry for him.

Almost, but not quite.

Lucy stood up. "I'm going home. I haven't had word from Connor tonight, and I don't know if that's a good thing or a bad thing."

"How about you show me around the lighthouse?" Brad asked me. "I still can't believe you have an apartment in here."

"Not tonight. It's late, and I'm tired, and I have a lot of things to think about."

With that, we all went our separate ways.

* * *

The following morning, Sam Watson called me shortly before the library opened for the day."Lucy said you want to speak to me, Nichelle. Can I assume it's about your father's case?"

"Cases, I guess we should say. What happened thirty-eight years ago and then three days ago. Yes, I've decided I need to know what happened, both times."

"I'll do what I can to help, as long as you understand I'm retired, meaning I'm not actively involved in the Brian Saunders investigation. Having said that, I know how things work around here, and I hear things. I might be able to give you some direction, but I don't want you to count on being able to solve it. If you intend to get involved, you need to talk with Detective Thomas. Not me."

"Understood."

"Let's meet for lunch then. How about Josie's at one? Be just like old times."

* * *

Josie's Cozy Bakery was a crowded place at one minute past one o'clock. A line stretched out the door reaching almost to the sidewalk, and a quick glance through the windows showed me a full room. In case Sam had arrived before me, I slipped past the line, saying "sorry, sorry" all the way, and stuck my head through the door. Across the crowded room, I saw him stand up and give me a wave.

"One of the benefits of being retired," he said once I'd taken a seat on the high stool at a table made out of a reclaimed ship's barrel. "I got here early enough to snag us a place. I'm sure you have to get back soon." He had an almost empty cup of coffee in front of him. "Plus, I have influence, so I took the liberty of putting the staff on stand-by."

None other than Josie herself appeared at our table. "Hi, Nichelle. How was book club last night?"

"Good, I think. I hope the members enjoyed it. Everyone had a lot to say."

She laughed. "I have no doubt about that."

"I was sorry to miss it," Sam said. "CeeCee dragged me to dinner with some of her arty friends to discuss the fall exhibit at the gallery. I have absolutely no idea why she thought I'd have anything to contribute, but I went anyway."

"Never hurts to be the supportive spouse," Josie said. "I only wish I had more time to be that for Jake."

"Says the woman whose idea of date night is chopping vegetables at his restaurant," Sam said.

Josie laughed again. "Then along come the kids, and a date night of any sort is nothing but a fond memory."

"I'm collecting recommendations for books to read over the next few months," I said. "Please, send me your suggestions, both of you."

"Will do," Josie said. "Now, on to more important things: the sandwich specials today are ham and Swiss cheese on a minibaguette with or without spicy mustard, or for a vegetarian option hummus on pita with a side of raw vegetables. Otherwise, we have a vegetable quiche, my homemade chicken noodle soup, as well as a range of muffins and pastries."

"The ham sandwich sounds good, with the mustard," I said. "And a latte please."

"Same for me," Watson said. "Heavy on that mustard. And another coffee."

"Coming right up." Josie slipped away.

I said nothing while Sam downed the last dregs of his coffee and put the mug on the table. He chose his words carefully. "I understand you have questions, Nichelle. Anyone would in your situation. I have a lot of experience as a cop, both on the street and then as a detective. First, in New York, then back home here in Nags Head. I've found that when folks ask questions, they often get answers they don't want to hear."

"Someone else told me that only yesterday," I said.

"Lucy?"

"Yes."

"She's right. Then again, when questions fester, that doesn't do anyone any good either."

"If it was just that Brian Saunders . . . my dad had been murdered, I'd leave it to the police. His disappearance all those years ago is obviously something that's hung over my life since, but not as much as you might think. Basically, I moved on. I had a life of my own and a family, and I did okay. What I'm wondering most of all is what brought him to the library the other night, and was his killing directly related to that."

"Here you go." A smiling young woman put our lunches on the table.

"Thanks, Alison," Sam said. "This is Nichelle, by the way. The new assistant director at the library."

"Pleased to meet you," Alison said. "I'm sure we'll be seeing you in here a lot. I hope so anyway."

"You will," I said. My sandwich looked absolutely fantastic. A crusty six-inch baguette loaded with thick slices of ham and thinly cut cheese topped by yellow mustard dotted with specks of black pepper. A salad of fresh baby greens sat on the side of the plate.

"Just like old times," Sam said once again, as he dug into his sandwich.

I did the same. It tasted as good as it looked.

When we both came up for air, Sam said, "Okay. Brian Saunders has largely been a model citizen. From what I could find out, he's lived in Nags Head almost forty years."

"All the time he was missing."

"Seems so. You have to understand, no one looked for him to be alive. The coast guard searched the shoreline; the police contacted other jurisdictions inquiring if a body had washed up or been taken to a hospital or morgue. It was assumed he'd gone for a swim, unwisely alone, late at night, having had a significant amount of alcohol, and been swept out to sea. Records show the tide was high that night and at the time he appeared to have gone for his swim, it was going out. It happens."

"But it didn't happen."

"Exactly. In the years since Bradley Sanderson walked out of that hotel with nothing but the clothes he was wearing and his bathing suit, and Brian Saunders died, the man did almost nothing to bring himself to police attention. Not even a speeding ticket. He moved quite a few times, from one rental house to another; he had several jobs, all of them seasonal and casual. Detective Thomas has spoken to people he worked with, some of his drinking buddies. His girlfriend. You know about her?"

"I do."

"None of the people Thomas spoke to have indicated he was involved in the sort of thing that gets a man killed."

"You said he did almost nothing to come to police attention. So there was something?"

He grinned. "You have some detective material in you, Nichelle. Yes. About a year ago, a man came into the office wanting to lay charges against Saunders."

"What sort of charges?"

"Embezzlement. This man claimed that Brian Saunders had befriended his mother under false circumstances and extorted money from her in exchange for this friendship. According to him, Saunders convinced this woman to give him a substantial amount of money to invest on her behalf in some scheme or another; she did so, and he claimed to have lost it all. When confronted by the son, Saunders refused to explain where he'd supposedly invested it, so the son came to the police."

"What happened?"

"An officer went around to the woman's house and spoke to her. She refused to lay charges. She said Brian was her dear friend, and sadly he'd also been duped by a fraudster. It was her money, plain and clear, not her son's money, so the son had no legal standing to try to get it back or to lay charges. The woman was fully capable of handling her own affairs, so the case was closed, no further action to be taken."

"Can I guess this woman was a widow or divorced and in her mid-to-late sixties?"

"You can. She's a summer resident, and she returned to New York City not long after this incident. I don't know if she's come back this year. From what I heard, she's of considerable means, and the money she gave to Saunders was nothing she couldn't easily afford."

I sighed.

"Didn't help the son's argument that, according to the woman, she and her son are estranged, and largely, again according to her, because of financial disagreements since her husband's death."

I sighed again. I was getting a bad feeling about this, but I'd been warned, more than once, that I might discover things I didn't want to know. Sam ate his sandwich and said nothing, allowing me to process the information. I poked at the lettuce on my plate. "I've been wondering about Brian's dating situation." I told Sam what I'd heard from Loretta Kowalski and Jo Harper. "Nothing wrong with a single man of that age wanting to meet women, except he supposedly has a much younger girlfriend. Whom I've met."

"They could have an open relationship," Sam said.

"Yes, and they could be running a scam together. Are you sure there weren't any more complaints of that sort against him?"

"I'm not working any more, Nichelle. I retired about a year ago. Please remember that. I was able to see the records from your father's disappearance because that happened a long, long time ago, and foul play was never seriously suspected. As for the current case, what little I know was told to me by Detective Thomas. She's not from around these parts and doesn't know all the players or the way we Bankers do things, so she comes to me for advice on occasion, and I'm glad to be able to give it. Nothing I've told you was told to me in confidence. If it was, I wouldn't repeat it."

"Fair enough."

"As for your question, the incident I mentioned is the only official complaint laid against Saunders that Detective Thomas was able to find." He finished his coffee and pushed his empty plate to one side. I'd barely touched my sandwich. "I have to be going. Lunch is on me. Some things never are solved, Nichelle, and some questions are never answered."

I nodded.

"Is your brother still in town?"

"Yes. He came to book club last night."

"Did he tell you Thomas has questions for him about his whereabouts last weekend?"

"He did."

"Good. For my final piece of advice, today anyway, talk it out with him. As I said, it never does any good when questions fester."

Chapter Twenty-Two

I asked Alison for a take-out bag for my unfinished lunch and drove back to the library, full of thought.

Had Sam Watson been telling me Brad knew more than he was letting on? If so, yes, I needed to know what that might be.

I was paying attention to where I was going with half a mind, but that half mind suddenly read a sign ahead I hadn't noticed before.

Gardner Beach Supplies. Propelled by the wind, a twelve-foot tall, long-limbed, garish pink inflated blow-up figure waved to passersby.

I turned the wheel so sharply the car behind me leaned on his horn. I gave an embarrassed wave of "sorry" and screeched into the parking lot. The front of the store in question was festooned with blue and red bunting and flapping flags hanging above lines of primary-colored plastic chairs and huge boxes overflowing with towels, beach balls, pail and shovel sets, and flip flops.

Brian Saunders had worked at Gardner Beach Supplies. It was possible this store was part of a chain and they had more outlets, but I thought it worth a try. Surely he'd made friends with some of the people he worked with, or at least talked to them during breaks. The police had been here, but people don't always tell the police everything they know. Not if they believed it was of no importance or they didn't want to speak ill of the dead. Some people didn't trust the authorities and some didn't want to get involved.

No harm in trying, I said to myself as I got out of my car.

"Hi!" A pink-cheeked, short, chubby woman in late middle age standing by the doors greeted me. "Welcome to Gardner Beach Supplies, providing all your vacation and beach needs. Can I help you with anything today?" Her teeth gleamed. The gleam did not reach her eyes. She was reciting the expected lines and clearly didn't much care whether or not I satisfied my vacation and beach needs. Instead her expression said her feet hurt.

I instinctively started to smile in return, and then I remembered why I was here. "Thank you, but no. My father died recently, and I was hoping to meet some people who knew him."

The fake smile disappeared, and her face flooded with genuine sympathy. "Oh, no. I'm sorry to hear that, honey. I don't know if I can help. I haven't been working here too long."

"Unfortunately, we'd been estranged for a long time, but I now find myself needing to talk to people who knew him. Brian Saunders?"

The sympathy disappeared to be replaced with outright curiosity. "Brian? Yeah, I knew Brian. The cops were in here asking about him. I heard on the news he was murdered. Do you know about that?"

"No. I mean, yes, I know about that, but I don't know why."

"Everything okay here, Martha?" A woman approached. She was dressed in a severe brown skirt suit that had most definitely seen better days. Her feet also hurt. Her name badge said 'Carol'.

"Fine, fine. This lady's Brian's long-lost daughter and she—"

"I'll take over, thank you, Martha." Carol looked at me, and not in a particularly friendly way. "The police have spoken to my staff. They've told them all they have to say."

"Of course. I'm sure they cooperated fully. I was hoping to talk to people who knew him on a personal, friendly level. I'm Nichelle."

"As you can see, Michelle, we're very busy."

I didn't bother either to correct my name or point out that the store was almost empty of customers. Martha had edged away a few inches, and the sole cashier was in danger of straining her neck if she moved her head any further in our direction.

"As for Brian Saunders," Carol, presumably the manager, said at last, "I told the police the same. At the time of his death, he was not employed here."

"When did he leave?"

"About two weeks ago."

Behind me, the doors swooshed open and a family came in. The kids immediately headed for the toy section. I stood my ground. Indecision crossed the brown-suited woman's face. The overwhelming desire to spread gossip won out over seeing to her customers, so she said to me, "Follow me, please. Martha, keep an eye on those . . . younger customers in case they need any assistance." Meaning watch them in case the kids started throwing balls around.

She led me through a door marked "Staff Only" into a dingy corridor. She didn't take me into an office or suggest we find seats. "I don't mind telling you this store is struggling to stay afloat. Our owner, Curtis Gardner, ran into some legal troubles recently and his brother, who Curtis handed control of the business over to, isn't as competent as one might like. What I'm saying is, we don't need trouble here, and so I had to let Brian go. I felt bad about it, but what else could I do?"

"What sort of trouble?"

"You're his daughter, right?"

I nodded.

"I see the resemblance. I overheard you tell Martha you were estranged, so you probably don't mind hearing about what happened. A man came in one day. It was a rainy Saturday so the store was busy. He demanded to speak to Brian and cornered him on the floor. Brian was serving customers at the time but the guy just started yelling. It would have been okay if Brian walked away, but he really got into it in return. We get kids in here, right? His language was not something I am going to repeat. They yelled at each other a couple of times, and then Brian punched the guy. Smack dab in the jaw. Not what you expect from a couple of old geezers like that. Everyone else started yelling and screaming, and some younger guy, a dad here with his family, had to separate them. The other man left, still yelling threats, and I told Brian to get his stuff and clear out. Right then and there. I don't know if that was the right thing to do, but at the time I was so angry. I later thought Brian might come back, either to talk me into giving him his job back or to threaten to sue the store, but I never saw him again. And then, not long after, I heard he'd died."

"Did you tell the police about this altercation?"

"Yeah, I did. I thought maybe the guy tracked Brian down, and they had it out once again."

"What was the argument about?"

"I'm not saying what the guy had to say was true, but Brian didn't deny it. He just told the other guy to mind his own business."

I nodded, encouraging her to go on.

"He told Brian to stay away from his sister. The way they talked, you would have thought they were in high school. As though the sister couldn't make up her own mind. Then again, maybe that's not entirely fair. The guy, I never did get his name, called Brian a cheat and a conman. As he was being hustled out of the store, he yelled that Brian had better return what he stole or else."

"Or else?"

"Or else. He didn't say or else what. I told the cops this."

"Had you ever seen this man before? You said you didn't get his name."

She shook her head. "Normal looking guy, late sixties maybe. On the short side and sorta thin. Dressed OBX casual, like most of the people we get in here."

"Thank you."

"I had grounds to fire Brian, right? Can't have employees exhibiting that sort of behavior in front of our customers. Particularly not little kids."

I realized she was telling me all this hoping I'd not get the idea of suing her for false dismissal. "I don't know much about employment law, sorry. Thanks for your time."

I headed for the exit, and on the way out I noticed a rack of toys for young children. Sidewalk chalk, bubble wands, water guns, inflatable balls, play jewelry, including bracelets with tiny pink beads.

* * *

I sat in my car for a long time. Sam Watson told me a man laid a complaint against Brian about a year ago. That man had been the son of the woman Brian was . . . whatever Brian was. Two weeks ago, he lost his job after a confrontation with another man about . . . once again whatever Brian was up to.

I was beginning to see a pattern. Yes, two incidents don't a pattern make, but in light of Loretta Kowalski saying something seemed "off" about Brian's attempts to date her, and Tim Snyder's accusations against Brian, I was beginning to put together a picture.

What to do about this picture, was the question.

* * *

I arrived at the library and was walking up the path when my phone rang. The display said it was Brad. "I can't talk for long, I just got back from lunch."

"Let's get together after work," he said. "I have someone I want you to meet."

"Who?"

"My alibi, because you seem to think I need one."

"I never said that."

"Not in so many words, but you thought it. How about six? Same place as the other night? We'll meet you there."

"Okay."

"Before you go, I went to that restaurant this morning, hoping to catch the regular breakfast crowd."

"What restaurant?"

"The Shrimp Shack. Where Brian met the woman who was at your book club last night."

"Oh, right. Great. What did you learn? Can it keep until we meet tonight?"

"I learned nothing. I showed his picture around. Everyone had heard about his death. Some people knew him, but only on sight or to exchange talk of the weather with. It's the sort of working man's place where the same people go day after day, year after year. Guys, and a few women, who work on the fishing boats or charters or at the docks. Brian came in for breakfast occasionally, but he wasn't what anyone would call a regular, and as far as anyone can remember, he was always on his own. He usually sat at the counter by himself, ate his bacon and eggs, drank his coffee, and left. One of the waitresses said he often seemed to be, in her words, 'down'."

"Down?"

"I took that to mean depressed. Sad anyway. I asked if he was a good tipper, and she said it varied a lot. Some days, he tipped almost the same amount as the bill. Some days, he left a couple of quarters. I asked if he ever came in with a woman, and she said not that she'd seen. The customers I spoke to said the same."

"All helps to build the picture. See you later then." I hung up without telling my brother what I'd learned about our father today. Until he told me the truth about why he'd been in Nags Head last Saturday, I wasn't entirely sure I could trust him.

It was not a pleasant feeling.

* * *

Shortly before closing, the library had an unexpected visitor.

The woman I'd met at Brian's house, Melissa Archibald, came in. She wore a form-fitting summer dress with a plunging neckline, cut just above her knees. Strappy sandals with three-inch heels were on her feet and a long silver necklace around her neck with matching earrings in her ears. Her blond hair hung loosely around her shoulders. I was behind the circulation desk, and she spotted me immediately. She gave me a bright smile and headed my way, heels tapping on the floor.

"Hi. Michelle, right?"

"Nichelle. With an N."

"Silly me," she giggled. "My bad. I hope you don't mind my coming in out of the blue like this but I found out that you work here, and I wanted to apologize for not being friendly the last time we met. It's a hard time for me. I'm sure you understand. Brian and I were very good friends."

The middle grade summer reading program was about to end in the children's library. Parents were arriving to pick up their kids. Not a few of the fathers took sideways peeks at Melissa. She was, in my admittedly biased opinion, pretty enough, but in a hardened way. Brittle might be the word I'd choose. Her eyes, rimmed in black liner, lashes coated in a boatload of mascara, showed no signs of recent tears.

"You took me by surprise showing up at Brian's door like that. His daughter. Imagine that. After all the time we'd spent together, I didn't even know he had a daughter. I hope we can be fast friends." She smiled at me.

Not a chance of that.

"How did you find out where I work?"

"After you left, I remembered seeing Mrs. McNeil in the paper. Her husband's the mayor so her picture's been in the local news with him at functions, as well as from some library events. I checked the library's website and there you were."

Children tumbled down the stairs, and stacks of chapter books were dropped on the desk in front of me.

"It's nice of you to stop by, Melissa," I said. "But, as you can see, I'm working right now."

"I don't mind. You carry on. I just wanted to say hi. I'm sure you're wondering what someone my age would be doing dating your dad, but I always say age is just a number. Brian was so much fun, anyone would have thought he was decades younger than he was. A soulmate is a soulmate, isn't that so, Michelle? We have so much to talk about, you and me. I can't wait to hear all about what he was like way back then. Talk soon, bye!"

And, with a wiggle of her fingers and a slight stumble on her too-high heels, she was gone. She did not check out any books.

That, I thought, was weird. Yes, I did wonder what a woman of that age would want with my father. Not to be a soulmate, for sure.

Louise Jane popped out from behind the staircase. "Ah ha! Perfect timing. As you will come to find is normal for me. Can I take a guess that was none other than Melissa Archibald?"

"You can," I said.

"I have my report ready. We'll talk after closing."

I was left wondering what Louise Jane had to report, as I checked out books and chatted to kids and parents.

A few minutes before closing time, Lucy came in. She'd been at a meeting all day with the directors of the other Dare County libraries. "Can you spare a few minutes after work, Nichelle?" she asked me. "I learned something you might want to know."

I was supposed to be meeting Brad at six. Louise Jane had a "report" for me, and Lucy had "something" to tell me. My brother would have to wait, and when I had the chance I sent him a text: *Delayed at work. Be there at 7.*

Eventually, closing time rolled around. Ronald bid us a good night, and I locked the door behind him. When I turned around, both Lucy and Louise Jane were watching me.

"What?" I said.

They glanced at each other. "Why don't I go first?" Louise Jane dropped into a chair at the computer station, and Lucy and I did the same. "Last night after book club, I put the word out on the family grapevine I was wanting info about Brian Saunders and Melissa Archibald. No one knew much about Brian, other than that they'd all heard about his death. My mother and grandma didn't know him. He didn't frequent the usual things in their social circles like the bridge or euchre clubs or volunteer at the hospital or anything else along those lines. But . . ." Dramatic pause.

"But what, Louise Jane?" Lucy said.

"Lest you fear my grapevine is in danger of letting us down, fear not. This morning, I heard from my cousin Kevin.

He owns a couple of bars in town, not the sort of places either of you are likely to frequent. One of which is Blackbeard's Cave. I vaguely knew that, but I didn't say anything earlier because I wanted to confirm before mentioning it. From what Cousin Kevin says, Brian Saunders was a customer there, as is Melissa Archibald. And she in particular is not entirely unknown in certain circles."

"Huh?" I said.

"Louise Jane likes to draw out the suspense," Lucy explained. "She means Melissa has a reputation of possibly being up to no good or at best knowing people who are possibly up to no good."

"Well put," Louise Jane said. "Kevin's main place, the one where he takes some bartending shifts himself, is none other than the hideously named Blackbeard's Cave. Kevin knows Melissa because she's done some waitressing there, although not recently. She still comes in, now and again. Has a couple of drinks, talks to people, leaves. Sometimes with men, sometimes not. Far as he knows, she hasn't held down a regular job in a couple of years."

"Is that significant?" I asked.

"Might be. Might not be. Kevin admits he doesn't know everything about everyone who comes in, but he keeps his ear to the ground, if you know what I mean."

I didn't, but I didn't say so.

"Not a regular job, but there are other types of jobs," Lucy said.

"Exactly!" Louise Jane said. "According to Kevin, Melissa's been dressing better lately, got herself some nice jewelry." I thought of the silver necklace and earrings. "She started going to a better hairdresser. She's even been buying her own drinks, which, according to Kevin, was not her habit in the past. And not only her own, but buying for other people too."

"Step back," I said. "Most men don't know anything about the quality or price of women's clothes, never mind their hairdresser. Why would he comment on that?"

"Fashion is one of Kevin's passions in life. He wanted to go to design school, but his dad died, and Kevin had to take over running the business. Anyway, I took the liberty of asking Kevin if Melissa ever came in with an older guy, and he jumped right on that." Louise Jane's eyes gleamed with the love of telling the story. I'd been warned she liked to take liberties with her paranormal knowledge. I'd need to be careful to take whatever she said with a grain of salt, but the bones of this story sounded real. Louise Jane continued, "Kevin had seen Brian's picture in the paper, and recognized him right away. Brian was a regular, he often came in when Melissa was there, but . . ."

"But?"

"Spit it out Louise Jane," Lucy said. "I have to get home and relieve Sofia."

"A good story," Louise Jane sniffed, "is worth telling well. But I concede your point. I told Kevin Melissa told the cops she was Brian's girlfriend, and he laughed outright. Not a sign of anything like that, he said. They were friends, that was obvious, and they got on pretty well, but nothing more. Melissa would flirt with guys she met, even leave with them occasionally, and Brian never seemed to mind."

"Did Kevin tell the police that?"

"He called them, said Brian drank at his place sometimes, but that was about all. A uniform came to talk to him, but he couldn't tell them anything more. Kevin last saw Brian more than a week ago. He couldn't remember the exact day, but he wasn't working last weekend. He told me the police sent a couple of officers to ask around at the bar about Brian's activities and when anyone last saw him, but it's not the sort of place that attracts the type of customers who talk freely to the cops, so they likely didn't learn much. Even if there was anything to learn."

"Why do you suppose Melissa is saying she was his girlfriend?" I asked.

"Wanting in on any inheritance maybe?" Lucy said. "She did have a key to his place. She might have gone there the time we saw her to help herself to what she wanted while she could."

"Why would she have a key if they weren't involved romantically?" I asked.

"Lots of people give friends keys, so they can water the plants when they're away, keep an eye on things, as a back-up in case they lose their own key."

"Kevin is now on our side," Louise Jane said.

"We have a side?" I said.

"We certainly do. He'll keep an eye out and report back to me on Melissa's activities and listen in if he hears any talk about Brian. Kevin might have wanted to be a fashion designer, but I don't think he would have liked it much."

"Why not?" I asked.

"Not enough gossip in the fashion world. Kevin likes to be at the center of all knowledge about the goings-on on the shadier side of Nags Head."

"I also have something to report," Lucy said. "When I got home last night I told my husband, Connor, what Theodore's mom and Jo Harper had to say about Brian. I hope that was okay?"

"Even if I wanted to keep it secret, which I don't," I said, "too late now."

"Marie, Connor's mom, told him a while ago about a friend of hers she was worried about. His mom's friend, a widow of many years, has an adequate but not lavish income, and she'd met this man."

"Brian Saunders?"

"Marie didn't tell Connor the name, so he's going to ask her today if she remembers it. An elderly gentleman, also widowed, supposedly looking for a companion. His mom got the feeling her friend was spending money she shouldn't on this man. A red flag went up when the friend told her she loaned the man money."

"I bet it did," Louise Jane said.

"What happened then?" I asked.

"Marie has never been one to suffer fools gladly. She asked her friend if that was wise; her friend got angry, and they've never spoken again as far as Connor knows."

"It can be awful hard for some people to admit they've been foolish," Louise Jane said. "Not something I myself can understand, but there you are."

Lucy coughed lightly but said nothing.

"Connor thinks this man might be Brian?" I asked.

"He has no reason to believe so. It's only that the story fits what we're talking about. With your permission, Nichelle, he'll call his mom and ask if her former friend might be willing to talk to you. You can take it from there, if it was Brian she was seeing, and if you want to pursue this."

I nodded. "I've come this far. There's clearly a pattern here, and I have to see it through." I told the other women what I'd learned today: about the man who went to the police to lay a complaint against Brian, and the reason Brian lost his job at the store.

"What do you suppose this has to do with Melissa?" Louise Jane asked.

"Maybe nothing, other than they knew each other from your cousin's bar. She couldn't pretend to be Brian's girlfriend in front of women he was trying to start a relationship with."

Lucy stood up. "I have to go. If Connor's able to get a name for you, Nichelle, and if she's willing to talk to you, I'll pass it on. Good night."

"Night," we called.

"I'm thinking of dropping into Kevin's place," Louise Jane said. "I've never been there. I'll check out the scene, see if anyone's willing to talk to me. Wanna come?"

"I can't. I have an engagement of my own to keep."

"Want company?"

"I would, but I fear that would not be appropriate under the circumstances."

Chapter Twenty-Three

My brother was sitting alone at a small table in a far, dark corner of the beachside restaurant. The music was loud, the patrons louder. The place was full of vacationers, many of whom were not on their first drink of the day. The scent of grease and beer hung over the cavernous room, and lights flashed from the giant TV screens mounted high on the walls.

Brad was watching for me and stood to lift a hand in greeting when he saw me hesitating at the doorway. He had an almost-finished mug of beer in front of him and a half-consumed plate of nachos, but nothing else was on the table. "Sorry," he said.

I sat down. "She's not coming?"

"Cold feet."

"What can I get you, hon?" the waitress asked.

"Just a lemonade, please, if you have something like that."

"No lemonade, but we have tea."

"Fine."

"Anything to eat?"

"No, thank you."

I looked around the room. This was unlikely to be one of Louise Jane's cousin's places. It catered mainly to the tourist crowd. Family groups ate burgers and fries; a toddler was stuffing pizza into her mouth while a baby bounced in a high chair. A large table of middle-aged women in loose T-shirts and baggy shorts, with sunburned noses and salt-encrusted hair called to the waiter to bring another bottle. "Make it snappy, kid. We're not getting any younger here." They roared with laughter at their own wit.

"I'm not the police, Brad," I said. "I'm not going to arrest this mysterious woman. I thought she wanted to meet me."

"She does." He pushed the plate of nachos toward me. The cheese had gone cold, the tortilla chips soggy.

I ignored the unappetizing mess. "So, where is she then?"

"It's complicated, Nichie. And more than just for her, okay. I'm embarrassed, get it? You like Maya, and I know she likes you. I don't want her to get hurt."

"You should have thought of that earlier," I snapped.

He held out his hands, palms up. "Some things aren't that straightforward."

"Some things are very straightforward. You're messing around on your wife, who I will openly admit I like very much. More than I like you, right now. Not only that, but you're messing around with a woman who is so afraid to admit it, she won't help clear you of suspicions of patricide."

His face hardened. "You don't know—"

"Here you go. One tea." The waitress put an enormous, ice-filled mug in front of me. "Get you another, buddy?"

"Yeah, sure," Brad said.

"I hope you're not driving anywhere," I said.

"You're not my mother, Nichelle."

"Maybe you need one," I replied. I took a long drink in an attempt to calm my nerves. Way too sweet.

Brad plucked idly at a strand of cheese. "Not everyone's life is as easy as you seem to think."

"Easy! You think things have been easy for me the last few years?" I sucked in a breath. I struggled to calm down. I wasn't here to fight with my brother about anyone's past, least of all mine. "Forget that. Tell me why I should believe you."

"I told you I've come down here a few times over the years since Dad disappeared. No reason really, other than I thought maybe I could find something the police missed. Some reason he'd . . . walk into the sea. Nothing like that ever happened, of course. I knew it wouldn't, but I guess I just needed to tell myself I tried. About three years ago, I met a woman. It had nothing at all to do with Dad. We had a fender bender. I was pulling out of a parking space. I didn't look behind me, and I hit her car. No damage to either of us other than a couple of dents and scratches. We exchanged insurance info and phone numbers. I apologized. She apologized for getting in my way. We went for coffee, talked for a long time, said good-bye, and I drove home. I found myself thinking about her, a lot, and so I called her one day. She said she'd been thinking about me too and asked when I'd next be in town. I said on the weekend. And . . . it went from there."

"This has been going on for three years? I suggest you both need to decide what you want out of life."

"It's more complicated than that. I don't want to go into details about my marriage to Maya."

"Spare me."

"My friend's husband is a prominent member of the community. He's a pastor at a big church. She married him when she was eighteen, largely because her parents pushed her into it. They've never had anything in the way of a real marriage, as in two people who love each other and care for each other."

"Cry me a river."

"Nichelle, I'm telling you the way things are. Not always cut and dried. Her husband knows about me. He doesn't care. He does care about his standing in the church and his status in the wider religious community. If word gets around she's seeing someone else, he'll destroy her."

"What does that mean, destroy her? This isn't the middle ages; he can't wall her up in his castle and throw away the key." It wasn't even the 1860s. I thought of Louise Jane's story of The Lady, confined to what was now my apartment.

"She has no employable skills, only the most basic education, and no money of her own. He controls it all. They don't have any kids, which is one of the reasons he doesn't care what she gets up to in her own time, as long as she plays the faithful, devoted wife on demand."

"Look, if she goes to Detective Thomas, explains why you were here last week, the cops aren't going to make it public."

"Not public no, but Thomas will put her statement and her name down on the record. Some of the people who work at the police station, cops and civilian clerks, are members of that church. They'll know, and they'll tell others quick enough. I don't know the details, but there's some sort of a power struggle going on in the upper ranks of the church, and her husband has his enemies."

"So, marry her, Brad. Take her away from this ogre of a husband of hers."

He studied the mug between his hands. At long last he said, "I don't want to lose Maya. I don't want my kids to hate me."

I stood up. "You want to have your cake and eat it too, Brad. At some point in time, and probably soon, you're going to have to decide. You don't want any advice from me, but I'll give it. If this lady friend of yours is more concerned about embarrassing her husband and losing access to his money than the possibility of you going to prison, maybe you should think twice about whether you even want to have that cake."

I walked out of the restaurant, my heart pounding.

Chapter Twenty-Four

Friday was my day off. I'd been looking forward to a lovely long lie-in, but when I went to bed I was so angry at my brother, I barely slept, and as soon as the morning sun touched the east-facing window, I got up.

Charles, not entirely approving of the early hour, opened one eye.

I looked at him and plopped down next to him. "I'm not sure what more I can do, little buddy. I can't tell the detective my brother had a reason to be in Nags Head on the weekend, but that reason won't talk to her. She's not going to believe me. I scarcely know if I believe it. You think you know someone, and it turns out you don't. Not really."

Then again, how well did I know my brother? We'd grown up together, as siblings do, but we'd never been close either as kids or as adults.

I had to admit, if only to myself, the idea that Brad had finally found our father, confronted him, and allowed a lifetime of anger to take control of him, was possible.

Had my pending arrival in Nags Head precipitated Bradley Sanderson Sr. to break out of the role of Brian Saunders, and thus enable Brad to find him?

"If so, that is absolutely not my fault," I said to Charles.

Charles exposed his belly to me as a sign of his total agreement. I rewarded him with the necessary rubs and scratches.

When I decided he'd had enough rewarding, I pushed myself to my feet. I put the coffee on, served myself a generous bowl of granola and yoghurt with a sprinkling of fresh blueberries and went online. A couple of friends from my previous life had sent emails with their news and asking how I was settling in. I scarcely knew what to say to them. I replied, trying to sound totally upbeat about my new life and my new job. When it came to the life and the job, I was truly feeling upbeat. It was only that pesky problem of what my father had been up to for the past thirty-eight years and what had brought about his murder that was bothering me, along with my concerns about my brother's honesty.

Correspondence over, I was about to check the local news when my phone beeped with an incoming text. With some trepidation, I saw it was from my sister-in-law, Maya. I hesitated to open it. What would I say if she asked me what I knew about her husband's visits to Nags Head over the years?

Maya: *Just checking in. Brad says you're okay, but you know men! If you need me to come down, I can take time off work.*

Me: *Thanks. I'm managing. Love the job! Fab apartment! More later.*

I then checked the local online news, but nothing new was being reported about the murder investigation. The police were still asking anyone who'd been in the vicinity of the library and the marsh late Sunday night or early Monday morning to come forward. I was surprised no one had yet reported that Brian Saunders wasn't who he claimed to be. I would have thought that would be a juicy story. Then again, local newspapers all over the country are either dying or dead. Likely there wasn't anyone left to dig into the details, and the police hadn't released that information.

Finally, I closed the laptop, finished the last cup of coffee, washed my few dishes, and headed for the shower. Not knowing what the day would bring, I dressed in white capris and a blue blouse. I'd love to get out and explore more of my surroundings, but before doing that, I wanted to hear if Lucy and Louise Jane had learned anything more.

I was letting Charles out—Charles never gets a day off—when the phone rang.

"Good morning," Lucy said. "I hope I haven't woken you?"

"I've been up for a long time. Things on my mind."

"I'm feeding Isaac and Lucas now. I'm off work today too, but I have something to tell you. Connor called his mom last night, and she phoned the friend I was telling you about. To cut a long story short, the friend said she was pleased to hear from Marie and apologized for her reaction to Marie's concern. She stopped seeing the gentleman in question not long after they last spoke, and she's willing to meet with you. She confirmed it was Brian Saunders she was seeing; she saw the news about him in the paper."

"Thank your husband for doing that."

"He's happy to help. Marie suggested you meet for lunch at Jake's Seafood Bar today at one. Does that suit you?"

"Yes, it does. Thanks again."

* * *

Judging only by the name, I expected Jake's Seafood Bar to be a casual beachside restaurant with cheap beer, great views, and clam chowder and hush puppies featured prominently on the menu. I was correct in two of those three categories. The restaurant was located on Roanoke Sound, looking across the water to Roanoke Island; clam chowder and hush puppies were the specialties, but the beer was most definitely not cheap. The restaurant occupied the higher end of the scale, a place for vacationers with money to spend to treat themselves to a nice night out, for locals to celebrate a birthday or an anniversary.

I wasn't too concerned about my clothes. It was lunch time in the Outer Banks in the summertime and just about anything went, just about anywhere, any time.

I gave the young woman at the hostess stand Connor's mother's name, and she led me outside to the spacious deck overlooking the calm waters of the sound. Being daytime, the lights were off, but I thought it must look wonderful at night, with the light from the large white globes strung from railing posts and the fairy lights above the outdoor bar. Sunlight sparkled on the windows of boats tied up at the docks on the far side of the sound; fishing boats drifted slowly past, returning to harbor. A few men were sitting at the bar in the main room, watching the bartender wipe glasses, but most of the customers were middle-aged or older, either couples or small groups of women.

The two people I was here to meet had arrived before me and been seated at a table for four next to the wooden railing. They were in their early sixties, one with short gray hair, the other dyed blond tied into a loose chignon, both of them well-groomed and nicely dressed with good but subdued jewelry. All they had in front of them were glasses of water and menus, clearly waiting until I arrived before ordering.

"Hello. I'm Nichelle Gilcrest. Thank for you agreeing to meet with me."

"My pleasure," the short-haired woman said. "I'm Marie McNeil, and this is my good friend, Karen Connelly. Please, do join us."

I sat down. I fluffed my napkin.

The waiter arrived. "Ready to order something to drink, ladies?"

Marie and Karen each asked for a glass of white wine. I was nervous as to what I was about to hear, but I wanted to keep my wits about me. "Water is fine, thank you."

Karen shifted in her seat. She was even more nervous than I was, and I could understand why. She'd acted foolishly (haven't we all at one time or another?) and broke off with her well-meaning friend, when her friend pointed her foolishness out to her. She was now here to confess to her mistake and that is never easy.

"I hope you're settling in at the library," Marie said as a way of opening the conversation. "I don't mind telling you Lucy's thrilled to have you. With the babies and then Bertie's sudden retirement and Lucy getting the promotion, she was worried about how she was going to manage."

"I'm thrilled to be here," I said. "Did she tell you this is my first ever library job? I went back to college at fifty. I'd been a bookkeeper for many years prior to that."

We chatted casually while the elephant squatted in the middle of our table. Marie showed me pictures of her twin grandsons (just as cute as could be), and I told her about the lives of my own twins. Karen concentrated on reading her menu and contributed nothing more to the conversation than the occasional nod, except to express her admiration of Lucas and Isaac.

The waiter brought our drinks and asked if we were ready to order food. I hadn't even looked at the menu yet, but Marie said, "The clam chowder here is wonderful if you're not wanting a full meal. They make it the OBX way, loaded with potatoes and clams in a clear broth rather than cream or tomato based. As for me, I'm going to have the crab salad."

"Salad for me too," Karen said.

"I'll try the chowder then." I handed the waiter my menu.

"Did you know, Nichelle," Marie said, "the owner and head chef here is Jake Greenblatt, who's married to Lucy's cousin Josie?"

"I didn't. It's a beautiful place."

"Hugely popular as well. It's not too busy now, in the middle of a lovely sunny day, but last minute dinner reservations can be hard to come by."

"I'll keep that in mind." I picked up my water glass.

Marie sipped her wine. "Connor tells me you have reason to believe the man who died on the weekend at the library might be your long-lost father."

"It's been determined that he was."

"My condolences. If you ever want to talk about it, I'm here for you."

I nodded my thanks.

"Connor also tells me you're interested in what that man had been up to lately."

"I'm trying to make some sort of sense of it all. What happened then, what happened now."

"Karen?" Marie prompted.

Karen put her wine glass down. It was almost empty although Marie had barely touched hers. She took a deep breath, gathering her courage around her. "Marie called me this morning, and I was so glad to hear from her. I behaved very badly toward an old friend, and later I simply didn't know how to properly apologize."

"I think you mean a friend of long standing," Marie said. "Not *old*."

Karen smiled for the first time. "Yes, I do mean that." She was an attractive woman, slim with well-defined cheekbones and a sharp chin. Her hazel eyes were round and clear, accented by a slight touch of mascara on her lashes. Her hands were smooth and manicured although not recently; the polish was chipped. "I apologized for my behavior, for the things I said."

Marie reached across the table and touched the other woman's hand lightly. "Friends of long standing might be one of the most precious things in all the world."

"Agreed." Karen smiled at her friend and then turned to me. "Marie told me some of why you want to know about Brian and what happened between him and me."

"Only if you want to tell me," I said.

She twisted her wine glass between her fingers, and spoke without looking at either me or Marie. "You never think it's going to happen to you. To be conned, scammed. You're far too clever for that, you tell yourself. My husband died four years ago. I miss him dreadfully. We had two children, who are married with children of their own. My son and his family live in Raleigh; my daughter is still in Nags Head. They have busy lives of their own, jobs, and families, responsibilities. I've hesitated to date, not wanting a replacement for Scott, my late husband, but I was feeling lonely. Sorry for myself, I suppose."

"That's perfectly normal," Marie said. "We all need companionship, perhaps even more so as we get older and friends and loved ones move on."

"I had a good job, one I loved. I was a primary school teacher, but when Scott got ill and then died, I lost all interest in it, and I took early retirement when it was offered to me. In retrospect that might have been a mistake."

"All anyone can ever do," I said, "is what seems right at the time."

She lifted her head and gave me a soft smile. "You are wise."

"Only through trial and error."

"The best type of wisdom," Marie said. "Tell Nichelle about Brian."

"I thought I'd try to venture into what passes as the dating pool for my age group in Nags Head. I have to say, it's a mighty shallow pool. I was about to forget about it and give up when I met Brian at a singles' dinner. We hit it off, and I was agreeable to seeing him again. He was at least ten years older than me, probably more, but all the men my age are interested in is women in their forties or less."

"Which is why they're still single," Marie said. "Never mind me, carry on."

"He was a nice-looking man, good manners, pleasant to talk to. He loved movies, as do I, so that gave us something in common."

I said nothing. My dad had also loved movies. With a pang I remembered how disappointed he'd been when first Brad, and then I, reached our teenage years and no longer wanted to go on the regular Dad-and-kids Friday night outing to see the newest blockbuster release.

"He told me his wife died ten years prior. We had a few dates, coffee at first, then lunch followed by a walk on the beach. A couple of dinners." She colored slightly, and I didn't ask if those dates led to anything more. "He never offered to pay for us both, and I thought that was just the way things are done these days. One night, when we went to a particularly nice place for dinner, he said he'd forgotten his wallet. I thought nothing of it and happily picked up the entire bill. We'd ordered, at his suggestion, a bottle of wine far more expensive than I'd normally ever get. The next time we went out, he told me the roof on his house was in bad shape. He'd been putting off getting it fixed for a long time, trying to save up the money, but he'd made some risky investments and this wasn't the time to sell them. If the roof got any worse, it was in danger of taking much of the house with it."

"Had you ever been to his home?"

"No. We always went to mine. Long story short, I gave him the money for the roof. It was just to be a loan, mind, but we didn't draw up any sort of agreement or contract. It wasn't more than I could afford, although I did have to sell some stocks to raise the funds."

"When Karen told me about that, I started to worry," Marie said. "I didn't say anything to her at the time. I should have."

"I should have realized what was going on," Karen said. "Not long after that I met his daughter, and she—"

"His daughter?" I said. "He had a daughter? Other than me?"

"He told me she was his daughter. We'd been to the Elizabethan Gardens in Manteo, gardening is a passion of mine, and Brian said he was eager to learn more."

"I bet he did," Marie muttered around a forkful of lettuce leaves.

"After touring the gardens we went to a lovely little place for a coffee. This woman came in and they greeted each other. Brian introduced her as Melinda, his daughter."

I started to see where this might be going. "Melinda. Can you describe this Melinda? How old was she?"

"Mid-forties, perhaps. Rather pretty, thin but not too skinny the way some women can be. She had nice blond hair. I didn't see any sort of a resemblance between them, but Brian joked that she got all her looks from her late mother."

Melissa. I'd bet my . . . something on it. "What happened then?"

"She'd popped in for a coffee before picking up the kids from school, but she was early so she joined us for a few minutes. Brian asked her how the kids were, and she said fine, but Rebecca needed braces, and they didn't know how they were going to afford it. She was a stay-at-home mom and her husband was a car mechanic, but he'd recently lost his job when the dealership he worked at closed. Then, hugs and kisses all around, a word to Brian not to worry, they'd manage fine, and she left. Whereupon Brian sighed, told me Rebecca, his granddaughter, was a lovely girl who wanted to be a singer, but she needed those braces soon or it would be too late."

"And you volunteered to pay."

"Yes, I did. Brian assured me he wasn't asking me to, just explaining the situation, but I insisted. I sent him the first five thousand that night."

"The next morning, Karen and I met for coffee," Marie said. "And she told me about it."

Karen waived to the passing waiter and pointed to her empty wine glass. I'd had one sip of my clam chowder before putting my spoon down. It was one of the best things I'd ever tasted, but I needed to keep my attention focused.

"I might have been a mite blunt in telling Karen I didn't think she was being wise," Marie said.

"Blunt is putting it mildly," Karen said. "I got up and walked out. Left Marie with the bill."

"I can afford two cups of coffee," Marie said.

"And two slices of cake, but never mind that now. We didn't speak again until this morning. It was meeting the daughter that convinced me Brian could be trusted, and the story of the girl needing braces, the poor but hard-working family struggling."

I wished I had a picture of Melissa to show her, but it wasn't necessary. Who else could it have been? "What happened next?"

"Nothing."

"Nothing?"

"Almost nothing. A few days later, I phoned him and left a message suggesting we have dinner. He replied, by text, to say he'd decided not to see me anymore. Some rubbish about complicated feelings, still mourning his late wife. I was confused. I didn't understand. I thought we were getting on well and no one had said anything about taking our relationship to the next level. I let it go for a few days, and then I texted to ask if the roof had been fixed, with what I thought was a subtle hint that if we weren't going to be seeing each other again, I'd like to start being repaid. As I believe the young people these days say, he ghosted me. I've heard nothing since."

Brian and Melissa had been smarter than I'd have expected. They got out when the going was good. Karen would have told Brian she had adult children, and he would have realized that before much longer her kids would want to meet him, and they'd eventually find out she was giving him money. "Did you think about going to the police or hiring a lawyer to get your money back?"

The waiter put the fresh glass of wine in front of her and Karen snatched it up.

"In the great scheme of things," Marie said, "it wasn't a lot of money."

"Enough to teach me a lesson," Karen said. "One I won't be repeating. To be totally honest, Nichelle, I'm embarrassed about the whole situation. The police will pretend to be sympathetic while they laugh at me behind my back. Getting a lawyer, going to court, would be throwing good money after bad. I never signed any sort of agreement with Brian. I handed over the money, freely. He could argue, if pressed, I said it was a gift."

I picked up my spoon and began to eat. Brian—whom I would not think of as my dad—was a scammer, out to cheat lonely older women. Melissa was not his girlfriend, but his business partner.

So far, the other women I knew about, Jo Harper and Loretta Kowalski, hadn't given Brian any money. One woman's son had tried to lay a complaint with the police that had gone nowhere as his mother refused to testify against Brian. Another man had shown up at Brian's place of work wanting to fight over Brian's relationship with his sister.

Who else might be out there? Had Brian and Melissa tangled with someone who, unlike Karen, didn't accept being cheated as a lesson? Had this woman sought revenge? What about sons and grandsons and brothers?

That opened a world of possibilities as to who might have wanted Brian dead. Loretta Kowalski didn't specifically tell me she hadn't given Brian any money. It had been only her word that she stopped seeing him because she found him "off." If she had given him money, did her son, Theodore, know about it?

"When did all this happen?" I asked.

"Over the winter," Karen said. "I last had contact with Brian in March. When I saw his picture in the news and read that the police were saying he'd been murdered, all I felt was sadness. Isn't that strange? I should have been angry; I should have been pleased that he got what he deserved. Instead, it was all just so sad."

Chapter Twenty-Five

As soon as I reached my car, I called Detective Thomas. She needed to know what I did. Karen had not gone to the police when she heard the news of Brian's death to tell the detective what happened between them, and it was possible none of his other lady friends had either. Shame and embarrassment are powerful deterrents.

If someone killed Brian because of one of his scams, that person most certainly wouldn't have gone to the police and thus drawn attention to themselves.

"Ms. Gilcrest," Thomas said. "I was about to call you."

"What about?"

"You first."

"I've been learning things about Brian you might not be aware of. It's possible some people believed they had a good reason to kill him."

"I'm heading into a meeting on another case. That shouldn't take long. I can come to the library in about an hour."

"I'm not working, but you're welcome at my apartment."

"An hour then." She hung up.

I drove back to the library. I hadn't made my bed this morning, and I hadn't washed or put away my breakfast dishes. Come to think of it, I hadn't emptied Charles's litter box either. There's a definite disadvantage to living in a one-room apartment when one is expecting visitors.

When I pulled up, the parking lot was crowded. People came in and out of the library and others walked the boardwalk and the marsh.

Ellen O'Malley was at the circulation desk today. She looked up when I came in and gave me a smile.

I returned it. "I had lunch at your son-in-law's place. It was wonderful. I'll definitely go there again."

"I'll let him know. He's worked very hard to make a success out of it."

"I can't imagine how he and Josie manage; their schedules must be totally different."

"It's not been easy. It still isn't easy, but they are two determined people."

"I'm expecting Detective Thomas soon. Can you send her up to the apartment, please?"

"Sure. Is she wanting anything in particular?"

"More questions about the murder."

"The longer these things drag on the harder it is for everyone," Ellen said.

I headed for the stairs in time to meet Louise Jane coming down. "Just the person I wanted to talk to," she said. "You might have noticed I have an uncanny ability to be in the right place at the right time. My great-grandmother says—"

"I'm not working today, and I have company coming shortly."

"Won't be a minute. I went around to Kevin's bar last night after we talked, but he wasn't there." Her face drooped in disappointment. "I wanted to talk to anyone who might have known your Brian—"

"He wasn't my Brian."

"Whatever. Some big game was on all the TV screens, and the score was awful close, so no one would talk to me, and a couple of guys even told me to hush. Can you imagine the cheek! I left without learning anything. I checked with Kevin, and he'll be in tonight if I need him to run interference. I'm going back later to try again. Eight o'clock will be a good time. Brian might have hung out at that bar, but he was an old guy. He would have headed home for beddy-bye most nights not long after nine, so I figure that's the best time to get his buddies. You said you were busy last night. Wanna come tonight?"

I spoke without taking time to mull it over. "Yes, I think I do."

"I'll pick you up. Quarter to eight. Remember, it's not a fancy place. Dress accordingly."

I ran upstairs and hurriedly began tiding up while I thought about what I could wear to a not-fancy place. Jeans and a T-shirt should do, with running shoes.

I was stuffing my pajamas into a drawer when a light knock sounded on my door. I put on a big smile and opened it to Detective Thomas.

She came in and glanced around with a nod of approval. "Nice apartment. Limited space but what there is, is used well." She crossed the room to look out the window. "Great view, but you don't have a balcony on which to sit and enjoy it."

"The window seat will do. Lucy says it's the best place in Nags Head to watch storms coming in."

"I can see that."

"Please, have a seat." I gestured to the two chairs around the tiny table in the kitchen nook. She sat. She studied me with her penetrating dark eyes and waited for me to start. Today's suit was gray, not brown, but the same fabric and cut, Shapeless almost. I suspected the style was deliberate.

"I'm not going to give you any names," I said. "If the people concerned want to come forward, it's up to them."

"Not necessarily, but that'll do for now. Continue."

I shifted in my seat. I hadn't done anything wrong, but that stare of hers was unsettling. I went into some detail about what Karen told me. "Sam Watson told me a woman's son tried to have charges laid against Brian, but they wouldn't stick without the cooperation of the supposed victim."

"You've been speaking to Sam about this?"

"Did you doubt I would want to find out what I can? We are talking about my father."

"No."

"If you're worried about police confidentiality, he didn't give me any names or other details. But enough so I'm starting to see signs of a pattern. Do you know why Brian was fired from his job at Gardner Beach Supplies?"

"I do. And yes, I am also seeing a pattern. It would appear that Brian Saunders was in the habit of befriending lonely women of a certain age with the specific aim of getting them to give him money. Extortion can be a dangerous business. Relatives, seeing themselves cheated out of their inheritance, can get mighty vengeful. Even the aggrieved can act badly when they finally realize they've been conned."

"Do you know of anyone in particular who might have been so inclined?"

She gave me a look. "Are you really asking me that? I wouldn't tell you if I did."

"I guess not. Can I make this personal, once again? Has anyone given you any indication as to why he came here that night? It has to have been to see me."

"No, but you must remember that everyone who knew him, workmates, friends, drinking buddies, knew him as Brian Saunders. He would have been unlikely to casually share that information, particularly not before talking to you and discovering your feelings regarding him."

"What about Melissa Archibald, the so-called girlfriend?"

"So-called. She insists she knew nothing about his past. Do you have reason to believe Melissa Archibald was involved in these schemes of his?"

"Most definitely. On at least one occasion, she pretended to be Brian's daughter in order to make him look more respectable to the woman he was with."

"She herself didn't ask the women for any money?"

"Not that I'm aware of, no."

"It's not a crime to tell someone you are who you are not." Something approaching a smile touched Thomas's mouth. "Jails'd be mighty full if it was. I appreciate you have some compulsion to find out whatever went on with Brian, why he was killed, but I'll tell you what I told Lucy McNeil. I do not care for civilian interference in my investigations. Do you understand?"

"I do, but—"

"No buts. You spoke to someone today who provided you with insight into the activities of Brian Saunders. I respect that you don't want to tell me this person's name, but I'd strongly advise her to come forward. Or I will have to formally ask you for the name. Do you understand that?" The intense stare drilled into my face.

"I do," I said.

"Glad to hear it. Now, as for what I wanted to speak to you about, we will be ready to release the body before too much longer. The situation is, of course, awkward as you and your brother are the next of kin but, mentally at least, you laid your father to rest long ago."

"We'll take care of the arrangements." I didn't want to even think about that now. What sort of arrangements? Should I even tell people back in Rochester, people who'd known Bradley Sanderson Sr., that he'd been found? What about my mom's relatives? Her sister and her children? Would they want to come to a funeral thirty-eight years after they believed the man had died?

"Has an autopsy been done?" I asked.

"It has."

"And?"

"And, I see no reason not to tell you the results, if you want to hear them."

I suppressed a shudder. "Yes, please."

I didn't suppress it well enough, and she said, "Are you sure?"

"I am. I saw him, remember. Nothing can be worse than that."

"Time of death has been established as roughly between 8 and 10PM on Sunday."

"Eight isn't too late for a social call. If that was his intention."

She nodded and then continued, "He was discovered, by you and Mrs. McNeil, shortly after 8AM Monday. As we initially suspected, he died almost instantly as the result of a blow to the back of the head by a metal instrument such as a golf club, hammer, tire iron etc. Whatever was used has not been located, which isn't surprising as there's a lot of water around these parts. He died where he was found. He was in moderately good health for a man of his age, meaning nothing immanently life-threatening, although he showed signs of a lifetime of alcohol abuse, and his liver was not in good condition, to put it mildly. The night he died, he'd had a fair amount to drink. Not enough to seriously incapacitate him, but enough that he would have been arrested for DUI if he'd been pulled over."

"He needed a shot of liquid courage to face me," I said. "Not flattering."

"We don't know the reason, of course, if there even was one, but at a guess I'd say he had enough to drink to slow his reflexes. Even if he saw danger coming, he might not have had the time or the sense to realize what was happening."

"Before it was too late."

She gave me a moment to think that over before continuing. "I also came here because I wanted to check in with you. Have you remembered anything new?"

"No. I told you everything I know. And it obviously isn't much."

"Does your brother remember anything he might not have shared with me?"

"Why are you asking me about him? He can speak for himself."

"And he has, but not with full and frank honesty. He says he left Nags Head Saturday morning and drove straight home to Rochester. It's about a twelve-hour drive, allowing for a couple of short stops."

"That's right."

"His wife says he arrived home late Saturday evening. That time corresponds with his account, but not the departure location he gave her. She says he was on a business trip to New York City. He, in turn, confesses to not being in New York, having lied to her about that, but he continues to insist he left Nags Head Saturday morning. No one, other than his wife, can place him in Rochester between Saturday night and Monday morning. He says he stayed at home all day Sunday and did yard work most of the day. He was seen at his office in Rochester on Monday morning, and shortly after that you phoned him. I have to point out that anyone leaving Nags Head at 8PM on Sunday would be able to make it to Rochester in time to show up at work Monday morning. When someone lies about one detail, I am always interested in the veracity of the second detail."

"He has his reasons."

"Yes, I know. A woman who will be compromised if she comes forward. A good excuse."

"I don't think—"

She lifted one hand. "Any statement by this woman won't mean much, if anything, Nichelle. Even if she says he was with her on Saturday morning, and she saw him drive away, that doesn't mean he wasn't still in town on Sunday night."

"But it gives him a reason for being here."

"It gives him a reason to come to Nags Head where he might have encountered his long-lost father. Your brother is a person of interest in this investigation. However, as long as no one can place him anywhere near this building at the time, or even in Nags Head on Sunday, and we can find no evidence to prove he was, then we don't have much of a case. Let me assure you, I will keep searching."

I had absolutely no doubt about that. "What about people Brian might have cheated? Lonely women or their relatives?"

"Also evidence I am still searching for."

She started to stand, but I quickly said, "Back to Brian, please. Before you go, can I ask what state his finances were in? I assume you've checked his bank records. The money he got from women like Ka—like the one I told you about. Was there a lot? I'm not investigating," I added quickly, "just curious."

"He had more money coming in than he earned at the store where he worked, yes. Not excessively large amounts. A few thousand here and there, occasionally a slight bit more. Either he wasn't greedy, or the women he preyed on weren't that well off. Or that gullible. His records show regular transfers to Melissa Archibald in varying amounts, but unless we can prove the money was illegally earned, and they conspired together to commit a crime, we can do nothing. Like anyone else, he was free to do with his assets as he wished. She denies, by the way, knowing he was dating other women; however, she says because of the age difference, they didn't have a totally committed relationship."

"What does that mean?"

"I suspect it means whatever she wants it to mean. They went to Atlantic City a couple of times a year, but I can find no evidence, so far, they were meeting with criminal elements there or engaging in illegal activity."

"Do you suppose they went to gamble?"

"I've heard there are other amusements in that city, but yes, to gamble. From what I can find, he had no big wins, nothing out of the ordinary going into his bank accounts, no purchases of a flashy new car or anything extravagant such as that. For him or her. Some withdrawals that likely account for losses, but nothing particularly outstanding there either."

"I wonder why he worked at that beach store if he had other sources of income, shall we say."

"Maybe simply for something to do. In season the job was part-time casual; not many hours over the winter. I know plenty of retired people who decide they don't like retirement all that much after all." She smiled, and I was startled to see a glimpse of the real human being peek out from beneath that crusty cop exterior. "My own grandfather comes to mind. Then again, his return to work might be because Grandma got fed up with having him underfoot all day. She still works out of her home office, and he kept sticking his head in to ask what was for lunch or if she needed anything from the store or how much detergent to put in the washing machine."

Chapter Twenty-Six

If I went to the bar where Brian Saunders was known to hang out could that be considered interfering in the police investigation?

I decided it could not. I wanted, I needed, to learn more about the man who had, once upon a time, been my father. That was all. Perfectly natural in the circumstances.

I considered asking Brad to join Louise Jane and me, but I soon dismissed the idea. Emotions might start running high, particularly if we found people who weren't overly fond of Brian and, although my brother was now a mature, responsible family man, he'd been a hot-head in his youth. I feared any sort of confrontation would release that hot-head. Plus, I had to admit only to myself, I was worried, very worried, about what Detective Thomas said. Rather than clearing Brad of the killing, even if his woman friend came forward, it would accomplish nothing but establish that he had a reason to be in Nags Head over the past few years.

I couldn't help asking myself if on one of those visits he'd seen our father. Had Dad approached him? Had they recognized each other? Had they decided to come together to meet with me, and rather than engaging in a loving family reunion, Brad killed the man who deserted our mother and abandoned his children?

The thought continued to niggle at the back of my mind as I awaited Louise Jane's arrival.

* * *

"This isn't a bar for well-to-do, middle-aged tourists," she said when I got into her car. She drove an Audi. An expensive car for someone on a part-time librarian's salary. I wondered if Louise Jane had outside income or a friend or relative wealthy enough to make such a gift.

Never mind the car, I felt quite insulted at her comment. "If you mean the way I'm dressed, it's the best I can do. And as for being middle-aged, there really is nothing I can do about that. And I am, I hasten to point out, not well-to-do."

"Well enough." In contrast to her usual work attire of comfortable pants and loose shirts, tonight Louise Jane wore a tight, low-cut, sparkly t-shirt and jeans so tight she must have poured herself into them. High heeled sandals were on her feet and her toenails were painted black. She had more make-up on than I'd seen her wear before, and her hair hung in limp strands around her face.

In contrast, I had on a nice pair of jeans and a black T-shirt with the Eiffel Tower drawn in beads worn under a denim jacket in case the air conditioning at our destination was turned up too high. I'd even gone to some trouble to make my hair look nice, put light pink lipstick on my lips and a swipe of blush on my cheeks.

"If we're trying to look like we're down and out, your outfit doesn't match this car," I said.

"We'll park a couple of blocks away and walk to our destination. We'll say you're my out-of-town cousin. Older cousin."

"Why are we saying we're anything?"

"I helped Lucy on some of her cases. This is what we call going undercover."

I bit back the thought of what Detective Thomas would have to say if she heard I was "going undercover."

"As I might have explained, I know just about everyone in the Outer Banks. Obviously that's a slight exaggeration. Case in point, I didn't know your father."

"Not my father. Not anymore anyway."

"Okay, Brian Saunders. My point is, I have never been to any of Kevin's bars and not many of my acquaintances have. If we do encounter someone who knows me, I will be playing me while you are playing the visiting cousin, not the proper middle-aged librarian."

"Do you have to keep saying middle-aged?"

"Aren't you?"

Nothing I could say to that, so I said nothing as we drove into town.

Our destination was as expected. A bar in a strip mall not on the beach. Blue and red lights flashed in the windows advertising brands of beer. A handful of bearded and goateed men milled about outside, smoking. They barely glanced at us as we walked past them.

Louise Jane pushed the door open, and I was overwhelmed by the smell of sweat, cheap perfume or aftershave liberally applied, stale beer, lingering tobacco, and grease. Something might have recently been on fire in the kitchen. I hoped it had been extinguished.

"Hey! There's my girl. Long time no see!" A man came around the bar, arms extended. He was short and lightly built, clean shaven, blond hair carefully styled and arranged to sweep across his forehead. A small gold hoop was through his left ear and a thin gold chain hung around his neck. He wore immaculate white pants, a pink linen shirt without a single fold or wrinkle, and leather loafers with no socks. He wrapped Louise Jane in a ferocious hug. She hugged him back. Many of the patrons stopped their drinking or conversation to watch.

Most of the people in the bar were men, working men and fishermen by the looks of them. Wind-blown cheeks, craggy faces, sunburned noses. The handful of women, middle-aged (that word again!) mostly, but a few younger ones, were also life-hardened with chapped hands and worn eyes. They all watched Kevin and Louise Jane with a smile. This was their place; it was where they belonged, with people they knew, and they were happy here.

Kevin and Louise Jane separated. "Everyone," Kevin bellowed. "This is my cousin, Louise Jane." Louise Jane waved, clearly enjoying the attention.

"Welcome," people called. "Nice to meet you, Louise Jane."

"Kevin talks about you all the time," a woman said. "You're the storyteller. I love hearing stories about the Outer Banks."

"Come to the Lighthouse Library one day," Louise Jane replied. So much for being undercover. "I'll pull out some of the historical records for you to have a look at and tell you stories you don't get in the books."

"I'll do that."

I shifted awkwardly, not sure of what I should be doing. If I was an out-of-town cousin, didn't that mean I was Kevin's cousin too?

A waitress emerged from the kitchen, her tray laden with burgers and fries and mugs of beer. "Outa the way," she snarled.

Kevin pulled Louise Jane outa the way. Then he turned to me. "You must be Michelle. Nice to meet you, Michelle. What can we get you? First drink in my place is always on the house."

I decided the quality of the wine might be risky, so I asked for a half-pint of whatever was on draft. Louise Jane ordered a local craft beer.

Kevin turned to two bearded men sitting at a nearby table for six. "You two, find yourselves someplace else."

They grabbed their drinks, leapt to their feet, and sought seats elsewhere.

"Ladies." With a bow and a whoosh of his right arm, Kevin indicated the now vacated chairs. I cautiously took one, and Louise Jane plunked herself in another.

A waitress brought our drinks. I took a hesitant sip. The beer was excellent, and I took a longer drink.

"Okay, everyone," Kevin said. "Listen up. Louise Jane and her friend here are looking for info on Brian Saunders. They're not cops," round of laughter, "so you can talk to them."

"I thought we were undercover?" I whispered to Louise Jane.

"I might have forgotten to mention to Kevin that we wanted to be subtle in our questioning. Probably wouldn't have mattered. Kevin doesn't do subtle."

"First up," Kevin shouted. "You, Bert. You knew Brian, probably more than most of us. Come over here."

To many cheers, a short, round, bald man stood up.

One after another, people came to sit with us. I felt as though I was conducting interviews for a job.

Not many had anything specific they could tell us. These people, I surmised, were Brian's drinking pals, not friends in the true sense. They shared sports news, talked about their cars, bragged about their kids, grumbled about their wives or husbands, complained about politicians, pushy tourists, and the condition of the roads.

Speculation was ripe as to who might have killed Brian, but no one knew anything, at least nothing they were prepared to discuss. Some talk about not-like-the-old-days and what's-the-town-coming-to, complaints about rude tourists and rich, spoiled college kids run amok. The general feeling seemed to be that some random tourist killed Brian for some unknown reason, and this person would be long gone by now.

"He did have that money from his winnings," a woman said. "Do you suppose it was a robbery that got out of control?"

"Nah," a man said. "He wouldn't have been carrying that much cash on him. People don't carry cash these days."

"I do," someone else said. "Don't trust those banks."

I was well into my third beer, and feeling it, unlike the first, the others had not been half-pints, but my ears pricked up. "Winnings?"

"He scored big in Atlantic City not long ago. Came in here when he got home, proud as a peacock. Bought drinks all 'round."

"When was not long ago?" I asked, smothering a hiccup.

My informant frowned, thinking. "Two weeks maybe?"

"About that," people agreed.

Detective Thomas told me Brian gambled in Atlantic City. She also told me he didn't seem to have ever won much. Then again, "scored big" means different things to different people. Maybe all he needed to feel like a winner was enough to buy a round of drinks for his pals.

"I remember that night," Kevin said. "He was mighty pleased with himself. Didn't stint on the drinks either. Come to think of it, Eddie, you came up twice. I turned you away the second time."

"Can't blame a guy for trying."

The woman snorted. "Typical. Not one of you bothered to ask him how much he'd lost over the years before this big win. Nowhere near enough to break even, would be my guess."

"Do you know Melissa Archibald?" Louise Jane asked.

"Yeah, I know her. She comes in now and again. Friend of Brian's, she was."

"Just a friend?"

"Yeah, just a friend. Why?"

"She told the police she was his girlfriend," I said.

The men laughed. The woman said, "Not a lie. She's a girl. She was a friend. Let the cops interpret that as they want. Maybe she thought there'll be something in it for her if folks believe that. Brian didn't have any family, did he?"

Everyone shook their heads. "Not that he ever talked about."

"I didn't know him well, mind," the woman said. "Just to have a beer and a laugh with, but I always had the feeling he was not a happy man."

"In what way?" I asked. My eyes were beginning to lose focus. The waitress put another pint in front of me.

"I didn't ask for this," I said.

"Complements of Randy over there."

A man with about as many teeth as strands of hair waved at me.

It wouldn't be polite to refuse, would it?

Fortunately, Louise Jane was driving, so after her first beer she declined any more.

"Hard to say," the woman continued. "In here, Brian could be cheerful enough, but there was something underneath, I always thought. Life weighing on him, maybe. Regrets. Things left unsaid. Debts never repaid."

Louise Jane looked at me. I put down my mug and struggled with my emotions. For the first time since all this happened, I felt tears well up behind my eyes. I burped.

"Never mind Joan here," a man said, "She watches too many of those soap operas."

Joan stood up. "Maybe I do. I thought he was a sad, lonely man, that's all. I take my grandkids to the library every Monday. See you around, Nichelle."

Busted.

* * *

"You're not accustomed to drinking much, are you?" Louise Jane said as she manhandled me up the twisting iron staircase, supervised by a concerned-looking Charles. When I'd been unable to unlock the front door, Louise Jane decided I might need some assistance.

I burped. "I'm fine. They kept pushing drinks on me."

"Two and a half beers, Nichelle. Good thing I was there."

"It was your idea. Oopsie, sorry Charles." The big cat nimbly leapt out of the way as my foot slid off the step.

Louise Jane tucked her arm under mine. "If you don't remember anything in the morning, rest assured I was listening intently the entire time, so I can fill in the gaps in your memory if needed. Oh, for heaven's sake. Give me that!" She took the apartment key out of my hand.

The door swung open. Louise Jane shoved me in. "From this point on, you're on your own. Charles, take care of Nichelle."

Charles ran ahead of me as I stumbled into my new home. The door slammed shut behind me.

* * *

When I awoke, for a moment I wondered where I was. Unfamiliar bed. Unfamiliar shaft of painfully brilliant light pouring through a tall window. Something warm and soft curled up next to me. A loud buzzing. Then my head started to throb, and I closed my eyes against the light.

Oh, right. Blackbeard's Cave. Kevin's bar.

I struggled to open one eye and focus on the bedside clock. It was eight, and my alarm was going off. Good thing, as I had to be at work at nine. I slapped the snooze button and rolled over. Charles leapt off the bed. No point in trying to snooze, my throat was desert-dry, my head was aching, and my stomach didn't feel all that good either.

I drank a great deal of water and stood under the shower for a long time.

My career as an undercover operative was not starting out terribly well.

When I finally came out of the bathroom, Charles gave me a long disapproving look. Then he tossed his head and walked, deliberately and ostentatiously, to his empty food bowl.

By the time I sat down to a breakfast of dry toast and extra-strong coffee, accompanied by more water, I was feeling fractionally better. Charles was feeling much better, and after a hearty breakfast, he was enjoying a brief nap before going downstairs for another strenuous day of being admired.

I'd compare notes with Louise Jane later, but I thought I remembered most of what transpired last night.

To sum it up, we learned nothing of any value.

* * *

Saturday is always a busy day at the Lighthouse Library, but particularly so over the summer when as well as the regular roster of children's programs, we have special events for visiting families. Today, an exploration of the marsh led by Ronald and a ranger from Cape Hatteras National Seashore. Various parents and volunteers would accompany the group to keep an eye on children who might decide to wander off to explore something even more interesting than what the ranger was talking about.

While the children were engaged, parents and grandparents stocked up on books, browsed the library computers, or relaxed in the magazine nook.

I was busy enough all day, I was able (sometimes) to ignore my upset stomach and headache. I kept a large glass of water close to hand on my desk.

Louise Jane wasn't scheduled to work today, but she bounded through the door shortly before ten. "Glad to see you're still alive," she said as though it were a matter of some doubt. "I called Ronald first thing to check if you'd come to work. He said you had and wanted to know why I was asking. You'll be pleased to hear, I didn't tell him what we got up to last night."

"What did you get up to last night?" Maureen Peterson asked. The first group of young naturalists was getting ready to head out. Mrs. Peterson would accompany them, and she was dressed as though off to explore the savannahs of Kenya in multipocketed and multizippered khaki pants and shirt and heavy boots. Binoculars hung around her neck, and she even had a pith helmet perched on top of her head.

"Nothing," I said.

"Girls' night out." Louise Jane gave me a broad wink.

"That sounds like fun," Maureen said. "Next time you do something like that, I'd love to join you. Now that my girls are growing up," (martyred sigh) "things seem so quiet at our house in the evenings."

"Okay, everyone," Ronald yelled as he came down the stairs. "We're ready to go! Outside for roll call."

The excited children and the equally excited Maureen Peterson filed out.

When the area around the circulation desk was momentarily quiet, Louise Jane leaned toward me. "Do you remember what happened last night?"

"I do. I think I do at any rate."

"Any gaps in your memory?"

"I don't know what I don't remember, but unless someone confessed to killing Brian, no."

"No one did. Unfortunately. Okay, what do you want me to do next?"

Earlier I'd briefly considered asking Louise Jane if she could locate the woman my brother was seeing in Nags Head so I could speak to her. I dismissed that idea almost instantly as far too intrusive on Brad's privacy. My brother and I still had some bonds of trust we needed to maintain. Detective Thomas was right. Even if the police found the woman, if she told them Brad left town Saturday morning, that wasn't much of an alibi for Sunday night. It was possible he told her he'd seen his long-lost father in town and wanted to meet up with him. It was also possible he'd been with her after the time he told the police (and me) he left. But I didn't think so. Maya told the police her husband had been at their home in Rochester Sunday evening, the time Brian died. I thought I knew my sister-in-law fairly well. I couldn't see her lying to the authorities to protect Brad, not from a murder charge. Then again, no one else really knows what goes on in other people's marriages.

"We hit a dead end last night," I said to Louise Jane. "I have absolutely no idea what else we can do."

"I'll keep my ear to the ground, let you know what I hear. Kevin said he'll keep asking people about Brian over the next few days. Everyone who knew him wouldn't have been at the bar last night."

"Lovely day, Nichelle." A patron put a huge stack of what when I was young we called "bodice-rippers" on the desk. "I hope they're not working you so hard you don't get a chance to get out and enjoy all the area has to offer."

"I've been showing Nichelle some of the local highlights," Louise Jane said. "Places not on the normal tourist trail."

"How nice of you to do that. There's nothing like true Outer Banks hospitality."

I went back to work.

Chapter Twenty-Seven

I'd been truthful when I told Louise Jane I had no idea as to what, if anything, I could do next. I was ready to abandon what passed for my feeble investigation when, conveniently, a clue came to me.

We were locking up the library at the end of a good day when the desk phone rang. I answered, "Bodie Island Lighthouse Library."

"Hello? I'm looking for a woman who might work there? She was in my store asking about a former employee. Brian Saunders?"

"I'm Nichelle Gilcrest and that would have been me."

"It's Carol here. I'm a shift supervisor at Gardner Beach Supplies, and we spoke recently. You didn't give me your full name, but when you left one of the clerks said you were the new librarian. If you're interested, the man I told you about, the one who argued with Brian in the incident that caused me to fire him, is here now."

"Here? At the store?"

"Yes, he came in a few minutes ago. He's asking about portable grills at the moment."

"I'd like to talk to him. It'll take me about twenty minutes to get there. If he looks like he's about to leave can you stall him?"

She chuckled. "We have a wide range of small grills to suit every taste and pocketbook."

I ran for the breakroom and snatched up my purse. "Ronald," I shouted, "I gotta go. Lock up, please."

A distant voice replied, "Sure but—"

I drove into Nags Head at a pace that could have had me pulled over by the police for speeding. I decided to take the risk. If the grill-purchasing customer at Gardner's Beach Supplies decided to leave without examining the full range of available products, there wasn't much Carol could do to stop him. I doubted she'd risk her job by knocking him to the floor and sitting on him until I got there.

I screeched into the parking lot, found a place near the doors, and ran inside.

Carol was waiting for me, eyes gleaming with the thrill of the chase. "He's still here. Martha's helping them select the perfect grill. Fortunately, Martha is completely up to date on the details and performance of all of our outdoor kitchen products. She's also very good at the upsell." She pointed toward the rear of the store, and I headed that way. Carol fell into step behind me.

The store wasn't too busy in the late afternoon, so I located my quarry easily.

A man and a woman in their late sixties, both of them short and thin, were staring vacantly into space and smothering yawns as Martha regaled them with warranty details, performance statistics, and assembly instructions for a range of small to medium-sized grills. They were both dressed in summer casual clothes, good quality but not ostentatious. She wore a diamond ring on her right hand, a thin tennis bracelet around her wrist, and small gold hoops through her ears. Her eyeglasses had colorful purple frames, and her chin-length brown hair was highlighted with streaks of caramel. His khaki trousers and blue golf shirt were clean and recently ironed.

"Did I tell you," Martha said as I came around the corner, "this one has been *Southern Barbeque* magazine's most highly rated in its price category for two years running?"

"You might have mentioned it, yes," the woman said. "We'll have to think about it. Let's go, Dennis."

"The size is okay, but I'm not sure about the color," the man said. "That bright green looks too feminine for my taste."

"Hi," I said. "I hope you don't mind me interrupting."

"As long as you're not here to sell us a grill," the woman said, "have at it."

Martha stepped back. Carol hovered a few feet away.

"This might seem like an odd question," I said, "but please bear with me."

"Are you doing a survey?" the woman asked. "We came in to get a portable grill for taking to the beach when my grandchildren come to visit next week, but I hadn't realized the choice would be so overwhelming."

"Don't care for green, myself," the man said. "Grills need to be black."

"It's not about grills, no. My name is Nichelle, and I would like to ask you about Brian Saunders."

The woman's face closed as though shutters had come down. The man's lips tightened and his eyes narrowed. "Never heard of him," he snapped. "Let's go, Tracy."

I turned to the woman. The features of these two were similar enough I took a wild guess they were siblings, not a married couple. When initially telling me about the incident that caused her to fire Brian, Carol told me the man who argued with Brian mentioned his sister. "Did you hear he died?" I asked. "Brian."

"I did. I was sorry about that. I don't know anything about it, though."

"We've got nothing to say about him," the man said.

"Do be quiet, Dennis. She obviously knows he and I were friends or she wouldn't be here."

"The manager of this store fired Brian when he got out of hand with me. I figured I'd return the favor by shopping here. My mistake." Dennis glared at Carol.

"Would you mind very much talking to me for a few minutes?" I asked. "I do have reason to be interested. A quick coffee at the place next door? It's on me."

"No thanks," Dennis said.

"I don't see that it would hurt," Tracy said.

I suspected she only agreed to accompany me because her brother didn't want to.

"What about the grill?" Martha asked. "If you pay for it now, I can put it aside for you to pick up later. We don't close until nine tonight."

"Don't want that green thing," Dennis said. "We'll look elsewhere."

"Yes, please." Tracy dug in her cavernous purse. "It's going to be my grill, Dennis. For the use of my family."

We trooped to the front of the store. Tracy paid with her credit card and tucked the receipt into her purse. Dennis grumbled about shopping around. Martha and Carol waved us a cheery good-bye.

The coffee shop in the middle of this strip of stores was part of a donut chain, nowhere near as nice as Josie's, but it was open and it was close, and I didn't want to give Dennis a chance to talk his sister into abandoning me.

The place was empty, and we chose a small table by the window. "What would you like?" I asked.

"Just a coffee for me, thanks," Tracy said. "Cream, two sugars."

"I'll have a coffee, black," Dennis said, "and one of those chocolate filled donuts. Make it two donuts. It's been a long time since lunch."

I placed the order, paid, and ferried everything to our table. I sat down and said to Tracy, "Brian Saunders?"

She gave me a smile, but the smile didn't reach her eyes. She twisted the ring on her finger. Her engagement ring, I suspected, moved to her right hand when she was widowed. "Dennis is making a huge fuss out of nothing. He's my older brother, you see, always far too protective." She threw him a disapproving look. He munched his donut and shrugged. "Not like you never needed looking after. Never did have an ounce of common sense, girl or woman."

"How do you know Brian?" she asked me. "And why are you wanting to talk to me?"

"I'm his daughter," I said.

"Oh, I'm sorry. I didn't realize."

"No reason you should. He and I didn't have any contact at all for many, many years. It's obviously far too late to reconcile now, but I would like to come to some understanding as to how he's been living these past few years."

Few years. I glossed over the fact that I'd believed he was dead for thirty-eight years.

"Perfectly understandable." Tracy spoke to Dennis rather than me. "My own dear George died two years ago. I miss him dreadfully, every day." Another twist of the ring.

"Good man, George," Dennis mumbled around a mouthful of donut.

"George and I had a long and happy marriage. Three children. I have six grandchildren now. Would you like to see a picture of the whole family?"

I didn't, but she pulled out her phone and held it up to face me. A smiling family group, infant to centenarian, all of them in party clothes. "This is us with the birthday girl at my aunt Susan's one hundredth birthday in the spring."

"Lovely family," I said. "You were happy in your marriage. You wanted to be happy again."

"Exactly!" she said. "You understand. Dennis didn't approve."

"Never matters whether Dennis approves or not," he said, starting on the second donut.

"How long did you and Brian . . . uh . . . spend time together?" I drank my coffee. Perfectly dreadful.

"A couple of months. We had a wonderful time; he was great company. He still drove, you know. We went to all the popular tourist sites, the places I haven't been to for years, decades maybe. We met for lunches and dinners. Such fun!" Her expression and her tone made a lie of the words. I didn't think she was lying to me, but to her brother.

"Why did it end?" I asked.

"Why does anything end?" she said with a deep sigh. "Life, responsibilities, get in the way. I'm retired now, but still so busy with my church and my charities, never mind the grandchildren. Brian was a manager at that store. It kept him so busy."

He wasn't a manager, but he wouldn't have been the first man to enhance his resume when he met a woman he hoped to impress. I wanted to ask if Brian asked her for money, but I didn't know how to do that. Fortunately, I didn't have to.

"The guy was a con artist," Dennis snapped. "I told her and I told her, but would she listen? No. Not until—"

"And as I told you, Dennis, more than once, I was happy to pay to enjoy our evenings out. If Brian was short of funds sometimes, it was only because he was trying to help his family." She turned to me. "You mentioned you and Brain had been estranged for a long time. Were you aware he had another daughter? She's a few years younger than you, so she must be from the family he started after he divorced your mother. So sad when families fall out, isn't it? Unfair to the children, most of all."

I nodded.

"His daughter, the other daughter, had been offered a promising new job, but she needed a new car if she was going to be able to get to it, and then one of the grandchildren needed a lot of dental care. Wouldn't anyone help a friend out? It was just a loan, as I explained, more than once, to Dennis."

Dennis snorted.

"Did you meet this woman? His daughter?"

"Yes, one time. Lovely girl. I don't see any resemblance between you and her, but you were only half-sisters, I suppose."

I didn't want to out and out lie, so I took another sip of my horrid coffee, letting her assume what she believed was true. "We ran into her in a coffee shop after an outing to the Wright Brothers."

"That was convenient."

"Wasn't it?" Her smile almost cracked at that point, but she struggled mightily to keep it in place. "I hope I'm not telling you something you didn't know. You did know he had another daughter, didn't you?"

"I know about her." I wasn't lying. What I knew about Melissa was that she wasn't Brian's daughter.

"Now that I'm looking, I can see the family resemblance between you and him. The other girl must have taken more after her mother."

I wished I could get rid of Dennis, but I decided it didn't really matter. Tracy might talk more freely without being subject to his disapproving stare, but I'd learned what I wanted to know. Tracy eventually realized Brian was using her, which was likely the reason she stopped seeing him. She might have given him more money than she could comfortably afford, or simply resented being cheated. If Dennis would stop with the "I told you so" attitude, she would be able to admit it, not only to me but to herself.

"Sadly, he died before he could repay the loans," she said. "Naturally, I wouldn't dream of approaching his daughter in her time of grief asking for money. I wanted to send my condolences, but I never did get her married name. Would you pass my regards on next time you see her?"

I was saved from answering by Dennis. "You claim to also be his daughter. You might want to consider that you have some responsibility to take care of his debts."

"Dennis, no," Tracy said. "I'll be fine. Nothing I couldn't comfortably afford." She almost choked on the words. "We didn't have any sort of legal agreement. I didn't see the point in making the loan official. I . . . trusted him."

Dennis's face indicated what he thought of that.

I stood up. "Thank you for talking to me. I'm sorry things didn't work out the way you might have hoped."

"I'm okay, Nichelle. Thank you for your understanding. Sometimes we learn lessons in life the hard way."

"And that Brian Saunders finally learned his," Dennis said. "Before he could do any more harm. Good riddance, I say."

Chapter Twenty-Eight

Dennis was still visibly furious at Brian. Tracy was doing a poor job of hiding her own anger. Had one of them, or both of them working together, followed Brian to the library that night, and acted on those feelings?

I had to admit, it was hard for me to imagine the diminutive, bespeckled, nicely dressed Tracy sneaking up behind a man and bashing him over the head.

Then again, I didn't know her, not at all, and one shouldn't judge by appearances.

Dennis? Yes, he might be able to do that. If Brian had been taken by surprise by the attack, it wouldn't have required a great deal of physical agility.

Which opened the possibility that any one of the women who'd been cheated by Brian or one of their relatives might have taken steps to get their revenge.

Better to go to the police, I would have thought, than to kill the man. I didn't know enough about the law to know if the women would have a leg to stand on, legally, to charge Brian. They gave him the money freely, not under any sort of threat, coercion, or blackmail attempt. Was lying to a friend about a child needing braces or a collapsing roof a crime?

Unlikely.

As I drove back to the library, I called Detective Thomas. "I'm not investigating," I told her when she answered, "but this information just happened to fall into my lap. It did, I promise."

She sighed. "What have you learned, Nichelle?"

I told her about Tracy and Dennis.

"Full names, please?"

"Oh. Sorry, I didn't think to ask them that."

"You are pointing me in the direction of a brother and sister as possible suspects in the murder of your father, but you didn't bother to get their surnames?"

"As I might have said, I'm not investigating. It was nothing other than a friendly chat. Not an interrogation. I've thought of one thing that might help—shortly after five-thirty today, Tracy paid for a small, green, portable grill at Gardner's Beach Supplies with a credit card. That'll have her name on it, right?"

"Any other noninvestigative information you have to share with me?"

"Not at this time."

"Keep me informed if you do." She hung up.

I pondered her words. Was Detective Thomas telling me to keep not-investigating?

Didn't matter if she was or not, I had nothing further to investigate.

It was a Saturday night; I was not young but I was fancy-free, and the evening stretched ahead of me. Not that such a situation was at all out of the ordinary for me. I hadn't yet made the sort of friends I could call on the spur of the moment to suggest a movie or meeting up for a drink. My brother was in town, but I was not in the mood to see him. I tried to reassure myself of Brad's innocence, but I still had niggling doubts regarding his activities last weekend.

I decided a walk on the beach would help clear my head. After that I'd go to the grocery store and do a big shop. When I was married and the girls were living at home, I'd always enjoyed cooking. I got out of the habit over the years I was in college, when my mind and my evenings were full of essays to write and books to read. The kitchen in the Lighthouse Aerie was tiny, miniscule by the standards of the big house in the suburbs of Rochester I'd shared with Dan. But it would do. I told myself I'd enjoy adapting some of my favorite recipes for one person.

I turned at South Old Oregon Inlet Road and found a place to park the car, not too far from the beach. I walked down the sand covered path and through long beach grasses and sea oats and climbed the dunes to see the rolling waters of the open ocean spreading out before me. I walked for a long time, enjoying the feel of the wind in my hair, the sand between my toes, the salt spray on my face, the cry of seagulls and the laughter of children in my ears. Not many people were still out, most vacationers having returned to their rentals or hotels for dinner, but a few family groups lingered, having picnics, watching kids chase sandpipers or skip through the edges of the surf. The houses lining the beachfront threw long shadows across the sand. A few fishing folk sat in beach chairs, watching their long poles arching over the water, beers in hand, coolers at their feet. Further to the north, brilliantly colored kites and streamers performed a ballet in the skies.

By the time I eventually turned back, I felt a great deal better. Grocery shopping could wait until tomorrow. There were things Brad and I had to discuss. Our father's final arrangements, most of all.

"I was hoping you'd call," he said when he answered. "I'm going home tomorrow. I've decided I need to clear the air with Maya. Time for honesty between us. If she wants to act on what I'm going to tell her, that's up to her."

"I'm pleased to hear that. It's the right thing to do. What about your Nags Head lady friend?"

"Finished. I took what you said to heart, Nichie. If she won't stand up for me when I need her to, what am I doing risking my marriage to be with her? I broke it off with her earlier. I have to confess she didn't exactly beg me to change my mind. More like, 'okay, have a nice life.'"

"I'm glad, Brad. Have you heard anything more from the police?"

"I spoke to Detective Thomas a short while ago to let her know I'm going home."

"Did she have any objections to that?"

"I've not been charged with anything, so any objections she might have don't matter."

"We need to talk about what we're going to do with Brian. Who was, like it or not, our father. In terms of a funeral, I mean. Do we let him stay here or take him back to Rochester? Do we bury Brian Saunders or Bradley Sanderson? What do we tell Mom's family?"

"I don't want anything to do with that, Nichelle. He chose to live here for half his life under a name of his own choice. His choice. Having said that, whatever you think best is okay with me."

Typical Brad. Leave me to make the tough decisions. "Want to meet for dinner?"

"Yeah, let's do that. I intend to get on the road early. How about—. Hold on, I have a call coming in I should take."

I stared into space listening to the empty sound of nothing. Then a click and Brad rejoined me. "You'll never guess who that was."

"I'm not in the mood for games, Brad."

"Melissa Archibald."

"What does she want?"

"To meet. She said she'd love to meet with me to talk about Brian."

"How'd she get your name and phone number?"

"You told her you were Brian's daughter, right? So she knows about us. Detective Thomas told me Melissa wanted to get in touch with me, and she asked my permission to pass on my number. Out of curiosity only, I agreed. I said I was free this evening, so we're meeting at the Ocean Side Hotel in half an hour for a drink."

"Did you tell her you were on the phone with me, right now?"

"No. I figure we can present a united front, right? I have no idea what she wants with me, but in case it's not on the up-and-up, you can be my wingman."

* * *

I had half an hour to kill, so I popped into a grocery store. I hadn't had time to make a shopping list so I could make some of my favorite meals, but I stocked up on basics for next week's lunches and quick dinners. I loaded my bags into the trunk of my car and then followed my phone's directions to the Ocean Side Hotel, arriving about fifteen minutes late, as planned. My phone told me the hotel had been built in the 1950s with the intention of recreating a grand old Southern plantation house. The effect was a striking three-story building of a soft pale yellow, with a white veranda complete with rocking chairs painted white and yellow wrapping around three sides and matching balconies on the upper floors. The pebbled parking area was outlined with huge iron urns overflowing with colorful flowers, ornamental grasses, and trailing variegated vines. A wide, sweeping staircase led to the imposing entrance, guarded by pillars crafted in the Greek style.

The hotel had valet parking, which I declined to take. As I searched through the crowded lot for a vacant spot I got a glimpse of a weather-stained boardwalk leading over the dunes.

I parked the car and went inside the hotel. The lobby appeared to have been updated not long ago, maintaining some of the Southern charm but refreshing it with new carpeting, good lighting and enlarged windows, and wide, soft chairs. The big round table in the center of the room held a vase full of long-stemmed red roses and delicate baby's breath. The lobby was busy with families or groups of friends heading out to dinner or returning from their day at the beach. A bank of elevators was at the far side of the room, staircase to one side. A hostess stand guarded the entrance to the restaurant. Brad said Melissa suggested a drink, so I assumed they'd be in the bar rather than the restaurant and headed that way.

I poked my head into the lobby bar and spotted my brother and Melissa sitting in comfortable chairs next to the fireplace, thankfully unlit at this time of year. He had a beer on the low table in front of him, and she sipped at a multicolored frothy concoction served in a wide-mouthed, long-stemmed glass.

I dropped onto the third chair at the table. "Hi. Fancy meeting you here."

Melissa's smile didn't reach her eyes. Brad looked nothing but relieved to see me. "Hi, Nichelle. I believe you've met Melissa."

"I have. Nice to see you again. I'll just have an orange juice, thanks," I said to the waiter. I still wasn't feeling all that well after last night's adventure with Louise Jane.

"Actually, Michelle—" Melissa said.

"It's Nichelle," Brad said.

"What?"

"My sister's name. Nichelle with an N. Not Michelle with an M. She was named after the original *Star Trek* actress."

"*Star Trek*? What's that?"

"Never mind," I said.

"Whatever. Nichelle with an N. I'm glad you're here. Brad told me he's going home to Rochester tomorrow, but I hope you and I can get to know each other better. You went to Blackbeard's Cave last night, I hear."

"Yes, I did." I wasn't surprised she knew about that. Louise Jane hadn't exactly been subtle and discreet; it was entirely possible one of Melissa's friends informed her of our visit.

"You had questions about Brian."

I hadn't told Brad about my failed attempt to go undercover, but he kept his face impassive, giving no sign of being in the dark. "My brother and I are both wanting to get at the truth."

"Dear Brian and I were good friends, very close in many ways, but he never talked about his past with me. I didn't know anything about you two, or his previous life in Rochester. I only learned all that when the police told me. I was totally shocked." She put on her shocked face and reached for her drink.

"How much of good friends were you?" Brad asked.

She laughed lightly, but the sound that came out was not what she intended. Instead of amusement, it was strained. Her eyes were narrow and calculating, making me wonder exactly why she wanted to meet with us. Meet with Brad I mean. Was she looking for another partner in whatever scheme she and Brian had going on? If he'd been her meal ticket, she'd need to find someone else, and quickly. Did she think Brad might take Brian's place? I couldn't see it. Any woman in her sixties or more who was approached by a guy of my brother's age would be instantly on the alert.

Melissa gave Brad a flirtatious wink that had me rolling my eyes. "Not what you're thinking, you naughty boy. We were friends. It is possible for an older man and a younger woman to simply enjoy each other's company."

"If you say so. How often did you pretend to be Brian's daughter?" I asked.

She blinked in surprise and hesitated, taking another sip of her drink while she debated whether or not to admit to it. "What makes you say that?"

I said nothing. Brad and I watched her. She let out another one of those forced light laughs. "Okay, I confess. We bumped into each other a couple of times when he was on a date, and it was simply easier that way. Some people," she gave me a tight smile, "don't understand the nature of a relationship between two people with the age difference such as that between your father and me."

"Not my father," I said. "Brian Saunders."

The waiter put a glass of juice in front of me. "Can I get you folks anything else?"

"I'll have another one of these." Melissa downed the contents of her glass.

"Despite what you implied to the police about the nature of your relationship with Brian, according to people who knew you both, you weren't his girlfriend," I said. "So why would you try to hide this nonrelationship?"

"People of *lesser minds* can be quick to leap to conclusions. I don't know why you two are being so aggressive. I suggested we meet tonight, hoping we could have a chat about my dear friend. You tell me about his youth, and I can tell you about his recent years."

"He ran out on his wife and his two children and disappeared for thirty-eight years," I said. "Nothing else to know."

"I understand that must have been very, very difficult, for Rosalee and for you two. But I can assure you, I had nothing to do with it." She forced out another laugh. "I was about five years old at the time."

She might have knocked a couple of years off her age, but I let it go. Plenty of women try to convince themselves, not to mention others, they're not as old as they are.

"I appreciate you calling me, Melissa," Brad attempted to smooth the waters, "and suggesting we talk, but Nichelle and I need to sort out our feelings before we can try to be friends."

"I don't need to sort out any feelings," I said, not wanting to smooth anything. "You worked with Brian to scam lonely, elderly widows out of their savings. From where I'm sitting you were not his dear friend," I put air quotes around the words, "but his partner-in-crime."

The waiter put Melissa's fresh drink in front of her. She looked at me with eyes that were no longer even pretending to be friendly.

"I suspect," I said to my brother, "Melissa came here tonight to present you with a business proposal, to suggest you take Brian's place in their nasty little scheme. Too bad, for her, you invited me to join you."

"Poor dear," Melissa said, taking a sip. "Do you search for enemies everywhere you go?"

"Maybe. Maybe not. If not seeking an actual business partner, you must have some interest in what's going to happen to Brian's estate, what little there might be of one. The police are looking into his bank records, and if there are hidden funds they'll find it. He rented the house he lived in most recently, but he might have had property elsewhere. Maybe he had a bank vault full of presents from his lady friends. We know he had two lives, maybe he had even more. Sorting out his estate is going to be a complicated legal process, but

I expect you will be far down any chain of inheritance, Melissa. Dear friends or not."

She consumed her entire drink in one swallow and stood up. "I didn't come here to make enemies. But so be it. As a final piece of advice, stay away from Blackbeard's Cave. You so clearly do not belong there, but I and many of my friends do. If you get my meaning."

She walked away, her heels tapping furiously on the carpet.

I collapsed against my chair. "Oh, goodie, a threat."

My brother stared at me. "What's gotten into you, Nichie? I have to admit I don't care for her either, but you went on the out-and-out attack there."

"All that boo-hoo let's be friends nonsense got under my skin. She wants something out of us, and I do not intend to find out what it is. Although, judging by the way she reacted when I mentioned any inheritance, that might be it. If she thinks she's entitled to anything, she won't be happy that we've appeared on the scene, not only revealing Brian's true identity but, if he didn't have a will, we're his heirs."

"You think he had money hidden?"

"No. I doubt there's anything like that. He was a small-time conman, that's all. She's equally small-time."

"You're angry at him, Nichie."

"You think? Yes, I am. Not only for leaving Mom and us, but for the way he lived these past years. I mean, really, extracting money from lonely women who only want some companionship in their old age?"

"I notice Melissa didn't offer to pay for her drinks. I also noticed she didn't hold back from ordering the most expensive thing on the cocktail menu."

"If it's any consolation, I don't think she enjoyed the last one much."

"Do you think she had anything to do with Brian's death?" Brad asked. "Maybe they had an argument, a falling out among thieves about dividing the spoils."

"I don't know. We have to assume he came to the lighthouse that night wanting to talk to me. I can't see him bringing her with him, or even telling her what he intended. She might pretend they were close, but they weren't so close he was going to involve her in something so important, not before finding out where I stood. I'm beginning to think one of the women he cheated or a relative of theirs saw him heading out of town after dark, and decided to follow. They took advantage of the opportunity to get their revenge and slipped back into the night from whence they came. If that's the case, this person, who is unlikely to be a master criminal, will slip up soon enough and Detective Thomas will have them." I began to gather my things. "Sorry, Brad, but I'm tired. I'll talk to you soon."

He stood up and wrapped me in a fierce hug. I settled into the embrace. How could I have ever thought my brother could kill a man?

When we separated, my eyes were wet and so were his. "You call me if you hear anything. I can come back if needed."

"Drive safe." Before I could move, my phone rang. The display said the caller was Detective Thomas. My brother and I exchanged a look and then I answered. He leaned close to me to listen in.

"Good evening," she said. "I thought you'd like to know we've opened the phone we found on Brian as well as his home computer and have accessed the contents. Our techies have been seriously overworked and backed up, so there's been a delay with getting around to Brian's, and before I could share anything I found on it with you, I had to go through his files, messages, and contacts. Other than the phone numbers of a good number of local women, whom we are in the process of contacting, I found nothing of significance that might help with the investigation, not yet anyway. But there are some items you might like to see."

"What sort of items?"

"I have personal plans this evening. Your brother is planning on leaving town first thing tomorrow, but if you ask him to delay his departure, I can meet you both at the station at nine tomorrow morning."

Brad nodded at me.

"Is this to do with our father's disappearance or with his death?" I asked.

"Mostly the former."

"See you tomorrow then."

Chapter Twenty-Nine

I met Brad at the police station at five to nine on Sunday morning. I'd been in Nags Head all of one week, but so much had happened, it felt much longer. My brother had checked out of his hotel and packed his car; he intended to hit the road heading north as soon as we were finished. We walked up the steps together. Detective Thomas was waiting for us, and she held the door to admit us to the inner sanctum. Her suit was an exact replica of the others I'd seen, although a lighter gray today. I wondered if she bought them all at the same time, or if a store somewhere was strictly dedicated to unattractive female cop attire.

She showed us to a small, nicely but plainly decorated interview room. A couch and two chairs surrounded a low coffee table, badly stained from years of water glasses and coffee cups. A box of tissues was discreetly placed on a side table.

I perched on the edge of the couch. Brad joined me, and Detective Thomas opened the file she was carrying. "I've made copies of the information I believe is pertinent to you both. We found photographs and old newspaper articles on his phone and his computer, as well an interesting search history. But first, I thought you might like to see this picture we found in a drawer in his bedroom."

She handed us a photograph of a photograph. The picture had been folded several times, was tattered at the corners, colors fading with time. A standard family shot of three people standing outside a house on a treed lot. The woman, presumably the mother, her clothes and hairstyle clearly dating from the nineteen seventies or eighties. A girl and a boy, both preteens. She wore orange shorts and a garish pink shirt. He was dressed in jeans. All three were smiling at whoever held the camera.

"That's us. With our mom," Brad said.

"I assumed so. The resemblance between the children in the picture and you two is obvious."

"Our dad kept this. All these years."

"He did. Nichelle, can you see what the little girl has around her wrist?"

I looked closer. A cheap toy bracelet. Pink beads to match her pink shirt. "That's similar to the bracelet he was holding when he died."

"Yes."

"What bracelet?" Brad asked.

"The police are keeping that detail under wraps," I said. "But he had a child's bracelet in his hand when he was found." I tapped my finger on the picture. "Not exactly the same, but similar to that one. We wondered why he'd be bringing me such a thing, if he was. It wasn't for me. It was an *aide memoire* for him. He must have had this picture on him when he . . . left the hotel that night. And he kept it. All this time.

Thomas put the file on the table. "I'll leave you two alone, shall I? Can I get you coffee or a glass of water?"

Brad and I shook our heads in unison. Restless, wondering what was in store for me today, I hadn't slept well and had risen early. I'd already had enough coffee to keep me awake for a month. The detective left, and I opened the file with a shaking hand. The topmost page was a printout of the recent library press release, welcoming me to the Bodie Island Lighthouse Library. The picture was a head and shoulders shot Isabelle took specifically for the library's "about us" information. The next page showed another photograph, the image taken from a social media site. In it, I carried a huge bunch of red roses and wore my cap and graduation gown from Syracuse. I smiled proudly. "Taken off Simone's account, I suspect," I said. "She should know better than to make her social media public."

Silently, Brad and I went through the folder. My brother and me going back over the years. Social media pages and online newspaper reports. I gasped when I came across our mother's obituary, and again when I found Isabelle's team picture from the high school cross-country championship and a mention of Brad's eldest son getting a college soccer scholarship.

We flicked through pages upon pages of computer printouts. Newspaper articles, social media posts, even team pictures copied from our children's high schools. Brad's wife, Maya, presenting a check on behalf of a charity she was involved in. Judging by her hair style, the picture had been taken ten years ago. Gradually, as we went back through time, the quantity of stuff lessened until it almost disappeared.

There wasn't much prior to the turn of the century, before the internet made everything available to everyone.

A note on NAPD letterhead told us alerts had been set on search engines for information about Brad and his family, and me and mine.

When we reached the end of the folder, I collapsed back against the couch. "Wow. So he didn't forget us."

"Didn't try to contact us either," Brad said.

"Do you think he regretted it—regretted leaving us?"

"Doesn't matter if he did or not." Brad stood up.

It did to me, but I didn't say so. If he'd come to regret whatever impulse had made him pretend he was dead, there would have been no way back. My mom moved on, made a good life for herself and for us. Brad and I had our own careers and our families. No place remained for Bradley Sanderson Sr.

The door opened and Detective Thomas and Butch Greenblatt came in. The eyes of both of them were kind. "Finished?" she asked.

"Finished. Once and for all," Brad said.

"There's more," Butch said. "I didn't want to overwhelm you, so I printed out a random sample from over the years. You can see the rest, if you want. We can have it all transferred to a thumb drive."

"No," Brad said. "I'm done."

"Maybe later," I said. "It's so overwhelming. Thank you for sharing this with us. It gives us . . . gives me . . . an insight into my father's last years."

"Before you go, Brad," Thomas said. "One thing in all those memorabilia is pertinent to my investigation. We now have definitive proof he knew Nichelle was coming to Nags Head, and she was starting work at the library that Monday."

"The library press release doesn't say so, but it would be easy enough for a local to guess the newest employee might get the lighthouse apartment," Butch said. "For anyone who wanted to talk privately with you, it would have been a matter of waiting until the library was closed and ringing the bell."

"We have one witness who says she thinks, although she can't be absolutely certain, Brian Saunders was on the lighthouse grounds shortly after sunset on Sunday," Thomas said. "She and her friends are birdwatchers, and they were heading for their cars when she saw a man matching Brian's description looking at the lighthouse."

"The lighthouse itself is a popular tourist attraction," Butch said. "Even when it's closed. Some people come out specifically at night to see the light from the lamp."

"We have to conclude he was there to see you, Nichelle," Thomas said. "I'm sorry."

I swallowed. Brad squeezed my hand.

"Doesn't explain why someone killed him," I said.

"No, it does not. I've spoken to Dennis McGregor and his sister Tracy Ireland. He was not happy with you turning him over, as he put it, to the police, but I assured him I had my sources."

"And?"

"And nothing. Not yet. He denies killing Saunders, as does Tracy. No alibi for either of them, but no alibi means nothing other than they were alone at the time in question. We're doing what we can to follow up on other women Saunders might have attempted to con, such as going back to the son who wanted us to charge him. Theodore Kowalski, who I believe is known to you, came in on his own initiative to repeat what his mother told us earlier. She dated Brian on two occasions, but she found him distant and cool, and so she cut the relationship off."

"I'm sorry things had to end this way with your father," Butch said. "It's never easy learning this sort of thing."

"No worse than I've thought a hundred times over the years," Brad said. "Now, if you've nothing more?"

"You're free to go, Mr. Sanderson." Thomas said. "But I remind you, you are required to notify the police if you intend to leave the country."

I glanced at Brad. The look he gave Thomas was not friendly. "I'll see myself out," he snapped. "I'll talk to you soon, Nichelle."

He stormed out of the room. Butch followed.

"My brother didn't kill our father," I said.

"That is still to be determined," Detective Thomas said.

Chapter Thirty

I spent a lonely, miserable Sunday. To match my mood, clouds were moving in as I left the police station and rain soon followed. Butch had been waiting for me at the door, presumably after seeing Brad off, and he walked me to my car. He gave me a warm smile. "A tough introduction to life in OBX. But I want you to know you are very welcome here, Nichelle."

"Thank you. That means a lot."

"I sent in some recommendations for book club reading."

"I'm sorry, with all that's going on, I haven't had a chance to go over them yet. I'll try to do that today and send out the list to everyone."

"Sherlock Holmes, mostly," he said. "I liked 'Murders in the Rue Morgue,' which we read not long ago. Maybe more Poe?"

"Poe's always a good choice. Let's see what the others suggest."

I drove to Josie's Cozy Bakery where I checked my library email account over a hot breakfast sandwich and a full-fat latte. Might as well live life on the edge.

The members of my new book club were, to put it mildly, an enthusiastic bunch. I'd been afraid I'd have to come up with all the suggestions myself. Instead, now I worried about how we'd ever manage to choose.

Thinking about all the books I'd loved over the years, plus a hearty meal, put me in a slightly better frame of mind. That frame died as soon as I stepped outside and got a bucket of cold rain in my face.I went home.

I spent some time sorting the book club's recommendations and putting them into a list to send to the members to vote on. I then made notes on ideas I had for updating the library's web site and read over various proposals for fall and winter events we might consider hosting. One thing I learned in my research before applying for this job was that the Bodie Island Lighthouse Library was the nerve center of local activities in this part of the Outer Banks, and they sponsored an enormous range of community events, author readings, and festivals for children and adults alike.

Work done, I made a cup of tea and settled into the window seat, Charles on my lap, reading my book. The tea, the view, the cat thoroughly relaxed me, and I was able to sink into the world of the novel. When I next looked up it was four o'clock, and the skies were clear.

"A walk would be nice, don't you think?" I said to Charles.

He didn't agree.

"That means you have to get up."

He didn't agree with that either, so eventually I had to pick him up and put him on the floor. He gave me a disapproving look and went to check out the contents of his food bowl. At the store earlier, I'd bought some cat grass seeds, and they were soaking in soil and water in a sunny spot.

I had no place in particular to go, so I decided to head for the stretch of beach I'd visited the other day. The national seashore, which was closer, was wilder and emptier, but somehow I didn't feel like searching out the wild places today.

I parked and headed for the busy beach. Like me, everyone who'd been cooped up all day had rushed out to take advantage of the break in the weather.

I walked for a long time. I didn't know what I felt about Brian—my dad—keeping track of us all these years. He might have been trying to convince himself he'd made the correct decision to leave us, but I didn't get that feeling from the pictures and articles I'd seen.

I remembered the woman at Blackbeard's Cave telling me she sensed a deep sadness in Brian.

Eventually, the beaches of Nags Head ended and the National Seashore began. The houses lining the beach were mostly of a type: brightly colored, multistoried, with rows of sparkling windows, numerous outside staircases, balconies on every level. One house, the last before the Nags Head town limits, was different from the rest. Covered in weather-worn, cedar shingles, two stories tall, with screened and roofed porches flanking two sides and a modern deck facing the ocean, steps leading down to the sand. This must be one of what was called the Unpainted Aristocracy, so called because the buildings were never painted, allowing the shingles to weather naturally. The houses were highly valued in Nags Head for the uniqueness of the architecture and their historical significance. As I admired the house, the sliding door onto the deck opened and a man and a woman came out, each carrying a blanket-wrapped baby.

Chapter Thirty-One

Lucy tucked Isaac into his bassinet and Connor did the same with Lucas. Colorful mobiles of puppet figures, handmade out of felt by Denise from the library, hung over the bassinets, swaying in the gentle wind. The babies stared up at their parents, wide eyed. Lucas gurgled and waved his legs.

"It would be nice," Lucy said, "if, for once, they would fall asleep at the same time."

Connor put his arm around her shoulders and held her close. "Someday we'll look back on these months and wish we had them again. Or so my mom tells me."

"Can't complain too much," Lucy said. "They did nap, on and off, at Ellen and Amos's, so we could enjoy our lunch. It was nice to see Ellie; I can't believe how fast she's growing."

"Maybe that's what my mom means. Babyhood doesn't last long."

"Thank heavens," Lucy said, as if by rote. Yes, babies—two babies—were stressful, exhausting, demanding, and the cause of constant worry. But the love she felt for these two little bundles of screaming helplessness made up for every lost minute of sleep.

"I'm getting a beer," Connor said. "Want anything?"

"Glass of tea would be nice."

Connor went inside. Lucy made a small adjustment to Lucas's blanket and was about to sit down, when she noticed a familiar figure standing at the edge of the waterline, flip flops in hand, surf washing over her toes. Lucy went to the railing and waved. "Nichelle! Nichelle!"

Nichelle started and looked around to see who was calling her. She spotted Lucy and waved back.

"Come and have a glass of tea! Meet my husband!"

Nichelle put her hand behind her ear and cocked her head. Lucy gestured and the new librarian raised her hand in acknowledgement and headed toward the house.

"Lucy, hi. Is this your home? I was admiring it. It's fabulous."

"Come up." Lucy opened the railing door at the top of the steps. "We've just gotten back from a late lunch at my aunt Ellen's and thought the boys could use some air."

Connor came out of the house with a glass of beer and another of tea. "Hi," he said.

Lucy made the introductions.

"Can I get you a drink?" Connor asked. "Beer, wine, tea hot or cold?"

"An iced tea would be nice, thank you. Are those your twins? How silly of me, who else's would they be. Can I see?"

"You can," Lucy said proudly.

While Connor went for her drink, Nichelle peered into the bassinets. Isaac and Lucus stared back. They had their father's blue eyes and what bit of hair was coming in hinted at their mother's wild curls. "They are so absolutely adorable. Identical twins?"

"Yes."

"We're dreading the preteen years." Connor handed Nichelle an ice-filled glass. "When they'll think it's great fun to pretend to be the other."

"My girls are identical too, and they tried that more than once. Hard to believe how different they turned out to be as they grew. I bet you already see some differences."

"We do." Lucy indicated for Nichelle to take a seat at the patio table, and she and Connor joined her. Connor asked how Nichelle was enjoying life in Nags Head, and she replied that it was all quite overwhelming.

"Exactly what I thought when I first moved here." A warm glow centered itself in Lucy's chest. "Best decision I ever made."

"Tell me about your house," Nichelle said. "It's gorgeous."

"It was built in 1923, in a style that is truly an Outer Banks original. Like most of the houses of this type, it would have been intended to be a vacation home for people fleeing the heat of the cities in the summer. Most of the Unpainted Aristocracy are located in a cluster nearer to the center of town, but the man who built this place was a notorious eccentric, and he wanted to be as far away from his neighbors as he could comfortably get."

"I can relate to that," Nichelle said. "Now that I'm living on the fourth floor of a lighthouse ten miles from everything."

"It has its advantages, for sure. An ancestor of Ralph and Jo Harper, whom you met at book club, built the house, and they grew up in it. For various reasons, Jo and Ralph didn't move back when their parents died, but they didn't sell it either. It was unoccupied for a long time and wasn't in particularly good shape when we bought it. Connor and his dad had a lot of work to do to get it ready for us to move in. Lots more still to get done; the upper level's boarded off until we can get around to it." Lucy was enormously proud of her house and all the work they'd done to make it a happy, loving home. Not that she'd done much herself, other than bring the working men glasses of tea or beer and sandwiches and make a dash to the store if they unexpectedly ran short of nails or screws.

When Lucy finished explaining the history of the Unpainted Aristocracy in general and this house in particular, Lucas was beginning to squirm. His little face scrunched up, and he let out a cry. "He might need changing." Lucy started to stand.

Connor beat her to it. He leaned over the baby and sniffed. "Yup, he does. I'll take care of it. You chat to Nichelle, honey." He lifted the baby, swung him in the air, and said, "You are one stinky little guy." Lucas gurgled in delight.

"Careful," Lucy said.

Connor gave her a kiss on the top of the head. "We'll go inside for some solid man-on-man time. Call me if Isaac wants to join us."

Isaac, however, had fallen fast asleep.

"I didn't want to mention it in front of Connor," Lucy said when Connor and the baby had gone inside. "Is anything happening with your father's case? Although I know you'd prefer we not call him that."

A seagull landed on the deck railing. It focused one black eye on the women, and finding them uninteresting, turned its head to stare out to sea.

"Things are happening, but I don't know if much progress is being made," Nichelle said. "Turns out he, Brian Saunders, wasn't exactly a model citizen."

"In what way? If you don't mind my asking."

Nichelle told her briefly what she'd learned.

"Louise Jane told me she dragged you out to the bar where Brian was a regular. She tried to imply it was your idea, but I know Louise Jane better than that. She means well, in work and in life, but she sometimes doesn't think everything through."

"What's with her and all that mysterious talk about popping back and forth to France and needing to keep a low profile?"

"Louise Jane is absolutely terrible at keeping secrets. Particularly when it's her own secret. She's seeing a man who, for reasons I will not disclose, lives in France and on the occasions he does come to Nags Head to see Louise Jane, he prefers his whereabouts not be known to certain people."

Nichelle's face twisted in puzzlement, but she didn't ask for any details. Lucy had her own reasons for keeping quiet about what she knew concerning the whereabouts and activities of Tom Reilly, Louise Jane's boyfriend for lack of a better word.

Nichelle sipped her tea and then she said, "He, Brian, was keeping track of us all these years. On the internet mostly. Me and my girls. Brad's family. He even had a copy of our mother's obituary notice on his computer, and he took an old photo of us, of the family, with him when he disappeared."

"How do you feel about that?"

"Conflicted."

Lucy hesitated. There's a fine line between wanting to be supportive and prying into things that are none of your business. "You've been on the job for a week, but if you need time off to make your father's arrangements, it's allowed by your contract."

"Thank you. That's going to be a mess. My brother left it to me to take care of, and I don't know what to do. Big funeral in Rochester with the family and those of the old friends I can locate, or small and limited in Nags Head with barely a mention of the man once named Bradley Sanderson?"

"Did he have many friends here?"

"Not what I'd consider close friends, not as far as I can find. Even his so-called girlfriend was nothing but a partner in his scams. We met with her last night. She tried to be all concerned, sympathetic, saying how hard things must have had been for Rosalee and Brad and me when Dad disappeared, but I didn't buy it."

Something tiny niggled at the back of Lucy's brain. Maybe her detective instincts hadn't completely disappeared with the arrival of the babies. "Step back a moment, Nichelle. Are the police saying anything about this woman? Partner-in-crime is usually a top suspect in any investigation."

"I don't think they're focusing on her. I considered it, but what would she gain by killing Brian? She never asked the women he was with for money. She pretended to be his daughter, told him she needed some financial help, and walked away, leaving Brian to close the deal."

"If he intended to approach you, as we know he did, might she have thought she'd be out financially?"

Nichelle shrugged. "Maybe, but an amount worth killing over? They made a couple of thousand here or there, maybe a bit more on occasion. Detective Thomas is looking, but she hasn't found evidence that Brian had money no one knew about. Doesn't mean there wasn't any, of course. That would be why no one knew about it. As for any other reason for her to kill him, they weren't romantically involved despite her calling herself his girlfriend, so jealousy or anything like that couldn't have been a motive."

Lucy struggled to grasp the thread of thought lingering at the back of her mind, teasing her to find it. Then, she did.

"You said you talked to her last night. Try and remember exactly what she said about your situation when your father disappeared."

"That she was sorry?"

"In detail. In her own words, if you can remember. "

Nichelle's eyes closed as she thought. "She said it must have been 'very, very difficult for Rosalee and you two.' meaning Brad and me." Her eyes flew open. "Oh, my gosh."

"I didn't know your mother's name," Lucy said. "You've always called her mom or our mother. Did you tell Melissa?"

"Almost certainly I did not. Not many people refer to their parents by their given names. I don't. Didn't."

"The question then is, how did she know?"

"Because Brian told her?"

Lucy nodded. "That would be the only reason. She might have seen some of these documents you told me he had on his computer, but the point is the same. Whether he told her or she pried into his private files, she knew about his real family before he died."

"Which means, when she pretended to be shocked to learn about his past, she was lying."

"When someone lies in one instance, it can be worthwhile to ask what else they might be lying about."

"Detective Thomas said that about a different person."

"You need to talk to the detective about this. I'll come with you if you—"

Lucas was sleeping peacefully. And then, suddenly he wasn't. He opened his eyes and bellowed. Inside the house his brother joined in the cry. The seagull took flight.

"Lucy!" Connor yelled. "I don't see any bottles in the fridge."

"Coming." Lucy jumped to her feet and picked up Lucas. His face was bright red, his little fists clenched, and he cried as though the end of the world was nigh.

"I have to see to these guys," Lucy said.

Nichelle stood up. "That's okay. I need to think this over. It's possible Brad told Melissa our mom's name before I met up with them last night."

Chapter Thirty-Two

I returned to my car at a considerably faster pace than I'd left it. My initial intention had been to call Detective Thomas, but as I walked and thought, I wondered if that was the right thing to do. It was a Sunday evening. The detective had a private life. Maybe a husband and children she wanted to spend a quiet night with. What, after all, did I know about all this? Only that Melissa knew my mother's name. I was pretty sure I'd never said it in front of her, but Brad might have when he met her in the bar of the Ocean Side Hotel before I arrived.

Detective Thomas would be unlikely to consider that to be a vital clue. Did it matter? Melissa lived life on the shady side, and any relationship she had with Brian was dubious at best. She might well have known all along he'd had a previous life, but she pretended not to so she could act all shocked and concerned when she met us.

I couldn't see any path from that to her killing him. Brian was likely more dependent on Melissa in their little criminal activity than she was on him. He was seventy-seven; not a lot of lively years yet. She was under fifty and still moderately attractive. Plenty of lonely widowers out there desperate for female companionship, if she ever decided to go into the "business" for herself. If she did decide to end their partnership, what could Brian do about it? Not much, unless he went to the police to confess their crimes. And, as I myself pointed out, Melissa hadn't done anything criminal. Unethical, perhaps, but not chargeable.

By the time I reached my car, I'd made up my mind. Rather than going home to think about it all some more, which was probably the most sensible thing to do, I headed into town. I didn't know where Melissa lived; I didn't know if she had a job; I didn't have a phone number for her, but I decided to take a chance she might be at Brian's. The house was a rental, but if it was paid up until the end of the month or longer, anyone to whom he'd given a key could continue to use it.

I was in luck. Melissa's car was parked in the driveway.

Before I got out of my own car, I phoned my brother. His voice mail answered. "Me, just checking in. Hope the drive's going okay. I'm in town, and I was near Brian's place, so I decided to have another talk with Melissa. Maybe she . . . uh . . . has something of his I'd like. A memento of a sort."

I hung up. That was a feeble excuse. I wanted absolutely nothing that would remind me of Brian Saunders.

I got out of the car. I looked at the house. I wiped my hands on the seat of my pants. I let out a long breath and changed my mind once again. *Let it go, Nichelle.* This was a bad idea. Bradley Sanderson Sr. was long gone, replaced by Brian Saunders. He was no longer my father, and that was his choice, not mine. Brian was not a nice man, and he eventually pushed one person too far.

I was about to get back in my car, when the front door opened. Melissa Archibald stood in the doorway, a dark outline framed by the light behind her. Dusk was settling over Nags Head. The streetlights were on, the sky to the east an inky black, to the west crossed by streaks of pink and gray.

"Are you stalking me?" she said. A bottle of beer was in her hand.

"Not at all. I was passing, and I wanted to see where he . . . where Brian lived."

"You were here a couple of days ago."

"One more time, then."

She was dressed in black leggings, baggy in the knees, and a loose sweatshirt. Her feet were bare, and she'd gone to no trouble with her hair or make up. It would appear she was staying here, and she intended to have a night in. She seemed to have read my mind and said, "Not all that impressive, I know, but it's nicer than the crummy apartment I've got, so I'm thinking of taking over the lease. For a while anyway. Not too much longer. It'll soon be time for me to leave this dump of a town, start over again."

"Have you always lived in Nags Head?"

"Why do you care?"

"Just asking."

"No, I haven't. I'm from some small town you've never heard of in the middle-of-nowhere North Carolina. If you're here because you're thinking Brian left me some money and you want to get your hands on it, think again. You can have his debts if you want."

And then I remembered. Atlantic City. The gambling winnings. Brian bragging to his bar buddies about his big win, a round of drinks at Blackbeard's Cave for everyone.

Was it possible Brian had more money than anyone believed? Did *Melissa* and Brian have more money than anyone was aware of?

"You knew about his previous life, didn't you?" I said. "About me and Brad and our mother. You knew he was going to the library on Sunday night. He wanted to meet me. To talk to me, after all these years. To apologize maybe, to make his excuses. It doesn't much matter why. I don't know how I would have reacted; I didn't get the chance. Thanks to you."

A woman passed, walking a small dog. She gave us openly curious looks. I was still on the sidewalk, Melissa in the doorway.

"Are you going to stand out there all night, sharing your business with the neighborhood?" Melissa stepped back. She lifted her bottle in invitation. "One thing I can say for Brian—he had good taste in beer. Still a few bottles of this craft stuff left."

I climbed the steps. I brushed past her and went into the house. Melissa shut the door behind me.

The house was as shabby on the inside as the outside suggested. Old furniture, tattered carpet, chipped plaster, paint peeling on the baseboards, a couple of prints of tourist-oriented paintings hanging crookedly on the lifeless beige walls.

Sad. Just sad.

There was no entrance hall; the door opened directly into the living room. A tiny dining area, a small galley kitchen beyond, a couple of closed doors leading off the main room.

Melissa watched me. "If you're expecting an inheritance, you're going to be mighty disappointed."

I didn't come here expecting to find answers, but I found myself asking the question anyway. "Why did he leave us, all those years ago? Why did he pretend to be dead? He didn't come to my wedding; he never met my children. He didn't even come to my mother's funeral. Her name was Rosalee. But you knew that, didn't you?"

"Yeah, I did. I guess I wasn't supposed to."

"No, you weren't. A woman at Blackbeard's Cave told me he was always sad. Was he?"

"Yeah, that's true enough. Brian was nothing but a sad, lonely old man. The only way he had of making friends was to buy drinks for people he never saw outside of a bar. I arrived in Nags Head two years ago. Met Brian the day I got here. Could tell he was a mark the moment I laid eyes on him. But, I soon realized, he didn't have enough money to be a real mark. I'm not in it for beer money." She lifted the bottle. She had not invited me further into the house, to take a seat, kick back and exchange memories of my father. I didn't mind. This wasn't a social call. "Get you one?"

"No thanks."

"Suit yourself."

"I assume the idea of him dating women to get money from them was your idea?"

"Yup. He needed a friend, so I became a friend. I suggested he start dating the sort of old women who don't mind paying to have a companion for a nice dinner out. After a couple of times doing that, I nudged him into asking them for money. A little bit at first, slowly increasing. I hate to break it to you, Nichelle, but he didn't need much nudging."

I wondered if that was true. Loretta Kowalski said he'd been almost relieved when she told him she didn't want to see him anymore. But, in the grand scheme of things, it didn't matter: he didn't have to keep doing it.

"He worked part time as a store clerk," Melissa said. "And whatever other odd jobs he could scrape together. He went to Atlantic City a couple of times a year. He was a good blackjack player, usually came out ahead. Enough to buy a couple of bottles of good beer now and again and pay for the cost of the trip. Not enough for a man who should be saving for his old age. Those women had plenty of money, why not give some of it to a friendly man who had nothing?" She grinned. It was not a good look. "You'd be surprised at how malleable some of them can be. Detective Thomas told me she's had calls from women Brian dated wanting to be notified of the funeral arrangements." Melissa chuckled. "There's an idea. I'll set up a charity fund in his memory. Plenty of those lonely old biddies would be glad to contribute."

"Sounds like you were onto a good thing," I said. "So why did you kill him?"

"Me?" She fluttered her eyelashes and pointed to herself. "Little old me?"

I waited.

"You want to know why he left you and your family? I'll tell you what he told me, one night when he'd had more of those beers he was so fond of than he should have. He started getting maudlin. I really hate it when men do that. Spewing all that rubbish about a wasted life."

"You were afraid he was going to back out of your business arrangements?"

"Not at all. He forgot about it the next day. That was starting to happen more and more. Him forgetting things I mean. Wouldn't have mattered if he had, by then I was ready to move on. We weren't making enough to keep both of us in style. He inherited a lot of money when his mother died, right?"

"He did, but that was a long time ago. When he was still with us. Still Bradley Sanderson Sr."

"Silly man. He was probably having one of his morose periods around then, when he left your mom, I mean. It was totally obvious to me, right from the beginning, he had an undiagnosed bipolar condition. Typical for a man of his age, he refused to do anything about his mental health." She tucked her chin into her chest, frowned deeply, and flexed her arm muscles. "I don't need no namby-pamby help. I can tough it out."

"What do you know about that? About his past?" I asked. I was no longer interested in whether or not Melissa had anything to do with the death of the man known as Brian Saunders. If she knew something about what he'd been thinking all those years ago, I wanted to hear it. I'd been waiting a very long time.

She shrugged. "I knew he had a family somewhere he'd left a long time ago. He never said much about it, and I didn't care enough to ask for more details. Then, one day, he read in the paper about you getting the job at the library. He was excited. I guess you like hearing that do you?"

"Go on."

"So he told me the whole sordid story. Sure you want to hear it?"

"Might as well." I tried to control the curiosity threatening to burst out of my chest. Did Melissa know the answer to the question that hung over me for most of my life?

"He knew he wasn't a good father or a good husband. He figured you guys would be better off without him."

That's what his fishing friends told Brad. They thought our father killed himself. Still didn't answer the question of why he would leave his entire life behind and disappear. Why not just tell Mom he was leaving and walk out the door?

"He inherited some money when his mother died. At first, he had grand plans of taking you all on a trip around the world, of moving to California and buying a big house on the beach. Then his morose mood took over and he realized it wasn't all that much. Not enough to allow him to throw everything aside and start living like some rich dude. He knew he'd end up squandering it, and your mother would let him." Melissa stared into the distance. "She must have really loved him."

"She did. She never got over losing him."

She focused on me again. "I bet the money helped though. He came down here with his buddies on their fishing trip, and he started thinking of not going back. With the money from the inheritance, Rosalee could start over, have a great life, give her kids what they deserved. If he wasn't around anymore. So he decided not to go home, simple as that."

"Not simple at all. To change identity? To disappear? To hide when people came looking?"

"He didn't say much more to me about it, but I got the feeling that soon enough, after supposedly drowning, he changed his mind—those mood swings again—but it was too late to apologize, and he didn't know what to say. So—he just stayed. He never did have anything in the way of initiative."

I believed her. She had no reason to lie about events of so long ago. By the way she was talking, it was obvious she was simply retelling details as someone had told her. An old story that didn't matter to Melissa herself in the least.

"Fast forward to last week," I said. "He heard I was moving here, and he wanted to meet with me."

"Soon as he learned you were coming, he started blathering on about the timing being a sign from God."

"Was he religious?" Didn't sound like it from what I'd heard but you never know.

"No, and he didn't start then. That's something people say, isn't it, to convince them to go ahead and do what they've already decided they want to do. He said it was time to make amends, time to do what he could do before it was too late."

"What did he mean by that?"

She'd slipped out of dry narration mode and something closed behind her eyes. She glanced away, avoiding looking directly at me. She shrugged. She lifted the bottle to her mouth. "I don't know."

That last statement was clearly a lie. She'd been open and, I thought, honest until now, but she'd reached the part of the story she did not want to be honest about. If Brian wanted to make amends to me and to Brad, did Melissa fear those amends would be financial? "But you do, Melissa, and I suspect I do too. Same as the reason he left us in the first place. He had money from his recent gambling winnings. He was going to offer it to me. To, in his mind, make amends. Although it would have done nothing of the sort. That was the good timing he thought had come from above. Him, having money for the first time in a long time. Me, arriving virtually on his doorstep."

As I spoke I watched her face. A muscle twitched beside her right eye. She studied her beer bottle in great detail. "What winnings? He'd already spent most of it on drinks for his buddies."

Another lie. There had to be more money involved than she was letting on. Enough to kill over?

"I don't think that's the case. I suspect he won more than he was letting on. A substantial amount, perhaps. Substantial to him, at any rate. And to you. I think you believed you were entitled to a share, and when you realized he intended to give it to me, in some feeble, far-too-late-attempt to make amends for abandoning my family, you killed him."

She looked up. "Seems like you believe a lot of things. Do you have proof of any of this?"

"No, but I'm sure the police will find evidence of those winnings soon enough, if they haven't already."

"Maybe. Maybe not. Even if he did win something, doesn't have anything to do with me. Everyone knew Brian was a braggart. He liked to spread his money around and show off. When he had any that is. Maybe he told the wrong person. Tsk tsk. He always was too trusting."

"Except that no one is going to kill someone for money he doesn't have on him. Not unless they know where it is and how to get it. You don't have an alibi for that night, do you?"

"Sure I do. I was at Blackbeard's all night until closing." The muscle beside her eye twitched again. I guessed she was telling the truth, but only in part. Busy bar, crowd of acquaintances, everyone coming and going, who would notice and remember if one person slipped out for half an hour or so? "Brian was there too, but he left. I didn't check the time, and I didn't know where he was going, didn't much care. He was weeping into his beer about what a bad man he was, and saying it was time to make amends. He was clutching some stupid flashy kid's bracelet he'd bought somewhere, like you were ten years old or something and going to be impressed by a cheap bauble. Sad, wasn't it, that ugly thing was all he had to hold in his hand at the end."

The pink bracelet he'd been clutching as he died. A bracelet similar to the one I'd been wearing in the photo of me and Mom and Brad he kept all these years. I didn't remember it at all, but he would have, if he looked at that picture a great deal, and judging by the wear on it he had. Had he bought a similar one recently, maybe even at Gardner's Beach Supplies? Did he need something to hold that would give him the courage to face me? Something he could show me so I'd know he hadn't forgotten me? If so, yes, it was beyond sad.

"You want to play that game?" Melissa continued. "I can play too. Did you kill him, Nichelle? You or your brother. That might be an avenue for the cops to explore. Did you think you were entitled to every cent Brian had, after all these years?"

Obviously she didn't know Brad was a suspect, although for reasons other than money. I wasn't going to let that idea fester any longer. "You just implied Brian was planning to give whatever he had to me outright, so why would I have reason to kill him? Which would have been a risky thing for us to do, with no guarantee of reward. Bradley Sanderson Sr. had been declared dead a long time ago. Brian Saunders might have had a will of his own, bypassing his children." I didn't even know if such a will would hold up. Would a will in a false name be valid? Would Brad and I be considered Brian's legitimate heirs regardless of any later heirs or wills?

Melissa yawned ostentatiously, lifted one hand, and tapped her mouth. She put the empty bottle on a side table. "I'm getting bored with this conversation, and I've finished this beer. Time for you to leave, Nichelle. Did I tell you that's a ridiculous name? Never mind." She made shooing gestures. "Off you go now."

"Don't worry about me. I'm going. To speak to Detective Thomas. She'll be interested in hearing what you told me tonight."

"I don't remember telling you anything."

I turned around and took hold of the door knob. Before I knew what was happening Melissa grabbed my arm and yanked me backward. I tripped on a patch of torn carpet and fell against the wall, hitting the back of my head. My vision swam.

Through bleary tears, I could see Melissa's angry face peering into mine. The muscle beside her eye was throbbing, her eyes were narrow slits, and her lips clenched. When she spoke, spittle flew. "Not so fast there." Keeping her gaze focused on me, she grabbed the beer bottle by the neck and swung it against the wall. It shattered, leaving her holding a formidable weapon. "Let's go for a drive. You and me. Get to know each other better."

I swallowed. My vision began to clear, and I forced myself to look past the shards of glass into her face. I didn't see madness in her eyes, nothing but anger and a touch of fear. She licked her bottom lip.

"No," I said.

"What do you mean, no? You have no choice. I'm not going to hurt you."

"You're brandishing a weapon, Melissa." I was surprisingly calm. "You want me to leave with you. What else am I supposed to think? I have no proof you killed Brian, although your behavior tells me pretty clearly you did. If you hurt me, kill me, the police will know. I talked some of this over with a friend before coming here. If I disappear or show up dead, that friend will tell the police what I told her. I texted my brother to let him know when I arrived outside this house."

She moved the bottle in a slow circle. "So. I'll tell them you left. I'll say you were as unstable as your father, poor thing. I couldn't stop you. We'll take your car. Move!"

"No."

Did Melissa intend to kill me? Yes, I believed she did. I was almost positive she'd killed Brian. They say a second killing is easier. I was not going to leave with her. Once we were outside on the street I might be able to get away, attract attention, but if no one was around . . . She was a few years younger than me, and likely substantially fitter.

"If you want to kill me," I tried to sound much braver than I felt, "you'll have to do it right here. On this dirty old carpet. Once they start looking for me, the cops will come straight here. Brian left blood on the library steps. I'll leave a lot more of mine on this carpet, and you'll never be able to get it out. What are you going to do with my body? Dump me on your steps? Wouldn't that be rather obvious? Drag me to my car and stuff me in the trunk? Think you can lift my dead weight? Think again. It's still light out, Melissa. People are in their yards or driving past. Someone might ask what's going on."

Indecision washed across her face. She started to lower the bottle. She raised it again.

I took one step away from the wall. My heart was beating so hard I feared she'd be able to hear it.

Melissa stepped aside, just a little bit but enough.

I didn't know whether to look at her face or at the broken glass clenched in her fist. I decided on the face as I edged around her, taking myself toward the door. Still facing Melissa, I gripped the doorknob. I slowly opened the door.

"Thank you," I said. I threw myself out the door, ran down the steps and across the yard, and jumped into my car. As I peeled away from the curb, I took a quick glance at Brian's house. Melissa stood in the doorway, framed by the light behind her. The neck of the brown bottle was still in her hand.

Chapter Thirty-Three

I drove directly to the police station as fast as I dared. I pulled into the parking lot, mostly empty on a Sunday night, and switched the engine off. I put my head on the steering wheel and simply sat there, breathing, trying to collect my nerves, to think about what had just happened.

I started at a sharp rap on my window. Butch Greenblatt peered at me and made a rolling movement. I fumbled at the switch to lower the window. The engine was off; it wouldn't work. I opened the door.

"Nichelle, are you all right?" Butch asked. "Why are you here? Is something wrong?"

"No. I mean, yes. I mean . . . I need to speak to Detective Thomas."

"She's not working tonight, but if you come inside I'll call her."

I nodded.

He reached out a hand and helped me stand.

"Melissa Archibald . . . I . . . I . . . She killed Brian Saunders."

To his credit, he didn't ask if I was sure, and that went a long way toward calming me down. "How do you know that? Did she tell you?"

"She didn't say it in so many words, but it was clear what she was saying."

"Can't take that to court," he said.

"She threatened me with a broken beer bottle. I believe she intended to kill me too."

Butch stopped at the bottom of the steps and stared at me. "When?"

"Now. Just now. I drove straight here."

"She threatened you because you accused her of the murder?"

"Because I figured it out, yes."

"Okay. Let's get you inside, and I'll call the detective."

Butch asked the officer at the front desk to bring me a glass of water and led me to the interview room.

Finally my legs gave out and I dropped into a chair.

* * *

Detective Thomas soon arrived. I tried to apologize for disrupting her Sunday evening, but she waved me off. Instead of one of her stern suits she was dressed in jeans, running shoes, a T-shirt and a leather jacket, which made her look far more human. "All part of the job. Officer Greenblatt tells me you believe Melissa Archibald killed the man known as Brian Saunders, and she tried to kill you this evening. Please take me through what happened tonight. Take as much time as you need."

"I might have said she tried to kill me, but that isn't factually correct. She threatened me with a broken beer bottle and demanded I get in my car with her and go . . . someplace. I don't know where she intended to take me, but when I refused, she didn't do anything more, and I walked out. I drove straight here."

Thomas studied me. "Were you harmed? Did you have a physical altercation with her?"

"She grabbed me, yes, but no more than that. I talked my way out of whatever else she might have had in mind."

"Still an assault, no matter how minor. Where did this happen?"

"At Brian Saunders's house. She's moved in."

Thomas gave Butch a sharp nod, and he slipped out of the room without a word.

"Continue," she said, and I did so. I tried to keep my voice steady and think before speaking. I wanted to relate the facts, as clearly as I could remember them, without the sort of overdramatizing and speculation she wouldn't appreciate.

Once, as I spoke, her phone buzzed, and she glanced briefly at it. She didn't tell me what it said, but simply nodded to me to continue.

I thought myself calm and in control, but as I related the final part of my story, about how Melissa had looked at me across the shards of glass of that beer bottle, delayed panic started to creep in. I grabbed my glass of water and drank deeply.

"Are you all right, Ms. Gilcrest?"

"I will be. I need a minute, that's all."

"Officer Greenblatt took another officer, and they went to Mr. Saunders' house, where they found Ms. Archibald. They asked her to come down to the station with them, and she freely did so."

"Was she arrested?"

"No. As of yet, all I have is your word as to what happened."

"Oh," I said.

Thomas stood up. "I'll have a talk with her now. I need you to remain here. Do you have a friend you can call who can come down and wait with you? This might take a while."

"My brother should be approaching Rochester by now, and I don't have any friends in the area. Not yet, I mean. I've scarcely been in town a week." I thought of Lucy, but dismissed the idea. She had enough responsibilities. Even if I was inclined to call her, Butch had warned me off involving her in anything to do with police investigations or murder cases. "I'm fine."

Thomas left, and a uniformed officer popped her head in to ask if I needed anything. I asked for a cup of coffee. She was soon back with a mug containing some thick, murky, dark liquid scarcely worth the name. I drank it anyway. I still had my phone with me, and I amused myself for a few minutes imagining what my daughters would have to say if I texted to tell them I was being held at the police station on a Sunday night. But I wasn't being "held," just asked politely to wait. I played some Sudoku, losing badly as I couldn't concentrate. I'd barely finished my horrific coffee before Detective Thomas was back, followed by the uniformed officer.

Thomas sat down; the officer stood by the door.

"Ms. Archibald denies killing Mr. Saunders as well as assaulting or threatening you. She says you came around to the place where she's staying, and you started throwing out wild, unfounded allegations. When she tried to calm you, you knocked a beer bottle out of her hand, causing it to break, and ran off."

I wasn't entirely surprised to hear that. I hadn't expected Melissa to confess. "What happens now?"

"You're free to leave, as is Ms. Archibald. I continue with the investigation. I'm interested in finding out more about this big casino win you believe Mr. Saunders had. If there's one thing I can say for casinos, their security is excellent, and they have cameras on everything at all times. No one gets into the place without being recorded, and they certainly don't get out the door with as much as a dollar in winnings without it being a matter of record. It's a place for me to pick up the investigation and if the amount Mr. Saunders won turns out to be substantial, I'll follow up as to what happened to the money.

"In the meantime, I'd advise you to stay well clear of Ms. Archibald. She has come to our attention on previous occasions."

"What does that mean?"

"It means stay well clear of Ms. Archibald." Thomas rubbed at her wrist and failed to hide a wince as she stood up.

"Are you okay?" I instinctively asked.

"Tennis injury sustained this afternoon. In college I had dreams of going pro. Now I play whenever I get the chance, which isn't as often as I might like."

"The bracelet!"

"What?"

"The bracelet. The girl's bracelet Brian had in his hand when he died."

"What about it?"

"I saw it, but I didn't touch it. You asked me about it, but I don't recall hearing anything about it on any of the news reports. You told me you were keeping that detail from the public. Like they do in mystery novels. I guess you do in real life too."

"Some things we keep back, and some details aren't worth mentioning in a tightly written news release. Why?"

"Melissa knew he was holding a child's bracelet when he died. How would she know that?"

"He might have told her he was going to give it to you," the uniformed officer said.

"Maybe. Maybe not." My excitement began to rise. "You said some details aren't worth mentioning, but she specifically mentioned it to me tonight. Why would she do that? Because it's stuck in her memory. He was holding it in his hand when he died, right? Even if she knew he had it with him, she would not know he'd taken it out of his pocket when he arrived at the library. Unless she'd been there."

Thomas nodded. And then she smiled. "She'll deny it, of course. She'll tell me she said no such thing to you. But over the years I've been doing this job, I've learned one thing: all you need is to find the slightest crack in the dam and the entire edifice of a false story comes tumbling down. You can go, Nichelle. I'll have another chat with Ms. Archibald before releasing her. I'll call you in the morning. You drove yourself here, Officer Greenblatt tells me."

"Yes."

"You're shook up, although you're trying hard to hide it, and I'd prefer you don't drive tonight. My officers are busy so I've called a friend for you."

"A friend?"

"A friend. We'll be releasing Mr. Saunders's body early this week. Shall I pass your contact information on to the necessary people?"

"Yes, please. I'll take care of the arrangements."

I found Sam Watson sitting in the lobby waiting for me. He stood up when I came in.

"I'm sorry you were bothered," I said. "I don't want to disturb your Sunday night. Despite what Detective Thomas might think, I'm well enough to drive myself home."

He grinned at me. "I don't mind. Reminds me of the old days, called out when Lucy managed to crack a case wide open. Shall we?"

Chapter Thirty-Four

When I got home I sent my daughters quick texts telling them nothing more than I hoped to be able to lay my father—their grandfather—to rest next week, and I'd be in touch with further details when I had them. I'd decided on a simple, small ceremony in Nags Head where he'd spent the last thirty-eight years of his life. As well as my daughters and Brad's family, I wanted to invite my mother's sister, to whom I was close, but no one else. I didn't want the merely curious or those hunting for gossip.

My daughters replied quickly.

Isabelle: *Don't make it a weekend. Tennis round robin finals.*
Simone: *Please make it a weekend. Don't want to take much time off work.*

I smiled to myself. Life goes on, and my daughters had never even known they had a maternal grandfather still living.

I then phoned my brother. He was still on the road, but we had a long talk. I told him what was happening, about Melissa and about the funeral arrangements, and he told me he intended to speak, openly and honestly, to Maya when he got home. "When I left the Outer Banks, I'd decided on total honestly. By the time I neared Fredericksburg, I changed my mind. I'd forget about it, and she would never need to know. As I drove into New York State, I changed my mind again. She might not ever know, but if someone is arrested for Brian's murder, there's going to be a court case, and I won't take the chance on being summoned and asked to account for my whereabouts. Better I confess straight to Maya's face than she hear it under those circumstances."

"I think that's wise, Brad. I'll keep you posted about the arrangements."

"I'm glad, you know."

"Glad about what?"

"At the end, he wanted to do the right thing. Yeah, it was far too late, but it's comforting in a way to know he didn't just walk away and forget all about us. Mom would have liked that."

"I'll be in touch."

"Love you, Nichie."

"Love you too, Bro."

While I'd been talking to my brother, texts had come in.

Isabelle: *Sorry about how that sounded. I can come anytime you need. Jonathan can go to tournament on his own.* 🎾♡

Simmone: *Work not that important. I can take whatever time off-needed.* 💞

* * *

I didn't hear from Detective Thomas again for a few days. Lucy told me that was to be expected. The detective had my statement; she had Melissa's statement. Her task from this point on would be to try to find a hole in Melissa's account. Or in mine, presumably, but Lucy didn't mention that.

Rhonda Thomas phoned the library on Wednesday afternoon, asking if I was available for an update.

As if I'd be anywhere else, or had anything more important going on.

She arranged to come in at six, after closing, and she brought an entourage. Sam Watson was with her as well as Butch Greenblatt. Thomas's face was as impassive as ever, but the sparkle in Sam's eyes and the grin on Butch's face told me what I needed to hear.

I had my own entourage, and Charles, Lucy, and Louise Jane joined us in the break room.

Chapter Thirty-Five

Lucy and Sam Watson exchanged secret grins. *Just like the old days.*

When Nichelle and Charles had come into her office at the end of the day to tell Lucy Detective Thomas was coming to give her an update on the Bradley Sanderson/Brian Saunders case, Lucy said, "If you think it might be unpleasant news, I can be with you, if the detective will allow it. It's obviously your business and entirely up to you."

"Please, do come," Nichelle said. "I talked the situation over with you, so you must be interested in how it turns out. I don't know what possible bad news she can give me. If Melissa isn't charged, I'll have to live with that. I got a text from my brother after she called, to let me know he and his wife will be here on Saturday, so she can't have had him arrested."

"Your brother?" Lucy asked. "After book club, he mentioned the police were interested in him, but I didn't realize an arrest was a possibility."

Nichelle winced. "I let that one slip. Guess I'm not much of a detective, am I? Yes, it was, for a while."

Lucy said nothing. Her own mother had been a murder suspect once, and she knew how hard it can be having a personal involvement in a murder case.

"Brad had been visiting Nags Head far more than he let anyone, including his wife or me, know, most recently only the day before I arrived and . . . what then happened, happened."

"Let's hear what Detective Thomas has to say, shall we?"

Charles narrowed his eyes and nodded in agreement. Shortly after coming to live and work at the Lighthouse Library, Lucy realized Charles was a great judge of character. That he'd taken so soon and so well to Nichelle, gave Lucy confidence she'd made the right decision in hiring the older woman.

"Police car pulling up outside." Louise Jane's head popped into the office. "They're probably here to talk to you, Nichelle. Don't worry, I'm here for you. Remember, if you don't want to answer their questions, you don't have to. Any unpleasantness, allow me to run interference for you."

Lucy got up from behind her desk. "I'm sure that won't be necessary, Louise Jane. The library's closed now so you're free to go. Have a nice evening."

Louise Jane waved her hand in the air. "Don't concern yourself with me. I've got nothing planned tonight. I'm happy to stay. I might be able to contribute. I've been getting regular updates from my cousin Kevin. The cops have been all over his place, talking to the regulars about what happened the night Brian died. They were there earlier, of course, but left without learning anything of significance. Kevin's regulars can be a closed-mouthed bunch, to the cops anyway. Now the dam's been blown open, Brian's friends are talking up a storm. Cops have been asking a lot of pointed questions about Melissa Archibald in particular. Most of the bar gang never liked her and never trusted her relationship with Brian. Some of them are remembering, now their memory's been prodded, she left the night in question not long after Brian did, and she was gone for about half an hour. There's the bell now. I'll let them in. Meet you in the break room."

Louise Jane bustled off. Charles followed. Nichelle looked rather stunned. Lucy felt rather stunned herself. She was supposed to be the boss here. She needed to remember that sometimes. She could simply order Louise Jane to leave. Bertie warned her that managing Louise Jane when Louise Jane didn't want to be managed would require the mental dexterity of a criminal trial lawyer. Lucy worried she wasn't up to the task.

"It's okay with me, if she sits in," Nichelle said. "She was of help getting people to talk to me in that bar."

"Let's do this then," Lucy said. "You go ahead. I'm going to call Sofia and tell her I've been delayed but I don't expect to be long."

Chapter Thirty-Six

"Melissa Archibald has confessed to the murder of Brian Saunders, aka Bradley Sanderson Senior," Detective Rhonda Thomas said when we were all sitting around the table in the Bodie Island Lighthouse Library break room. Charles had found a spot on the counter from where he could watch everyone and hear everything.

I hadn't expected an arrest, not so quickly. I thought it would be a long, drawn out battle of wits between Melissa and the detective.

"Will her confession hold up in court if she withdraws it?" The ever-practical Lucy asked.

"It shouldn't matter if she withdraws it or not. I'm confident I have enough to take it to court. I have plenty of footage from a casino in Atlantic City of her and Brian Saunders from two weeks ago. He played blackjack and had a good night."

"How much is good?" Louise Jane asked.

"Winning an amount in the mid five figures. Not a lot by some people's standards, but a great deal for others. We have an image, although no sound, of Melissa and Brian in the line at the cashier's office. They appear to be arguing. Notably, the line was long and moving exceptionally slowly. Eventually, Brian throws up his hands and simply walks away. Melissa follows. Meaning they did not cash in the chips before leaving the casino. I suspect he was either just too impatient to wait, or he needed to get back to Nags Head."

"Can you do that?" Lucy asked. "Take the chips away with you?"

"The rules vary by jurisdiction and the individual casinos, but at the one they played at, yes it's permitted to leave with them. Of interest, anyone can exchange them for the money at any time, as long as they present them at the establishment where they were won. They don't expire."

"Seems unwise to me," Lucy said. "A bag of casino chips? Suppose you lose them or someone steals them?"

"Or someone kills you for them," Louise Jane said.

I sat quietly, not saying much, simply absorbing it all. My father had been murdered for not much more than fifty thousand dollars? What a sad, sad end.

"Are you okay, Nichelle?" Sam asked. "Do you need some time to yourself? We can talk again tomorrow."

"No. I'm fine. Please, Detective Thomas, continue."

"We found a bag of chips marked from the casino in question in a drawer in the bedroom of Mr. Saunders's house. At first, Ms. Archibald claimed she knew he'd won at blackjack, but she wasn't aware he didn't bank the money. When presented with the camera evidence, she switched to saying she didn't know he kept the chips in his house. I pointed out his house would have been the logical place to put them, as he didn't have a safely deposit box at any bank we know of. Not to mention that she had a key, so after his death she had more than enough opportunity to search for them, and they weren't particularly well hidden."

"He could have used an out-of-state bank," Louise Jane said.

Butch grinned. "Yes, he could, but it's details like that where people's stories begin to fall apart, and we have them. When the evidence starts piling up, it takes a mighty quick-witted person to think up counterarguments on the fly. Ms. Archibald didn't think to ask if we'd checked with every bank up and down the Eastern Seaboard."

"She could have simply clammed up," Sam Watson said. "It's our job to prove what we're saying, not theirs to disprove it, but I've found over the years that once people start explaining themselves, they can't quit. And thus, they dig a hole deeper and deeper while trying harder and harder to climb out of it."

"Why do you suppose she didn't return to the casino to cash them in after he died, and put the money in her own bank account?" Lucy asked.

"In the immediate aftermath of his death, that might have attracted unwanted attention," Sam said. "She was spoken to concerning her relationship with him and the circumstances of his death, so she might have believed we were watching her. She would have had to drive to Atlantic City, and she had no way of knowing if we were keeping an eye on her banking activities. Likely she intended to lie low for a while and then start cashing them slowly."

"And then, once we had a solid idea of motive, it was a matter of finding opportunity," Thomas continued. "People at the bar she and Saunders had been at that night suddenly remembered her slipping out after he left. Again, all she had to do was claim to have gone for some air or to run an errand, make us prove she followed him. Instead, she admitted following him part of the way to the library. She claims she turned around once she realized where he was going and that he was determined to speak to his daughter." Thomas's dark eyes were kind when she looked at me. "To you. And so her story is that she drove back to the bar, leaving Brian Saunders alive and heading to the lighthouse."

"And?" Louise Jane asked.

"A matter of asking her how she knew information the police had not released, meaning the item he'd been holding in his hand."

"The bracelet," Lucy said. "I saw it, but you never released that detail to the public."

"I did not. Yes, the child's bracelet. Melissa tried to argue she'd seen him with it at the bar, and she simply assumed he'd have it in his hand."

"All she would have had to do was deny telling you that detail, Nichelle," Sam said. "Your word against hers."

Charles nodded sagely. Clearly Charles was also accustomed to how the police worked around here.

"And that was that," Thomas said. "I told her we'd be taking prints of the treads on her vehicle and comparing them to some we found at the library."

"Can you do that?" Lucy asked.

"No. We didn't get any useable prints."

Louise Jane snorted and threw a ferocious glare at Butch. "Unlike that time I myself was under suspicion of murder simply because my van had been in the parking lot at the time in—"

"We're not here to rehash that old story," Butch said. "We had reason to follow up your movements on that occasion and so we did."

How many murders have taken place at this library? I filed that thought away to consider another time.

"And then," Thomas continued, "Melissa Archibald nailed her own coffin shut. She started with the excuses and the justifications. She didn't mean to kill him; she only wanted to talk things over with him. It was her money as much as his; more hers than his as she paid for the trip to Atlantic City. He owed her for all she'd done for him this past year; he was going to give it all away to some . . . never mind some *what* Nichelle, but we knew she meant you."

I sat quietly for a long time. I was aware of Butch Greenblatt shifting in his seat and Louise Jane standing up and getting something out of the fridge. Charles scratched behind his right ear. Lucy put her hand on mine, and left it there, warm and comforting.

Finally, Detective Thomas said, "That's enough for now. I wanted to fill you in on where we're at. I'll have to interview you again, Nichelle, about what transpired between you and Melissa at Brian Saunders's house Sunday night, but that can wait until tomorrow. Doubtless I'll have further questions as the case progresses."

Sam and Butch got to their feet. Lucy followed. Louise Jane and Charles settled back down again.

"Before I go," Detective Thomas said, "I'd like a word with Nichelle in private."

"I need to be off home," Lucy said. "My babysitter has an appointment later tonight and Connor has a dinner meeting. Nichelle, call me if you need to talk. Anytime."

"I will, thank you."

As Lucy and Butch left, he said, "Steph wants to come around to your place soon and see the babies again, Lucy."

"Weekends are best. Call ahead to be sure they're awake."

"I don't mind telling you, I'm worried she's getting broody. First Josie and Jake, now you and Connor."

"Is Steph getting broody, Butch, or would that be you?"

"Louise Jane?" Sam Watson said.

"What?"

"Let's go."

"Nichelle has no secrets from me. I'll stay in case she needs my support."

"She does not. Come on."

With much huffing and puffing, Louise Jane got to her feet and left. Even Charles ran out the door, leaving Rhonda Thomas and me alone.

"Melissa Archibald was on our radar for the killing," Thomas said. "But we had nothing concrete on her. It was your statement about your confrontation with her that blew the case open, and I thank you for that."

I smiled at her, a nice warm feeling of pride at a job well done rising in my chest.

"However, if you ever interfere in one of my investigations again, I will have you arrested and charged. Do you understand, Ms. Gilcrest?"

The nice warm feeling turned to ice. She was not smiling and the kindness had disappeared from her eyes. "I said, do you understand?"

I nodded rapidly. "Yes. I mean, yes, I understand."

"See that you do." She walked out.

Chapter Thirty-Seven

Thursday was another pleasant summer's day at the Bodie Island Lighthouse Library. Patrons, young and old and all ages in between, came and went. Books flew off shelves and others were returned. The computer stations were busy with young people checking job vacancies or the elderly needing help corresponding with distant family. Upstairs, the floor shook as children danced in time to a musical story, and Louise Jane thundered down the spiral staircase and ran down the hallway in pursuit of what I never did learn. Charles joined the elderly ladies gossiping in the magazine nook and graciously allowed them to shower him with praise as well as scratches and pats. One of the women might have even surreptitiously snuck a cat treat out of her pocket.

Last night the police announced that Melissa Archibald, of Nags Head, had been arrested for the murder of Brian Saunders, aka Bradley Sanderson Sr., and all day people had been asking me what I knew about it.

"Nothing more than you," was my standard reply.

Theodore Kowalski came in with his mother, Loretta. "I keep telling Mom and telling her, she might have been killed!"

he told everyone who was interested, and many who were not. "Goodness only knows what that woman would have been capable of if she got my mother in her sights. Suppose Brian married her and Melissa decided she wanted my inheritance!"

Loretta looked at me and rolled her eyes. "As if. I said all along something was off about that man, didn't I?"

"You did." I said. As far as I knew no one outside the police and my circle of colleagues knew the nature of my relationship with Brian Saunders. Word would get around soon, particularly as the funeral approached, and Bradley Sanderson Jr. and his family arrived. My brother and I had decided to bury our father under his real name.

"I like to think it was because he wasn't truly a bad man." Loretta lowered her voice. "I'd had a hard day prior to the last time we went to dinner together, and I might have complained too much. Nothing that wasn't true though. The house is getting too much for me to handle. It's an old house, and I've got to make some expensive decisions soon, if I'm going to keep it. I keep putting that off. I'm not yet seventy, but I've been thinking about moving into a senior's residence. I'm worried whether or not I can afford a nice place. They're all so dreadfully expensive, and I can't ask my Teddy to help me out. He has his own life to live. I confessed my worries to Brian, and it was then his attitude toward seeing me seemed to turn, to the point he was almost relieved when I told him I didn't want to date any more. If dating is what you can call it."

"Thank you for telling me that," I said. "You obviously have good instincts." Whether or not hearing about her financial worries was the reason Brian hadn't tried to talk Loretta into going out again, I wanted to believe it was. That he understood she couldn't afford even the small amounts he intended to ask her for.

She gave me a big wink. "I like to think I've learned a thing or two in all my years. I'd better collect my son before he starts telling everyone I was on the point of signing my life savings over to Brian. As if I'd be that much of a fool."

We can all be fools for love.

One of the women who'd been at the book club meeting the other night put her books on the desk. "How's your brother doing, Nichelle?"

"Fine. Why do you ask?"

"Not too bothered about Patricia moving away, I hope?"

"Patricia? I don't know who that is."

"Patricia Reingold. Pastor Reingold's wife. He's been transferred to another church, about as far away from Nags Head as they can send him. The higher-ups are hoping to get ahead of the scandal, but," she laughed, "impossible to do and the knives are coming out awful fast now."

"Pastor's wife? You don't mean—?"

"I've never met your brother, but I recognized him when he came to the book club. Everyone in town knows Patricia has an eye for a nice man, and it was no secret she was sneaking around with him. Among her other conquests. Hard to keep track sometimes of what that girl gets up to. Wasn't even a secret to Pastor Reingold. Especially not to him. I was surprised to hear one of Patricia's 'special friends'," she put quotation marks around the words with her fingers, "was your brother though. Small world, isn't it?"

"Are you talking about Pastor Reingold?" Another woman joined us. "He finally made the mistake of trying to start an affair with a woman who was not prepared to accept his advances. Nor was she prepared to keep quiet about it."

"Everyone knows about this?" I asked.

"Heavens, yes, dear. Why else do you think we go to that church? Not for the quality of the sermons I can tell you, and the draft in that place in the winter is something fierce. There's a thought. Margaret, will we have to find another church for services? I hate having to start over."

"I'll keep my ear to the ground," Margaret said. "Oh, here's Charles. Let me see, I might just have a little something in my pocket."

She held out the treat to Charles, who accepted it without hesitation. The women took their books and left, calling goodbye over their shoulders.

I stroked the big cat as I watched the activity swirling around me.

I smothered a laugh. Oh yes, living and working at the Bodie Island Lighthouse Library was not going to be boring.

Author's Note

The Bodie Island Lighthouse is a real historic lighthouse, located in the Cape Hatteras National Seashore on the Outer Banks of North Carolina. It is still a working lighthouse, protecting ships from the Graveyard of the Atlantic, and the public is invited to tour it and climb the 214 steps to the top. The view from up there is well worth the trip. But the lighthouse does not contain a library, nor is it large enough to house a collection of books, offices, staff rooms, two staircases, and even an apartment.

Within these books, the interior of the lighthouse is the product of my imagination. I like to think of it as my version of the TARDIS, from the TV show *Doctor Who*, or Hermione Granger's beaded handbag: far larger inside than it appears from the outside.